PRAISE FOR LISA GRAY

"Lisa Gray explodes onto the literary stage with this taut, edge-of-the-seat thriller, and her headstrong protagonist Jessica Shaw, reminiscent of Lee Child's Jack Reacher, delivers a serious punch."
—Robert Dugoni, *New York Times* bestselling author

"Mazey Los Angeles noir for fans of Sara Gran. I'm liking it a lot."
—Ian Rankin, bestselling author of the Inspector Rebus series

"*Thin Air* is an exciting whodunit that kept me guessing until the end. PI Jessica Shaw is so capable and strong, I couldn't get enough of her!"
—T. R. Ragan, bestselling author of the Lizzy Gardner series

"One of this year's best new thrillers . . ."
—*Evening Standard*

"You'll find this one hard to put down."
—*Daily Record*

"The very best sort of detective fiction: gritty, real and gripping with a brilliantly realized main character."
—Cass Green, *Sunday Times* bestselling author

"A fast-paced, perfectly plotted killer of a thriller with a fantastic female lead and a cracking premise."
—S. J. I. Holliday, author of *Violet*

"If you like your mysteries full of twists and turns then look no further than *Bad Memory* . . . I couldn't put it down!"

—Jane Isaac, author of *A Deathly Silence*

"*Thin Air* is an assured and fast-paced debut with a compelling central character and plenty of twists to keep you guessing until the very end."

—Victoria Selman, author of *Blood for Blood*

"An assured and explosive debut with a premise that grabs you by the throat and refuses to let go. The pace never drops as it hurtles to a stunning conclusion."

—Craig Robertson, author of *The Photographer*

"Smart, sassy, and adrenaline-fueled, this kick-ass debut is a must-read for thriller fans."

—Steph Broadribb, author of *Deep Down Dead*

"Lisa Gray's thriller is so assured it's hard to believe it's a debut. It's so fast-paced it should be pulled over for speeding!"

—Douglas Skelton, author of *The Janus Run*

LONELY HEARTS

ALSO BY LISA GRAY

Thin Air

Bad Memory

Dark Highway

LONELY HEARTS

A JESSICA SHAW THRILLER

LISA GRAY

THOMAS & MERCER

Published by Thomas & Mercer, Seattle

www.apub.com

Amazon, the Amazon logo, and Thomas & Mercer are trademarks of Amazon.com, Inc., or its affiliates.

ISBN-13: 9781542021166
ISBN-10: 1542021162

Cover design by Dominic Forbes

Printed in the United States of America

For Scott and Alison—with love

PROLOGUE
1989

It was Friday night at Mike's Tavern, and the lighting was low and the hemlines were high.

Most of the patrons looked like they were on a date or trying to hook up with someone for the evening. Devin Palmer was in neither camp. She sat by herself in a booth at the back of the room, the pulsating beat from the speakers thrumming through her body, eyes fixed firmly on the door. Each time it opened, the new arrivals brought with them a gust of cool March air and more disappointment. None of the faces were the one Devin was hoping to see. She glanced at her Swatch watch for the hundredth time and sighed. An hour late now.

Face it, Devin, you've been stood up. And by your own sister, no less.

Devin and Erika had always been close growing up, what with there being just over a year between them. Best friends, as well as sisters. But things had changed since Erika had left home last summer to go to college in the Valley.

Tonight was supposed to be a chance for them to catch up and reconnect over a couple of drinks. They'd agreed to meet at Mike's as it was nearby the Los Angeles Valley College's main campus and

Erika had a study date after class. She would head to the bar straight from the library as soon as she was free. Devin consulted her wristwatch again with a frown. But her sister shouldn't be *this* late.

Devin's legs turned to Jell-O as she got out of the booth. That would be the two dirty martinis. She wasn't legally old enough to drink alcohol, and usually stuck to light beers when she did, but this was the Valley, not Newbury Park, and all the other women were drinking cocktails. Thankfully, the waitress had barely glanced at Devin, let alone requested to see her fake ID. Hadn't busted her for being underage.

She pushed past the sweaty bodies on the busy dance floor and made her way to the payphone situated next to the restrooms. Pulled a crumpled piece of paper from her purse with the address and phone number of the small apartment Erika shared with her roommates, Cindy and Debbie. Slid some quarters into the slot and punched in the digits.

"Hello?"

The voice on the other end of the line didn't belong to Erika. Devin didn't know if it was Cindy or Debbie. She stuck a finger in her ear to block out Whitney Houston.

"Can I speak to Erika, please? It's Devin."

"Who?"

She had to shout over the thumping beat of the music. "Devin! Her sister!"

"Right, sure. Erika isn't home right now, Devin. She's on a date."

"Yeah, she's supposed to be meeting me at Mike's. She hasn't shown up yet."

"No, I mean a date-date. You know, with Todd. He picked her up earlier."

Heat rushed to Devin's cheeks that had nothing to do with the two cocktails. Tears pricked at her eyes, threatening to ruin the makeup she'd spent a half hour applying. Had Erika forgotten they were meeting tonight? Or had she deliberately blown her off after receiving a better offer? Either way, she'd left Devin on her own, in a packed bar, like the world's biggest loser.

"Hey, Devin?" Cindy or Debbie said. "Are you still there?"

"Um, yeah. I guess I'll catch up with Erika later."

Devin hung up the phone. She was supposed to be crashing at Erika's place tonight. Now what was she supposed to do? She'd only met Cindy and Debbie once before, right after Erika first moved to Van Nuys. Devin returned to the booth, tried to figure out what to do next. The waitress glided past and swooped up her empty glass onto a tray in one smooth motion.

"Same again?" the waitress asked.

Devin hesitated a beat, then said, "Sure."

Why the hell not?

While she waited for the cocktail to be delivered, Devin's gaze drifted around the room and landed on a guy also sitting on his own. He was almost movie-star handsome, mid-twenties, maybe a shade younger. Drinking a beer and so relaxed he could be sitting on his sofa at home. Definitely not a loser who'd been stood up. Probably waiting for his model girlfriend to join him.

Devin's drink arrived and she took a big gulp and watched as a glamorous blonde at the next booth—fueled by vodka and encouraging noises from her girlfriends—sashayed over to the guy with all the confidence of an extra from a Robert Palmer video, before sliding languidly into the seat facing him like she was slipping into bed. A few moments later, she got up and returned to her girlfriends with a slight shake of the head, and padded shoulders that were definitely more slumped than they had been a few moments ago.

The guy locked eyes with Devin and he tilted his head slightly to one side, as though regarding a curious artifact in a museum. She dropped her gaze to her drink. Figured she must look like a total idiot, sitting there all by herself.

She shrugged on her denim jacket, threw some bills on the table to cover the tab, and pushed out of the booth. Cussed under her breath as her brand-new turquoise pantyhose snagged on the wooden seat's rough edge.

Outside, the bite of cold air felt good on her flushed cheeks. It had rained while she'd been in the bar. Oil-slick rainbow puddles pockmarked the parking lot tarmac like little bruises under the glow of the bar's neon sign.

There was no way Devin could drive back home tonight. Her dad would be mad at her for drinking—and mad at Erika for ditching her. There was a road map in the car's side pocket so she could map the route to Erika's apartment, which she knew wasn't too far from Mike's.

She started toward the old Ford Pinto. Behind her, the door opened again and a burst of music briefly shattered the quiet night. Save for the neon sign, the lot was dark, the auto-repair shop and coin laundromat on either side of the bar shuttered for the night, or maybe forever. The heel of her stiletto caught on a pothole and she stumbled, pain tearing through her ankle.

"Whoa, steady there." Strong arms caught her and steadied her before she fell. "Are you okay?"

It was the hot guy from the bar. He was even better-looking up close. Eyes as intensely blue as a gas flame.

"Um, yeah, thanks," Devin said, embarrassed. She disentangled herself from his arms.

"Do you have a ride?" he asked.

Devin gestured to the Pinto. "I'm parked right over there."

The guy frowned. "You think it's a good idea to drive?"

"Sure, I'm fine."

"It's just that you seem a little . . ."

"Drunk?"

He laughed. "I was going to say 'unsteady' but, yeah, drunk."

"I don't have far to go. Delano Street. That's nearby, right?"

"Right." He raised an eyebrow at her. "Doesn't mean you won't get pulled over by a cop on the way though. And I think they'd be a little more interested in how old you are than the bar staff at Mike's."

An image of being driven home in the back of a patrol car flashed through Devin's mind. Her dad would totally freak out.

"Maybe you're right. I should go back inside and call a cab."

"I'm headed in the same direction. I can drop you off, no problem."

Devin was wary. Sure, this guy could totally give Johnny Depp a run for his money in the looks department, but he was still a complete stranger.

"Thanks," she said. "But a cab is fine."

The guy's frown deepened. "I wouldn't feel right leaving you here on your own. And it saves on the cab fare."

He had a point. Those cocktails had been expensive and he did seem real nice. Plus, her ankle hurt and she really just wanted to crash on Erika's sofa with a couple of Advil and a big glass of iced water. "I guess . . . as long as you're sure it's no trouble."

"No trouble at all."

They headed for his truck. Devin climbed gingerly into the passenger seat, her ankle throbbing like a heartbeat. The truck's cab was surprisingly clean and tidy. No fast food wrappers, no clutter in the center console. The air freshener hanging from the rearview mirror smelled of lemons. Devin thought of the twisted lemon-peel garnish in her cocktails and her stomach roiled. Definitely too much booze tonight.

She noticed the guy staring at her pantyhose and her fingers self-consciously brushed the rip in the stretchy fabric. "Snagged them on the booth's seat." She laughed. "I guess it really hasn't been my night."

The guy slammed his door shut, killing the dome light, and turned the key in the ignition. The radio burst into life at top volume. He twisted the knob to reduce it a couple of notches. "That guy's a real jerk, you ask me," he said, backing out of the parking lot.

"What guy?"

"The guy who stood you up."

"Oh, no. I wasn't on a date. I was meeting my sister. I guess she just forgot about me."

"That sucks too."

"Yeah, it does. I'm hoping things will be better between us when I go to college too this year."

"Same school as your sister?"

"That's the plan."

"What're you gonna do there?"

Devin made a face. "Business administration. Not exactly my dream major but everyone says it's important to know about computers and stuff these days."

"That's true. What would you rather do?"

"In an ideal world? I'd love to be an actress. I know, I know. How lame does that sound, huh? But I've performed in a bunch of school plays and it's something I enjoy. It must be so cool to be Winona Ryder or Meg Ryan and appear in all those great movies, and wear gorgeous dresses on the red carpet, and have people wanting to take your photo all the time. For the whole world to know your name. Although, *obviously*, it's all about the craft, not the fame."

The guy smiled in the gloom of the truck's cab. "I'm sure you have real talent. What's your name anyway? You know, in case you do wind up being famous one day."

"Devin. Devin Palmer."

He nodded. "I'll be sure to look out for you in the newspapers."

They drove in silence for a while. The gentle heat blowing through the vents and the rhythmic thrum of the engine were like chewing on a sedative. Devin felt her eyelids begin to droop. Her chin dropped to her chest. She told herself she'd rest her eyes just for a minute . . .

Devin's head snapped back and her eyes flew open. The tree-lined streets and houses were gone. They were on the highway. They shouldn't be on the highway. The warm booze haze was instantly replaced by stone-cold panic.

"Why are we on the highway?" she demanded. "Where are you taking me?"

"Chatsworth," the guy replied calmly.

"*Chatsworth?*" Devin asked in disbelief. "My sister's apartment is in Van Nuys, same as the bar. Why the hell are we going to Chatsworth?"

He glanced at her and grinned. "You like the movies, right? I thought I'd show you something cool."

Devin's head hurt and her stomach felt bad, like she might hurl all over the spotlessly clean truck. "Please, just take me home. I don't feel too good."

"It won't take long, I promise. And it'll be worth it. You'll see."

A half mile later, he flipped the blinker and eased the truck onto an exit ramp.

The chart tunes on the radio gave way to the serious voice of a newscaster with the ten o'clock headlines. The bulletin's top story was an appeal for information after the body of a young woman had been discovered in Stoney Point Park four days earlier. She had been named as Mary Ellen Hardwick, a twenty-one-year-old college student from Canoga Park. The guy reached over and turned off the radio. He made a few more turns then slowed the truck to a stop by the side of the road.

Devin stared out of the window. She saw nothing but the shadowy outlines of hills and rocks and overgrown shrubbery. From the road signs they'd passed, she guessed they were someplace in the rocky foothills of the Santa Susana Mountains.

"You know, this whole area used to be a movie ranch," he said. "One of the most shot-up locations in town. You don't recognize it?"

Devin shook her head.

Seriously? He brought me all the way out here to look at some dumb rocks?

He went on, "They filmed scenes from classics like *The Lives of a Bengal Lancer* and *Wells Fargo* and *The Bride Wore Red* out here."

"Um, I've never heard of them. Sorry."

"I used to watch old Westerns with my dad on Sunday afternoons when I was a kid," the guy said. "It's one of the few memories I have of him."

There was an air of sadness about him as he spoke now, and Devin felt bad for him. "I'm so sorry," she said. "Did your dad pass when you were young?"

"No. He had to go away."

Devin waited for him to elaborate. When he didn't, she said, "Look, I really should be getting back—"

"Let's go get a better look."

Before she could protest, he swung open the driver's-side door and got out of the truck. Pain shot through her busted ankle as Devin jumped down from the cab. She limped after him as he headed toward a towering rock formation.

The wind whipped her hair around her shoulders like wildfire. Her head pounded worse than her ankle, like tomorrow's hangover had arrived early. Even in the twin glow of the truck's full beams, she didn't see anything worth seeing. Just an empty landscape with some twinkling lights off in the distance, probably the mobile-home park they'd passed earlier. Other than the truck, the road was empty, a black ribbon disappearing into the night.

"I really should be getting back now," she said. "Erika will be worried about me."

The guy said nothing. Just stood there with his back to her, as though staring at the mottled hillside. Devin heard a sharp snap, followed by another.

"Did you hear me? I said I want to go home."

He turned around. He had a strange expression on his face. She noticed his hands were unnaturally white. It took a beat for Devin to realize he was wearing latex gloves.

"What the—"

The stranger smiled at her. "Don't worry, Devin. Soon the whole world will know your name. Just like you always wanted."

1

JESSICA—PRESENT DAY

Jessica Shaw puffed warm air into latex gloves as though she were blowing up balloons at a kid's birthday party.

She quickly shoved her hands inside the inflated rubber and slipped a disposable face mask over her nose and mouth. Then she dumped the contents of a stranger's trash bags onto the walkway outside her motel room door and got down onto her knees to inspect the debris.

The garbage belonged to a man by the name of Martin Nelson, a work-from-home financial adviser who lived in Sherman Oaks with his wife of twenty-two years.

Six hours earlier—at around three in the morning, when his street was as dead as a week-old corpse—Jessica had swapped two of the motel's trash bags for the ones inside the garbage cans outside the Nelson property. They'd already been moved to the curb for the early Monday morning collection—meaning, legally, their contents were fair game for Jessica or anyone else. The switcheroo was to avoid arousing suspicion that someone was taking an interest in Martin Nelson.

She'd never met the man, but a month of bird-dogging, as well as three weeks of trash covers—PI lingo for rummaging through other folks' garbage—meant she knew plenty about him. Martin Nelson enjoyed a nice bottle of Chablis at least three times a week, his favorite takeout place was the Cheesecake Factory, he took prescription meds to lower his cholesterol, and he had a very tidy sum stashed away in his savings account (as you would expect from a financial adviser).

Jessica also knew he was having an affair with a woman called Sherry Scott, who was one of his clients. She just needed to prove it. Hopefully she'd hit pay dirt among the garbage this time.

Ignoring the strange looks from other motel guests, she meticulously examined each discarded item. The ancient ice machine clunked and whirred and the late-summer sun beat down on her back. Warm weather was always the worst for this kind of job.

Jessica was halfway through the second bag when she found the golden ticket—or rather Martin Nelson's credit-card statement. A quick scan of the account-holder's name and transactions told her it wasn't the paperwork for the card he shared with Mrs. Nelson.

"Tut-tut, Martin," she murmured to herself. A financial adviser really should know better than to dump paperwork instead of shredding it. The only things likely to be getting shredded now were Nelson's nice suits once his wife had confirmation of his infidelity. Jessica slid the single sheet of paper into a clear Ziploc bag and pulled off the latex gloves. Tugged the face mask down to her chin and tapped out a text to her partner, Matt Connor.

You owe me ten bucks.

He replied almost immediately: No way! What did you find?

Jessica: Credit card statement. For the plastic the wife doesn't know about. Two hotel stays, a hundred bucks' worth of lingerie at Victoria's Secret, and dinner at Lucques on Melrose.

Connor: Damn! I really did think the wife was just being paranoid. Nice work, Shaw.

Jessica: Paranoid? Despite Nelson and Scott showing up at hotels all over West Hollywood within 20 mins of each other for the past month?

Connor: He's a financial adviser. Could've been completely innocent—work meetings in the business suite.

Jessica: Yeah, right. Looks like my gut feeling was correct. I guess I'm getting better at spotting cheating rats.

It was a low blow and Jessica wasn't surprised when he didn't reply. When she'd first started working for Connor, they'd gotten real close before she discovered he had a fiancée he'd conveniently forgotten to mention while he'd been kissing Jessica in a motel pool at midnight.

Jessica had been a fully fledged, card-carrying PI back in New York but still needed to clock up more hours on the job for a California license, so she'd reluctantly agreed to keep working for MAC Investigations. They'd come to an agreement that suited them both. Connor would work out of his Venice Beach office and look after cases in the Westside, while Jessica took care of business in Hollywood and the surrounding areas. It had worked out well enough so far.

Her cell phone lit up with another message from Connor.

I've sent a new client your way. Christine Ryan. She stopped by the agency earlier, wants you to track down a long-lost friend. Nice and simple. She'll meet you at your day office at 11.

Day office. That was one of Connor's little jokes. Jessica didn't have an office. She didn't even have a home, although her peripatetic lifestyle was through choice rather than circumstance.

She'd been staying at the Ace Budget Motel for a while now, which wasn't to be confused with the more famous and much fancier Ace Hotel on Broadway. But it did have a small, well-stocked bar on the premises and a diner right next door which served the best cheeseburgers around. She met with clients at the diner during regular office hours, while the bar served as the after-hours meeting spot.

Jessica heard footsteps approach along the walkway behind her, followed by the sound of someone clearing their throat in the dramatic way folks do when they want your attention, rather than to unblock some phlegm. She turned around on her haunches and raised a hand to her eyes to block out the fireball sun. An older woman was standing there. She was thin, with cropped platinum hair a couple of shades lighter than Jessica's own chin-length peroxide dye job, wearing a sleeveless blouse and wide-leg pants.

"Are you Jessica Shaw?" the woman asked.

"Depends who's asking? If you have cash and you need to find someone, or your husband's been acting suspiciously, I'm your gal. If you're a traveling salesperson, I'm not interested." She glanced at the Nelsons' garbage. "Unless you're selling air freshener, that is."

"The man who works at the diner told me I'd find you here. He said you'd be the one out back sorting through the trash. I thought I'd misheard him. But here you are."

Jessica got up. "And you are?"

"Christine Ryan. Your partner at the detective agency sent me."

"You're an hour early."

"I drove straight here from Venice. Didn't see any point in wasting time."

Jessica nodded slowly. "Fair enough. Let me finish up here and go get cleaned up. Grab yourself a coffee at Dustin's next door and I'll meet you there. Tell Woody to seat you at my usual booth. I won't be long."

She watched Christine Ryan retrace her steps back along the walkway and down the stairs to street level, then snapped on the gloves again and pulled the face mask back into position. She added two more incriminating items to clear plastic bags and deposited the rest of the trash in the motel's dumpster. Then she headed to her room for a quick shower and a change of clothing.

Twenty minutes later, Jessica found Christine Ryan in the back booth at Dustin's cradling a mug of coffee. The table was Jessica's favorite because it provided plenty of privacy for discussing delicate situations, while offering the best view of the restaurant, which was currently empty save for two tourists on the other side of the room.

Old black and white framed photos of Rat Pack stars hung above the counter and, while Jessica seriously doubted the likes of Frank Sinatra and Sammy Davis Jr. had ever frequented Dustin's, if it made the patrons happy believing they were dining with the ghosts of celebrities, who was she to argue?

Woody had bought the place fifteen years ago but was too cheap to replace the buzzy, red neon sign outside or the tired decor inside. He didn't mind having another man's name above the door and Jessica didn't mind the patched-up light blue leatherette seats or the tattered menus or creaking counter stools. It lent Dustin's a certain kind of charm that she liked.

She ordered a late breakfast of pancakes, while Christine declined the offer of food.

"Keep the coffee refills coming," Jessica told Woody. "My body clock is all out of whack, what with these middle-of-the-night trash covers."

"You got it," he said. "Pancakes won't be long." Woody was as bald as a baby with a smile as infectious as a yawn, but he also knew to keep the chat to a minimum when Jessica was working. He made his way to the kitchen with the order.

Christine wrinkled her nose. "Don't you find it disgusting, raking through other peoples' trash?"

Jessica shrugged and swallowed some coffee. "There are worse jobs, believe me. I did most of them while at college. And at least you know I'm thorough." She removed a notepad and pen from her shoulder bag, turned to a fresh page, and clicked the pen in preparation for taking notes. "Tell me about this friend you want me to find."

"Her name is Veronica Lowe," Christine said. "That's Lowe with an 'e' on the end. I haven't seen her in more than fifteen years. Probably closer to twenty. We're the same age, so she'd be forty-six now too."

Jessica tried not to show her surprise. She'd pegged Christine for a decade older. Her pale face was lined and the skin on her neck wrinkled, dark circles standing out like ash smears under tired eyes. Even her perfume was old-fashioned.

Jessica had had a friend at school whose mom always wore Chanel No. 5, and Christine's scent, while not the same, was another one of those classics only worn by women of a certain age. It wasn't to Jessica's personal taste but it was definitely an improvement on the stench of Martin Nelson's trash, that was for sure.

Christine went on, "We'd been best friends since we were babies. Even shared a crib when our moms babysat for each other. We grew up on the same street and did everything together—ballet class as kids, double dates as teenagers. Never out of each other's houses. Pretty much inseparable."

She took some photos from her purse and passed them to Jessica. They were old, their once glossy surfaces dulled to matte by years of fingertip touches. They all featured two little girls. One was fair, the other had red hair. Both were skinny, wearing summer tans and matching outfits, posing and laughing for the camera.

Jessica's pancakes arrived and she poured a generous helping of maple syrup onto the plate while Woody topped off their mugs. She speared a piece of pancake with a fork and popped it in her mouth, and washed it down with black coffee. Waited until Woody was out of earshot before turning her attention back to Christine.

"So, you and Veronica were inseparable as kids but then you lost touch? Why?"

Christine dumped the contents of a sachet of sugar and two plastic creamer containers into her mug. "I guess we just drifted apart. We were in our mid-twenties by then and our lives were moving in different directions. There was no big fight as such, no major falling out. Not really. Sure, there were things we didn't agree on but that had always been the case. One day, I guess we just stopped calling each other."

It was a sad story but Jessica knew how easily it could happen. She hadn't really kept in touch with anyone from her old life in New York, other than her former boss, Larry Lutz.

She wiped her mouth with a paper napkin and swapped the fork for her pen. "Okay, I'll need whatever information you can give me—last-known address, place of work, and so on."

"The last time I saw Veronica, she was doing some waitressing jobs. She was renting an apartment on Micheltorena in Silver Lake. I tried calling her once on the old landline, after coming across those photos of us as kids while clearing out junk for a yard sale. A stranger answered the phone, said Veronica didn't live there anymore. There was no forwarding address. I wondered if maybe it was a sign. It didn't stop me checking Facebook and Instagram over the years but I never came across her."

"What about her family? Would she likely still be in touch with them?"

Christine shook her head. "Veronica's mom passed a few years ago. There was an obituary in the newspaper. She never really knew her dad. He took off when she was three or four. I don't remember him at all."

Jessica put the pen down on the table and met Christine's eye. "I'll do my best to track Veronica down but you do understand that not everyone wants to be found? Some folks from the past want to stay in the past."

"Sure, I get it. She might not want me in her life. I just need to know that she's okay. That she's safe."

"Why now? Why hire a private investigator after all these years?"

"Something happened. Something really bad. And now I'm worried I might not be the only one looking for Veronica."

"What happened? Who else is trying to find her?"

The woman reached into her purse again, this time for a sheet of paper. It was a newspaper article, old and yellowed by age. She pushed it across the table toward Jessica.

"Someone who wants Veronica dead."

2

VERONICA—1999

Veronica was listening to "Everybody Hurts" by REM on repeat when two loud raps on the front door made her start.

It was Saturday night, just past eight, and she wasn't expecting any visitors. Maybe if she ignored whoever was at the door, they'd take the hint and go away.

There was another knock. Louder this time.

Or maybe not.

Veronica sighed and got up from the spot on the couch where she had spent most of the last twenty-four hours wallowing in self-pity and sad songs and Cheetos. She brushed powdery orange crumbs off her pajamas.

There was more banging, like a fist was being used now.

"*Okay*, I'm coming," Veronica muttered.

Maybe it was Allan, come to grovel and beg her to take him back. If so, he'd likely take one look at her and run a mile. She hadn't bothered to shower this morning or get dressed or even brush her teeth. She patted down her lank hair as she padded down the hallway in her fluffy slippers. Peered through the peephole and saw

Christine standing on the landing. Even through the tiny, distorted lens, Veronica could see the impatience on her best friend's face.

She was disappointed it wasn't Allan and that made her disappointed with herself. Veronica tried to convince herself it was only because she wanted an opportunity to shout at him, swear at him, maybe even slap him. Do all the things she should've done in the restaurant last night. But she knew it wasn't true. Knew if Allan wanted her back, she'd probably say yes. She plastered a smile onto her face and opened the door.

"Finally. I thought I was going to have to break the door down." Christine frowned when she caught sight of Veronica in her ratty PJs. "Please tell me you weren't still in bed?"

"Um, no. Just chilling, listening to some music."

Christine narrowed her eyes and cocked an ear in the direction of Michael Stipe's melancholy voice. "Is that REM? Just as I thought—you're not chilling; you're moping. And, if you're going to have a pity party, I figured you might as well have some company."

She had a bottle of white wine in one hand—clearly straight from the liquor store refrigerator, judging by the sweat rolling down the glass—and two DVD cases from Blockbuster Video in the other. She pushed past Veronica into the apartment.

"Come on in," Veronica muttered, closing the door.

She followed Christine into the living room and returned to her spot on the couch, sinking back into the warm ass-shaped dent in the faux leather. She heard her friend rummaging through the drawer by the kitchen sink, followed by the pop of a cork. Christine prided herself on never drinking screw-top wine, claimed it was for winos and college students, even though she never spent more than five bucks on a bottle.

Christine emerged from the small kitchen with a full glass in each hand and set them down on the black glass and chrome coffee table, next to the DVD cases. Veronica didn't even bother to berate her for not using the coasters.

"Scooch over," Christine ordered, dropping down next to Veronica. She kicked off her boots and tucked her feet underneath her. "I can't believe Gray Allan had the nerve to dump you. Tell me everything, sweetie."

"Gray Allan" was Christine's nickname for Veronica's boyfriend—or ex-boyfriend, as he was now—because she claimed he was every bit as boring as the color.

Veronica took a big gulp of Chardonnay. It tasted good and the booze quickly turned her tense muscles to liquid mush. She drank some more and then told Christine what had happened the night before.

"We went out to dinner at Casita Del Campo. You know, the place on Hyperion? Allan said he had something he wanted to discuss and he seemed real nervous. Barely touched his beef tamales, which isn't like him at all because he sure does like his food. I thought he was going to suggest moving in together, what with us dating for almost a year. Then, between the main course and dessert, he told me things weren't working out and we should call it a day."

"Wow, what a jerk-off." Christine shook her head and reached for her wine glass. "Doesn't he realize he was punching well above his weight by bagging someone like you in the first place? It's you who should've been doing the dumping."

Veronica managed a small laugh. "He actually said the words 'It's not you, it's me.' Can you believe it?"

Christine rolled her eyes. "Sadly, I can. What did you say?"

"I told him of course it was him—why on earth would it be me? After all, he's the one who's prematurely balding, still has his mother do his laundry for him, and who has a personality as dull as the gray suits he wears. Hence the nickname 'Gray Allan.'"

Christine looked shocked, then impressed. "No way! Did you really say all that?"

"Of course not." Veronica's shoulders slumped. "It wasn't until I was in the cab home that I thought of all the things I wished I'd said."

"I hate when that happens. What did you actually say?"

"That we should get the check and skip dessert."

"Did he at least pay for the meal?"

Veronica raised an eyebrow. "What do you think?"

Christine made a disapproving sound. "That asshole's wallet is harder to get into than Fort Knox. That's another thing you should add to his list of faults for that fantasy conversation of yours."

They both started laughing and kept on laughing until tears were rolling down their cheeks. Once they'd composed themselves, Veronica said, "Thanks for coming over and cheering me up, Chrissie. God knows I needed it."

"That's what best friends are for, isn't it?" Christine drained her glass and reached for the DVD cases. "Now, what do you fancy watching?"

"What are the options?"

"*Con Air* or *Snake Eyes*. In other words, Nicolas Cage as a convict or Nicolas Cage as a corrupt cop."

Veronica made a face. "Seriously?"

"To be fair, I was trying to avoid the rom-com section. Figured you wouldn't be in the mood for any boy-meets-girl movies or anything with Sandra Bullock in it."

"I don't mind Sandra Bullock."

"No, but I do."

Veronica sighed. "*Con Air* it is then."

"Or," Christine said, a wicked glint in her eye, "if you're in the mood for dangerous men, I have another suggestion for tonight's entertainment."

"Uh-huh?"

Christine fished in her purse and pulled out a cheap-looking booklet with glossy pages. The words "The Lonely Hearts Club" were emblazoned in big black letters above a garish, red love heart, which, inexplicably, had a set of handcuffs across the front.

Veronica groaned. "No way am I signing up for a dating agency. And definitely not one for kinky weirdos."

"It's not a dating agency," Christine protested. "Well, okay, it kinda is. But there's one big difference. All of these men are in prison. Isn't that fantastic?"

Veronica stared at her incredulously. "Have you lost your mind? Please tell me you're kidding?"

"Nope." Christine tossed the booklet at Veronica. "Have a look while I go grab some more wine. And, for God's sake, change that sad-ass music to something more upbeat before I stab myself with the corkscrew."

Veronica got up and swapped REM for a No Doubt CD. She returned to the couch and picked up the booklet, licked her finger, and flicked through the pages. Sure enough, they were filled with photographs of convicted criminals.

Some of the scanned pictures had apparently been taken prior to incarceration, while the clothing and backdrop in others suggested those ones had been captured inside the prison walls. Each image was accompanied by a reference number, incarceration and expected release dates, crime(s) committed, star sign, age, and a paragraph about hobbies and interests. Some had been circled with a ballpoint pen, presumably the ones that had caught Christine's eye.

Christine emerged from the kitchen with the bottle of wine and refilled their glasses.

"You aren't seriously planning on writing these guys?" Veronica asked.

"Sure I am. Why not?"

Veronica read aloud the details of one of the circled profiles. "Clay is a Leo who's serving a ten-to-twelve-year sentence for the distribution of narcotics. He's now found God and yoga, and would like to connect with a woman with a big heart."

Christine sipped some Chardonnay. "Admittedly, a ten-year stretch does require a certain degree of commitment that I don't possess but he isn't looking for anything serious. It says so right there on his profile."

"Just so long as Clay isn't expecting a serious relationship, then I guess that's fine."

"Sarcasm doesn't suit you, sweetie. Now drink your wine and listen while I tell you how it all works."

Veronica bit back a smile. "Okay, go ahead."

"So, the men pay a fee in order to be listed in the brochure. The cash supposedly goes toward helping to rehabilitate prisoners upon their release although I suspect the founder, a Southern broad by the name of Bibi Durrant, pockets the lot. The men can write you directly or, if you don't want to give out your home address, you can also pay a small fee for all of your correspondence to go through The Lonely Hearts Club's own PO box, so the guys don't ever have to know where you live.

"In other words, you get all the danger and excitement of writing a guy in prison, without having to worry about him showing up on your doorstep when he gets paroled. There are also 'socials' where you can meet up with other 'Lonely Hearts' for lunch, drinks, and to swap tips and hints on being a prison bride. Yep, some of them end up marrying their pen pals!"

"Are we really that desperate, Chrissie? Sure, the talent at the bars on Sunset isn't always the best—but convicts?"

"It's just a bit of fun, Vee. Where's the harm in it?"

"I guess," Veronica said doubtfully.

Christine was on a roll now. "Pen pals are encouraged to send a photo of themselves. Not Polaroids though—for some reason those are banned." She pulled a single-use camera from her purse. "I *was* going to suggest we take some pics of each other tonight but . . ."

"But what?"

"Please don't take this the wrong way, sweetie, but I think you need a shower and some makeup before I let you anywhere near a camera. Even the biggest desperado in Lompoc likely wouldn't respond to you looking the way you do right now."

Veronica eyed her friend. Christine was wearing bootcut jeans slung low on the hips, and a tight satin and lace camisole. Burgundy lipstick and matching lip liner, and her blonde hair teased into loose curls. "I did wonder why you were all dressed up for a girls' night in. I guess I could go and . . ." Her words trailed off as one of the photos caught her eye. The guy was in his early thirties and had the most intense blue eyes, which seemed to jump right off the page despite the poor quality of the scanned picture.

"What? What is it?" Christine craned her neck to see what Veronica was staring at.

"What about this guy? He's gorgeous. Looks like a movie star." Veronica held up the page for Christine to see, her finger tapping the photo.

Christine snorted. "Travis Dean Ford? Yeah, right. That's like sending fan mail to Matthew McConaughey and expecting a response. Travis Dean Ford is famous. Or infamous. You do know he strangled, like, fifteen women, don't you?"

"He doesn't look like a murderer."

"They never do, sweetheart."

Veronica couldn't tear her eyes away from the photo. Travis Dean Ford. A weird kind of electricity flowed through her veins, way more intoxicating than the cheap white wine. "It's like you said, Chrissie. It's just a bit of fun. What's the worst that could happen? He doesn't write me back?"

When her friend didn't immediately respond, Veronica glanced up from the page. Christine was frowning, and Christine hardly ever frowned because it led to premature wrinkles.

"What?" Veronica asked.

"Maybe he *would* write you back. And I'm not sure that's such a good thing."

"Why?"

"I remember reading an article about this guy after they finally caught him," Christine said, her tone unusually serious. "His victims were all slim, with long red hair and fair skin. You're just his type, Vee."

3

JESSICA

"Why would someone want Veronica dead?" Jessica asked.

"Read the article," Christine said.

Jessica picked up the old newspaper cutting. Other than the discoloration and a single crease where it had been folded in half, it was in good condition. No rips or tears or smudges, not tattered in any way like the menus at Dustin's, as though it had been carefully preserved in a photo album or between the pages of a book for a long time.

Jessica found the date in the corner of the page and quickly did the math. The article was from seventeen years ago. It was prominently illustrated with a photo of a very attractive man in his thirties, who was sitting alongside a pretty, younger woman. A cute toddler wearing honey-blonde bunches and a princess dress was between the couple, smiling shyly for the camera.

Just a normal family photo. Except it wasn't.

The man was wearing prison scrubs and the backdrop wasn't a park or a restaurant or a backyard. It was the plain cinderblock wall of a cold and impersonal visiting room. Jessica had visited with a Death Row inmate at the women's prison in Chowchilla a while back and it had been a daunting experience.

The little girl was clearly far too young to have any real appreciation for where she was but the woman, slim with long center-parted red hair and an easy smile, seemed pretty relaxed in the institutional surroundings, as though she were no stranger to that kind of environment.

The headline above the photo was big and bold and provocative: "PICTURE EXCLUSIVE! VALLEY STRANGLER ENJOYS FAMILY TIME ON DEATH ROW WITH 'SECRET LOVECHILD.'"

Jessica read the photograph's caption and felt a jolt of surprise when she realized who the people in the photograph were.

"Serial killer Travis Dean Ford enjoys a visit from his lover Veronica Low and 'daughter Mia.'"

Jessica was vaguely aware of the name Travis Dean Ford, in the same way she was vaguely aware of the names Ted Bundy and Son of Sam and Jeffrey Dahmer. She knew, like the others, Ford was a notorious serial killer, but that was as far as her knowledge went. She didn't know how many times Ford had killed or who his victims were or how and when he had been apprehended. And she didn't really want to know.

She saw enough of the dark side of humanity in her job without inviting it into her downtime. She didn't watch true-crime documentaries or listen to podcasts or even read crime novels. If she wanted to chill out, she'd do it with some good Scotch and *Friends* reruns.

Jessica noted that Veronica's surname had been spelled incorrectly, while the use of quotation marks around the words "secret lovechild" and "daughter Mia" meant the newspaper had likely been unable to verify that the child in the photo was, indeed, Ford's daughter. She wondered if what the newspaper was claiming was even true.

"Is this right?" she asked, glancing up from the page. "Veronica had a child with this Travis Dean Ford guy?"

Christine nodded curtly in confirmation, her mouth set in a tight line of disapproval. "No doubt about it. The little girl was the spitting image of her daddy. Same bright blue eyes."

Jessica could see what Christine meant. She read on. There wasn't a whole lot of detail in the piece, just the basics about Ford and his crimes and what little the newspaper knew about Veronica and Mia. Only that the mother was a waitress from Silver Lake. It was clear the photograph was the main draw for their readers.

It had been taken at San Quentin, where Ford was being held on Death Row for the murders of fifteen women between 1988 and 1993 in the Valley area of Los Angeles. The women were aged between eighteen and twenty-five and all had been strangled with their own undergarments—pantyhose, stockings, or bras—which led to him being dubbed the "Valley Strangler" by the media. Ford's reign of terror finally came to an end when would-be victim number sixteen managed to escape from his vehicle and alert the police.

According to the newspaper's "source," Veronica and Ford initially began exchanging letters, before she started making occasional visits to the state prison north of San Francisco. It was not known how Ford and Veronica were able to conceive a child together while he was on Death Row. The story ended with a quote from the father of one of the victims expressing outrage that the killer was "enjoying family time" with his young child, while the man's own daughter had been brutally taken from him at the hands of Ford.

"What happened to Mia?" Jessica asked.

"She's missing too," Christine said. "She vanished along with Veronica."

"She'd be, what, eighteen or nineteen now?"

"That's right."

Jessica sighed. She thought of Connor's text. So much for a nice, simple case. A long-lost friend was one thing; the missing lover and daughter of a serial killer was something else entirely.

She guessed the woman might have gone off-grid with the kid through choice. That she didn't want to be found back then when her private life became very public property, and she probably didn't want to be found now if they'd managed to carve out a new life together. A new life someplace away from the intrusive glare of the unforgiving public eye and the hurt and anger of Ford's victims' families—like Lou Hardwick, the man quoted in the story. But it didn't explain Christine's sudden concern for her friend—unless Ford had somehow secured his release from prison recently and was now a threat to the family he apparently hadn't seen for years.

"Did Ford get out? Do you think he's looking for Veronica and Mia? That he's out to hurt them?"

Christine shook her head. "No. Ford is dead. He was executed in 2006."

Jessica frowned. "This all happened a long time ago, Christine. Why would Veronica be in danger now?"

"That article was just to provide a bit of context, some background on what was going on in Veronica's life back then. There's something else you need to see."

The woman picked up her cell phone from where it had been sitting on the table next to her coffee mug. She tapped the screen to activate it and pulled up a web page, then slid the phone across the table to Jessica.

"I have Google alerts set up for Veronica and Mia, as well as Travis Dean Ford," Christine explained. "I got the alert late last night, just as I was getting ready for bed. I've barely slept all night."

The phone's display showed another article, this one from an online news site. Today's date was next to the reporter's byline and a time stamp showed the story had gone live shortly after midnight. There was another big, splashy headline: "MURDER PROBE LAUNCHED AS 'VALLEY STRANGLER' WIDOW FOUND DEAD AT HOME." The sub-heading underneath read: "Cops are treating the death of author and activist Jordana Ford as homicide."

Jessica picked up the phone and scrolled through the story, while trying to ignore the annoying animated pop-up ads for hand-guns and funerals. There were two photos. The first was Jordana Ford at a book-signing event, smiling over a bundle of hardcovers. Her age was given as fifty-three and she had clearly looked after herself. She wore lots of makeup and her dark hair was profession-ally styled. Freshly manicured nails rested on the books. The other photo showed a modest, but pretty, villa cordoned off by crime-scene tape.

According to the report, the woman's body had been discov-ered at her home on Morello Drive yesterday morning. The cause of death was unconfirmed at this time but was believed to be sus-picious. There had been a large police presence at the property throughout the day. Jordana lived alone and had no children. She had married serial killer Travis Dean Ford in a prison wedding in 2003, just three years before the so-called Valley Strangler was executed at San Quentin where he had been on Death Row for thirteen years.

Ford's wife had been a long-time advocate of his innocence and a passionate voice against capital punishment, and something of a controversial figure. She was the author of several books and regularly appeared in the media and on true-crime documenta-ries. Her latest book, *Lockdown Love: A Death Row Romance*, had just been published. The homicide investigation was being led by Detective Jason Pryce from Hollywood Division. The LAPD had been contacted for comment.

Jessica's hand froze above the phone's display.

"Pryce?"

She didn't realize she'd even spoken his name out loud until Christine answered her.

"Yes, the detective is how I found out about you."

Pryce had once been the best friend of Jessica's father but she had only gotten to know the cop a couple of years after Tony died of a massive heart attack, and following her move to LA from New York. He was one of the few friends she had here, along with his wife, Angie, and daughter, Dionne. Pryce had also saved Jessica's life not so long ago, so there was that too.

Jessica stared at Christine. "What do you mean, 'found out about' me?"

"When I read about Jordana's murder, I knew I had to find Veronica but I didn't have the first clue where to start. I guess it's possible Jordana's death had nothing to do with her relationship with Ford, but what if it did? What if Veronica is in danger too? When I tapped on the 'related stories' links, as well as older articles about Ford, there was one about Detective Pryce and you; about a case in Eagle Rock you were both involved in a while back. When I read that you were a private investigator, I figured maybe that's exactly what I needed to track down Veronica. I found the address of the agency where you work and drove down to Venice first thing this morning."

"And you think the person who murdered Jordana could come after Veronica next?"

"That's what I'm worried about. They were both involved with Ford and they both met him through The Lonely Hearts Club."

"The Lonely Hearts Club?"

"It's a pen-pal service for women who want to write men in prison. Veronica and I were both members in the late nineties. Jordana was too."

Jessica still thought it was a bit of a leap. Okay, both women had been in a relationship with Travis Dean Ford but that's where the similarities ended. Jordana sounded like someone who had craved the spotlight, whereas Veronica appeared to have done all she could to avoid it for almost two decades.

Christine picked up on Jessica's doubts. "Look, I know I'm probably worrying about nothing. What happened to Jordana could have been the result of a burglary gone wrong or a domestic dispute or a hundred other different things. But it's better to be safe than sorry and I know I'll sleep better knowing Veronica is okay. What do I have to lose? Best-case scenario, I spend a few bucks on a PI, everything is fine, and I get my best friend back."

Again, Jessica thought of Connor's text. *Nice and simple.* Yeah, right. As well as two possible missing persons connected to a notorious serial killer, she now had a homicide and Pryce thrown into the mix.

"Would you excuse me for a moment while I step outside and make a call?" Jessica said.

"Of course."

Jessica returned Christine's cell phone, grabbed her shoulder bag, and slipped out of the booth. She signaled to Woody to refill their coffee mugs as she headed past the tourists on her way to the front door. At least, she hoped they were tourists. Both women were middle-aged and wearing matching Mickey Mouse ears and t-shirts.

Jessica stepped outside. The traffic trundled past noisily on Sunset. Across the street, there were lines outside the Hollywood tours ticket place and the payday loans shop. The fantasy and the harsh reality of Tinseltown right there, on a single block, squatting side by side.

Jessica fished in her bag for her pack of Marlboros and a lighter, and lit a cigarette. She pulled up the recent calls on her cell phone and tapped on a contact. As she waited for the call to connect, she turned and looked in the window of Dustin's. Christine was staring straight ahead at the wall behind where Jessica had been sitting. Not texting or scrolling through her phone or even drinking the coffee Woody had topped off.

"Pryce."

"Why do you always do that?"

"Do what?"

"Answer the phone like you don't know it's me who's calling even though my name flashes up on the screen?"

"It could be a concerned passerby using the cell of a crazy lady who's gotten herself into trouble. Again."

"Good point," Jessica laughed.

"Is this a social call?"

"Nope."

"Didn't think so. What's up?"

"I'm looking for some advice on whether or not to take on a new client. I'm with her just now."

"Okay. What's the problem?"

"Are you working a homicide case? A woman by the name of Jordana Ford?"

There was a surprised silence. Then Pryce said, "I am. How did you know about Jordana Ford?"

"The story is online."

"Already? Shit."

"I'm afraid so. Bad news travels fast. The thing is, this potential client wants me to find someone. Veronica Lowe. She's an old girlfriend of Travis Dean Ford and had a kid with him while he was on Death Row. The friend is worried Veronica could be in danger too."

"Has this Veronica woman been threatened?" Pryce asked. "Is she concerned for her safety? If so, she should go to the police."

"No, she's been off-grid for more than fifteen years. The friend—her name is Christine Ryan—lost touch with her and wants me to find her. That's the job. She read the story about

Jordana's murder and now she's worried about Veronica. They both got involved with Ford through some prison pen-pal service called The Lonely Hearts Club."

"Was Veronica Lowe reported missing back then?"

"I'd need to check but I don't think so. My guess is she chose to go off-grid with the kid because of some publicity about her and Ford at the time. The thing is, I don't know if Jordana's murder even had anything to do with her being Ford's widow or if it was a random attack."

"You know I can't go into details about the case, Jessica. But . . ."

"But?" Jessica prompted.

Pryce sighed. "Yes, we have reason to believe Jordana was targeted because of her marriage to Ford."

"Shit. Do I take the case or not?"

Pryce was silent a moment. "Take the case," he said finally. "And keep me posted on Veronica Lowe."

"You got it."

She ended the call. The line for payday loans was now longer than the one for the tours. Inside Dustin's, Christine was still staring at the wall. Jessica thought about Pryce's words.

Targeted because of her marriage to Ford.

Jessica had considered the possibility that Veronica had chosen to disappear all those years ago. Now she wasn't so sure. She stubbed out the cigarette and returned to the diner.

4

JESSICA

Once the paperwork had been completed, and Christine had ponied up the retainer, Jessica returned to her motel room and set about putting together a makeshift evidence board for the new case.

This wasn't nearly as impressive as it sounded and mostly involved propping a piece of sturdy cardboard on top of the dresser.

It was the kind of thing you could purchase for a few bucks at Staples for a school project but it did the trick all the same. It had to be foldable so that Jessica could easily dismantle it and lock it in her suitcase whenever she left the room. It wasn't so much that she didn't trust Marie, the housekeeper, not to snoop when changing the bed sheets or emptying the trash—and good luck to anyone deciphering Jessica's crazy, looping handwriting in any case. It just didn't feel right, having folks' personal information on show for anyone other than Jessica to see, so her evidence board had to be mobile.

At the top of the new board, she pinned a photo of Veronica Lowe. Christine Ryan had offered up two photographs before leaving the diner. One had been taken at Veronica's 21st birthday celebrations and the other on holiday when she was twenty-four, according to the dates and locations written on the back. Jessica had returned the birthday snap, held onto the most recent photo, and had made several copies on her printer.

The photo showed Veronica in a big sunhat and a colorful swimsuit. A burst of freckles stood out across the bridge of her nose, as bright as a neon sign. She held an elaborate cocktail in a curvy glass with lots of crushed ice and fruit and a paper umbrella. She was slim and pale-skinned, with very light blue eyes and long, straight red hair.

Jessica also added photos of Mia and Travis Dean Ford to the board. The former was a cropped version of the one from the newspaper article; the latter was printed from a Google Images search that had produced hundreds of results.

Under each photo, she wrote their respective names and DOBs with a Sharpie. For Veronica and Mia, she added an estimated date of disappearance, as well as the age they'd have been then and now. In Ford's case, she wrote his age at time of death and the date of his execution by lethal injection.

Jessica stepped back and looked at the board. It wasn't much to go on.

Before getting down to some serious work, she opened the front door to let fresh air into the motel room—or as fresh as you could get in LA. She heard the rumble of traffic on Sunset and splashing in the motel's pool in the courtyard below, and the muffled drone of Marie's vacuum cleaner in another room. The collective noise soothed Jessica. It was one of the reasons she'd decided to make a motel on a busy thoroughfare her temporary home. Silence set her on edge and unnerved her.

She settled into an uncomfortable high-backed chair at an old wooden desk scarred by cigarette burns that looked like they'd been made both before and after guests were allowed to smoke in the room. A tap of the space bar sparked her laptop into life and she brought up a bunch of searchable databases that were usually the starting point when trying to locate a missing person.

Christine had mentioned an apartment on Micheltorena in Silver Lake where Veronica had lived in the mid to late '90s. Her driver's license had subsequently been registered to an address on Beverly Boulevard in Larchmont and had never been renewed after expiring in 2003.

Jessica compared the date when the address had been updated on the DMV's system with the date of the newspaper article with the photo of Veronica and Mia with Ford in prison, and frowned. Veronica *had* ditched the Silver Lake apartment soon after the article was published—but she hadn't gone off the radar at that point as Jessica had initially suspected.

Instead, she had moved on to Beverly Boulevard.

Jessica sat back in the chair and ran her hands through her hair. Outside, the vacuum was getting louder as Marie worked her way through the rooms. What had happened to make Veronica and Mia vanish into thin air? Not the family prison photo that had appeared in the press, that was for sure.

Jessica tried a bunch of other searches but couldn't find a more recent address anywhere for Veronica Lowe. She pulled up a telephone database and found a handful of listings for the apartment block in Larchmont for residents who still had a landline connected. There were no individual apartment numbers and none of the names listed was "Lowe." Jessica didn't hold out much hope that Veronica would be on the other end of any of those numbers but she had to give it a shot at least.

A couple of residents didn't pick up and the ones who did had never heard of Veronica Lowe. Either it wasn't a particularly friendly neighborhood or she was long gone.

Jessica got up and went over to the evidence board and added the Beverly Boulevard address underneath Veronica's name. She would have to go knock on some doors before eliminating it completely but, before she even set foot outside her motel room, she'd need to run Veronica's details through the death file. There was no point pounding any sidewalks if the woman was six feet under at the local cemetery.

The Social Security Administration's Death Master File was the one database Jessica always hoped would fail to produce a hit because she'd always prefer to find a missing person alive rather than dead. Sure, it would make her job easier in terms of legwork but it was never the news you wanted to deliver to a client.

Thankfully, there was no death data for Veronica Lowe or Mia Ford. Neither were listed on the DMF.

A trawl through online newspaper articles for unidentified dead bodies matching the descriptions of either mom or daughter also drew a blank. Ditto the Doe Network and the Charley Project and everyplace else Jessica could think of to look. If Veronica was dead, her death wasn't official as far as public records were concerned. If she was missing, no one, other than Christine Ryan, had tried too hard to find her through the usual channels.

Jessica rolled her shoulders and neck, the knots of tension crunching like a pretzel under a boot. She got up from the desk and locked the room door behind her, and made her way along the walkway and downstairs to the soda machine.

Young families fooled around noisily in the pool and old folk sat on plastic chairs quietly smoking cigarettes under a dirty blue sky. The end of summer was fast approaching but there was still a lot of heat in the air.

Jessica fed some quarters into the slot and crossed her fingers. It was fifty-fifty whether a trip to the front desk would be required to rescue a jammed soda bottle or packet of chips. She fist-pumped the air triumphantly when an ice-cold bottle of Dr. Pepper thunked into the bin. It must be her lucky day.

She went back upstairs and leaned on the walkway railing outside her room, and shook out a cigarette and smoked and drank her soda.

The motel would be cheerfully described as "no frills" on its website if it had one, its two stars proudly displayed on the outside of the building as though they were Michelin stars instead. The place might be basic but it was clean and well-maintained and run with care. The railing she rested against now was surprisingly ornate and the white paintwork was fresh. More importantly, the after-dark lighting outside her room worked a treat and came on at eight every night like clockwork.

When she'd first checked into the Ace Budget Motel weeks ago, Jessica had insisted on a room on the upper level, right in the middle of the walkway. That way, no one could get in through the bathroom window at the rear of the building and any attempts to access her room through the front door or window could potentially be witnessed by any one of two-dozen other guests whose rooms all faced into the same courtyard.

The desk clerk had been bemused by her demands but it meant less chance of an unwanted visitor in the middle of the night. Jessica had been in that movie before and wasn't keen on a repeat viewing of the scene where she woke up to find a man in a ski mask pointing a gun at her.

Jessica's back pocket vibrated and she placed the soda at her feet and pulled out her cell. It was Connor. She swiped to answer.

"Hey," she said, through a haze of cigarette smoke.

"Hey yourself. How was the meeting with Christine Ryan?"

"Surprising."

"Really? In what way?"

"In the way that I was expecting a long-lost friend case. Nice and simple. That's what you said, right? Turns out, not so nice and simple."

Connor groaned. "Ah, shit. What happened?"

"Let me see . . . our misper was in a relationship with a famous serial killer, somehow managed to conceive a child with him while he was on Death Row, then vanished without a trace along with the kid years ago. Oh, and his widow has just been murdered and Pryce is lead on the homicide. How's that for surprising?"

"Jeez. You took on the case though?"

"Sure. You know me, I'm all about the adventure."

"And you charged her extra for a more complex investigation?"

"Of course. Don't worry, you'll eat this month."

"Who's the serial killer?"

"Travis Dean Ford."

Connor whistled. "Damn."

"My thoughts exactly."

Jessica pinched the end of the cigarette and tucked the Dr. Pepper under her arm. Went back into the motel room and dropped the dead butt into the toilet bowl and flushed.

"Jesus," Connor said. "You're not on the throne, are you?"

"Nope. Just disposing of the evidence."

Connor sighed. "Still smoking, huh? What about those patches I got for you?"

"I flushed those too."

Another sigh. "So, you're good to go on the case? No problem with it?"

"Apart from all of the above?"

Connor didn't bother trying to hide the amusement in his voice. "Let me get this straight, you're pretending to be pissed because your long-lost friend case suddenly became a lot more interesting than a simple ten-minute database search or scroll through Facebook? Don't give me that pouting shit. Admit it, you're in your element."

Jessica suppressed a smile, even though Connor couldn't see it. He was right. "I guess it does beat background checks and insurance claims," she admitted, grudgingly.

"Exactly! I'm a little jealous, truth be told. If you need an extra pair of hands, I could help out. I'm pretty quiet right now as it happens."

"Back off, Connor. This one's all mine."

Connor laughed. "You got it, Shaw. Let me know if you change your mind and you do need a wingman."

Jessica's smile disappeared. Connor had recently taken to calling her Shaw, as though she were his buddy, one of the boys. She figured that was exactly the point he was trying to make. They were friends—and that's all they would ever be. They still worked cases together occasionally, when there was a lot of legwork involved or tag-team surveillance was required. Sometimes they hung out together after work too. A bite to eat or catching the game in a bar. But only when his fiancée Rae-Lynn was at work.

Then, a couple of weeks ago, Jessica had done something really dumb. She'd only met the woman once before and had wanted another look at her. It'd been spur of the moment, her curiosity getting the better of her. Big mistake. So far, she didn't think Rae-Lynn had reported back to Connor. If she had, he hadn't mentioned it.

Jessica said goodbye to Connor and turned her attention back to Travis Dean Ford. She studied a photo montage of his fifteen victims on the laptop screen. Memorized their names and their stories. They had all been young, slim, pretty redheads. Jessica glanced at the photo of Veronica on the DIY evidence board. The women Ford had murdered all bore a startling resemblance to the one he had chosen to have a child with. If that wasn't very fucking weird, then Jessica didn't know what was.

A tap of the keyboard replaced the gallery of victims with a big, full-color photo of the man who had prematurely snuffed out their lives. Ford had been good-looking, no doubt about it. Some people were just undeniably attractive and there was no debating the fact. No "They're not really my type" or "I don't see the attraction myself." They had that elusive X factor you couldn't fake or acquire. Something you were born with. Like Cary Grant or Audrey Hepburn or Angelina Jolie or Paul Newman. Ford had it. Connor did too, although Jessica would rather punch herself in the face than tell him as much.

The difference with Ford was that he was a convicted killer, which made his many fans, stalkers, groupies—whatever you wanted to call them—certified loonballs in Jessica's book.

She swapped the photo for his Wikipedia page, which made for interesting reading, especially the section on his family background. It seemed like murder ran in the Ford family.

Back in '72, Corbin J. Ford (what the "J" stood for remained a bigger mystery than his actual crime) was jailed for the rape and murder of Shelley Purcell, a twenty-six-year-old woman he'd met in a bar in the desert city of Lancaster.

Her body had been discovered in scrubland not far from the bar the next day. A few hours later, Corbin J. Ford was found in a nearby motel, her blood still on his knuckles from where he'd beaten her to death. The old black and white photos showed the victim to be slim and pretty. The newspaper reports filled in the blanks: Purcell had been a natural redhead with fair skin.

Like father, like son.

Nature versus nurture.

It was the kind of stuff psychologists had wet dreams about. And, sure enough, a quick peek on Amazon confirmed at least ten books had been written on the subject by so-called professionally qualified therapists, most of whom also had regular slots on daytime TV shows. Pages and pages devoted to speculation about whether Travis Dean Ford had been born a killer or had become one as a result of his father's incarceration. Ford Senior had died in prison courtesy of a fellow inmate's illegal shank before his son had even hit puberty.

The thing that intrigued Jessica most about this case, however, was Mia Ford. Another fascinating branch of a warped family tree.

She'd be a young woman now and almost certainly living under a different name to the one she'd been born with. Did she know who her father was? Did she have any idea about her backstory? Or was she like Jessica? Living a lie? No idea who she really was? Jessica had grown up unaware that she was the daughter of a murder victim. Until recently, she'd believed her mother had died in a car accident when Jessica was a baby. The truth was far more sinister. Jessica's biological mom, a woman by the name of Eleanor Lavelle, had been brutally killed in her own home. Jessica was a toddler at the time and had been abducted the same night. It had taken twenty-five years for the truth to finally come out. Now she wondered—had Mia Ford grown up not knowing she was the daughter of a murderer?

Jessica wasn't the only one intrigued by the little girl in the prison photo. Not by a long way. There were dozens of Reddit threads and theories and plenty of online articles. "Where is Mia Ford Today?" "What Happened to Travis Dean Ford's Secret Daughter?" "TikTok Teen Claims to Be Ford's Girl." Jessica had never used the social networking platform but she was pretty sure the "TikTok Teen" wasn't Mia Ford. One clickbait headline declared "Everything We Know about Mia Ford" and Jessica succumbed to temptation only to be disappointed when it became obvious they didn't know shit about Mia Ford.

The printer rattled and whirred and spat out pages for Jessica to add to her evidence board. Looping arrows made connections between people and places, names were highlighted in neon yellow and pink, lists of potential interviewees and places to visit were drawn up. Her belly rumbled and she silenced the growl of hunger with bags of chips and another Dr. Pepper from the machine downstairs, which was, miraculously, still playing ball.

Then she turned her attention to The Lonely Hearts Club.

Back when Christine and Veronica and Jordana had dabbled, new members were recruited through personal ads in the back of local newspapers. Prisoner profiles were printed up in booklets and mailed out to those who responded to the ads. Payment checks and most of the correspondence between inmates and TLHC members were sent to a PO box in Culver City. All very retro.

These days, it was all online. Profiles, photographs, forums, advice, message boards—they were all right there on TLHC's snazzy website, with its animated heart and handcuffs logo and newsletter sign-up pop-up. You could still write a prisoner via snail mail if you were old-school or favored the personal touch, but many inmates also had access to email via the likes of JPay—a company offering corrections-related services, such as money transfer, email, and video visitation.

Jessica was still having a hard time understanding why anyone would turn to correctional institutions to find the next great love of their lives, or even just friendship. A half hour later, it was a little clearer. According to academic research cited by TLHC, prisoners who established, and maintained, positive contacts outside of prison were less likely to reoffend upon release. A lot of the inmates were into fitness or education, a surprising number claimed to write or read poetry, and many just wanted some sort of contact with the outside world after being deserted by friends and family.

Some of the profiles tugged at her heartstrings:

Jamil Tooles, 41, CA: "I did some bad stuff but that doesn't mean I'm a bad person. I still got a lot to offer. I want a life outside these prison walls with someone who

can help me be the best individual I can be. I want some-
thing to show for my life other than a DOC number."

Robert Brewer, 28, TX: "Please don't judge me on the
mistakes I made. Judge me on the person I want to be. I
just want to bring a smile to someone's face, brighten up
their day, and have them do the same for me."

Jenni Voight, 46, FL: "I'm funny and open-minded and
I like to read romance novels. If you know how to treat a
woman right, please shoot me a letter or email."

Jessica could empathize with Jenni Voight, who'd probably had shit luck with men in the past. After all, her own previous relationships had sucked big-time, a depressing mix of not available enough (the cheaters) and too available (the stalkers). She also had a lot of sympathy for Jamil and Robert too.

But what about the victims? After all, there weren't many victimless crimes that landed you in jail. The sweet spot between rehabilitation and punishment was a tricky one and Jessica didn't envy the lawmakers whose job it was to strike that balance.

Then there was the likes of Travis Dean Ford. A career killer. No mistakes there. Apart from the ones that had landed him on Death Row.

Jessica clicked on the website's "About" tab. The Lonely Hearts Club had been founded in 1990 by a woman called Bibi Durrant, whose own husband was in jail for murder.

Bibi was a salty-looking fifty-something with dark hair backcombed high on the crown and a plaid shirt with enough buttons undone to create a plunging neckline as deep as a valley and offering a teasing hint of ample bosom. She was smiling in the photo

46

but Jessica thought there was a "don't fuck with me" edge to the smile.

The big difference between Bibi and the rest of the Lonely Hearts was that she'd known Denis "Doc" Durrant before his incarceration.

They'd been high-school sweethearts back in Arizona, before he moved to California. Then he'd shot a liquor store owner during a robbery that went bad in 'Frisco and Bibi had started writing him in prison at San Quentin. That's where the idea for TLHC came from, after Doc told her mail call was often the hardest part of the day for the guys with no one to write. Bibi had then upped and left Arizona for Los Angeles when Doc Durrant was transferred to Lompoc a couple decades ago.

Jessica added Bibi Durrant to the list of people she wanted to speak to. Then she glanced at the photo of Veronica Lowe in the sunhat and swimsuit on the evidence board.

It was time to go pound some pavements.

5

JESSICA

Veronica Lowe's last-known address was a ten-minute drive from Jessica's motel. East along Sunset, dropping south onto Cahuenga, and then a short hop along Beverly. They'd practically be neighbors if the woman still lived there. Jessica didn't hold out much hope.

The building was in the heart of a residential area alongside a ton of other apartment blocks. Many were shiny and modern and clearly thrown up in the last decade. This one was older, a three-story jaundiced rectangle with a distinct 1970s feel. Each apartment had a covered patio or balcony, accessed via a sliding door, with apparently not much to look at apart from other folks' homes. There was gated underground parking and some effort had been made to prettify the entrance with a giant banana palm and some shrubs in a small, well-tended landscaped area.

Next to the building stood a vacant plot of land, fenced off by graffiti-tagged boards, that likely wouldn't stay vacant for long in this neighborhood. A green metal bus bench sat in front of the plot, displaying an ad for a criminal-defense lawyer.

Jessica circled the block before finding a parking space on a side street around the corner. She strolled around to the front entrance on Beverly and climbed the stone steps to the door and noticed a panel of buzzers to the side. Not ideal. She tried the door anyway but, as expected, it was locked. She had three options: Wait for someone to exit or enter the building, which could take a while. Hit random buzzers and claim to be a FedEx delivery and hope the resident who provided access then didn't appear at their door expecting a package. Or—she produced her picklock set from her bag—her preferred option.

Jessica casually gazed around. Road traffic was steady but foot traffic was almost non-existent, other than a lone jogger who huffed past without a glance in her direction. Ten seconds later, there was a satisfying click and she was in.

The lobby was dim after the glare of the sun, with exposed brick walls and brown painted panels and industrial carpeting that smelled of floral Carpet Fresh. There were a lot of potted plants, and a stairwell to the right, and a bank of metal mailboxes to the left. Five apartments to a floor, fifteen in total. Most of the mailboxes displayed handwritten names on paper slipped under strips of plastic. None of the names was "Lowe." Two mailboxes had no names at all, just the apartment number, providing a small glimmer of hope that one belonged to Veronica, although the most likely explanation was empty units or new arrivals who hadn't gotten around to personalizing their mailboxes yet.

Jessica hadn't completely thought through her strategy, other than to start banging on the doors of the homes of those she hadn't spoken to on the phone earlier, asking after a woman who'd resided in the complex almost two decades ago. It wasn't a great strategy. She was pleased to note there was an on-site manager based in apartment 1A, according to one of the mailboxes. Under the word "Manager" was the name "Dorfman, H." She recognized it as one of those listed in the telephone directory who hadn't picked up during her ring around.

An alcove led to a landing with five doors, as well as a rear exit which probably provided access to the parking lot. Apartment 1A was the closest to her. Jessica stepped forward and pressed an ear to the door. She could hear the muffled burble of television voices and smell something cooking with garlic. Seemed like Dorfman was home now and about to sit down and have lunch in front of some daytime trash on TV. She rapped hard on the door.

The door opened and the smell of garlic was almost overpowering, as though Dorfman was expecting a vampire to show up on his doorstep, rather than a nosy PI with half a lead to follow. He looked late fifties or early sixties, which was a good sign. Jessica didn't know how long apartment-building managers usually stuck around for but at least there was a chance he'd have been running the show when Veronica moved here in the early 2000s.

The man was extremely hairy. Silver-gray fuzz appeared to sprout from everywhere—his head, his ears, his nose, his arms, a broad chest where his short-sleeved white shirt was undone at the top. Only his eyebrows were untouched by time, two fat, black slugs squatting above equally dark eyes. He wore light chinos and a pair of flip-flops. Even his toes were hairy. He was very tan and thirty pounds overweight, and a cigarette dangled precariously from the corner of a wide mouth surrounded by thick stubble.

"Hi there," Jessica said. "Are you Mr. Dorfman, the building manager?"

Dorfman's eyes widened and he pincered the smoke between his forefinger and thumb and shoved the cigarette hand behind his back as though Jessica had never spotted it. Smoke escaped from the side of his mouth as he asked if she was here about the unit upstairs. Jessica had been right about at least one of the mailboxes with no name. A vacant unit rather than a woman trying to hide the fact she was still living here. Another apartment off the list of potentials.

"Actually no, I'm not here about the apartment upstairs. Although I'm sure it's a great building and a fantastic neighborhood, and if I'm in the market for a rental anytime soon, I'll be sure to keep it in mind."

"Damn." Dorfman sighed in a weary way, as though Jessica had just ruined his entire day. "You know, units in this building used to get snapped up as soon as they became available. Not anymore. If you're not here about the condo, what can I do you for?"

Jessica noticed Dorfman had started smoking the cigarette again, now that she wasn't a prospective tenant. She flashed her business card. Connor had insisted on having them made up after she started working for MAC Investigations. He didn't seem to think it was professional to write her number on scraps of paper or body parts.

"I'm a private investigator and I'm trying to track down a woman by the name of Veronica Lowe. An old friend of hers wants to reconnect. I believe she used to live in the building. Maybe still does?"

Dorfman sucked on the cigarette and shook his head. "Name isn't ringing any bells. Definitely not one of the current residents. But lemme check the files for you. Come on in."

He swung the door open wider. Jessica stepped into the narrow hallway and her senses were immediately assaulted by the stench of garlic again. "I hope I'm not interrupting your lunch, Mr. Dorfman."

"Nah," he said, with a wave of his hand. "Just a pot of soup on the stove. It'll keep. Unless you'd like a bowl?"

Jessica's stomach growled as though on cue but she figured she was unpopular enough at the Ace Budget Motel—what with her trash dives—without breathing garlic fumes everywhere. "I just ate," she lied. "But thanks anyway."

"Follow me," he said. "And call me Harry."

51

Judging by the open doors off the hallway, the place was a two bed, two bath. Bamboo flooring throughout and an open-plan living and kitchen area. Nice little patio off the living room. Dorfman muted the TV, an episode of *The Young and the Restless*, and invited Jessica to head on through the open sliding door out to the patio while he fetched some iced tea. He returned a few moments later with a sweaty highball glass for Jessica and nothing for himself.

"What was the name you were after again?"

"Veronica Lowe. Spelled L-O-W-E. She had a kid. A little girl by the name of Mia. They lived here around 2003."

"Can't say I remember them but lemme check. My memory ain't the best these days. If you asked me what I had for dinner last night, I'd struggle to tell you."

Jessica guessed it'd be something with too much garlic.

Dorfman padded off down the hallway to his home office, his flip-flops slapping a staccato beat against the wooden floor. Jessica drank the iced tea and enjoyed the sun's warmth on her skin and inhaled the woody scent of junipers in the air.

"Here we go!"

Jessica turned to see Dorfman emerge onto the patio with a file held aloft triumphantly in a meaty hand.

"Turns out I *do* remember your Ms. Lowe after all. She was a lease skip. That's not the reason I remember her, though. It doesn't happen a lot in my building but it does happen. No, the reason I remember her is because she upped and left all her furniture, and her things too. As though she'd left in a real hurry with the kid. Talk about a pain in the ass. I had to hire a company to clear the place and then bill the owner, who wasn't best pleased, let me tell you. And guess whose ass got kicked?"

"That would be yours?"

"Exactly right."

"I don't suppose any of her furniture or things were kept here in the building? In a communal storage area?"

"'Fraid not. Her stuff would've been sold or trashed. We do have some basement storage but that's strictly for rent-paying residents."

"You said it looked like she'd left in a hurry. Were you concerned for her safety at all? Worried she may have come to harm? Was her disappearance reported to the police?"

Dorfman frowned and consulted the file again. Flipped a page and read a handwritten note tucked among the more official-looking pages. He shook his head. "No need. According to my notes, I spoke to Glo Goldson in 2C at the time and she confirmed Ms. Lowe had moved on. Ms. Lowe had apparently left a handwritten letter in Glo's mailbox apologizing for not saying goodbye before she left. Nothing bad happened to the woman, she just skipped out on the rent. I vaguely remember Glo Goldson being quite upset though. They'd been friendly, despite the age difference."

Jessica felt a prickle of excitement. Goldson was the other name listed in the phone directory who hadn't picked up earlier. She hoped the directory was up to date. "This Glo Goldson," she asked, "does she still live here?"

"Oh, sure. Glo's been here longer than anyone, including me. I figure she'll outlive us all."

"Would she remember Veronica, do you think?"

"I'd guess so. She makes Keith Richards look like he's in the first flush of youth but she's all there up here." Dorfman tapped the side of his head and Jessica realized he'd sparked up another cigarette.

"Do you think she'd talk to me? When would be the best time to catch her at home?"

"She wasn't out front on the bench when you arrived? Old, silver hair, smokes more than I do?"

"Not that I noticed."

"I keep telling her, 'Glo, it's okay to smoke on the patio, you don't have to go outside every time you want a cigarette.' But she won't listen, apart from in the winter, when she does stick to her patio. Otherwise, it's the bench outside. I think she likes to keep an eye on what's going on in the neighborhood, truth be told."

"I'm pretty sure the bench was empty. I'll try her apartment."

"What day is it?" Dorfman asked.

"Monday."

"What time?"

Jessica checked the time on her cell phone and told him.

"Ah, she'll be in Larchmont Village. You know the place?"

Jessica shook her head.

"It's not far from here. Shops, food places, a plaza. Popular with the ladies. Glo will either be shopping in the boutiques or most likely having lunch with one of her buddies. They meet up twice a week for bridge at the community center, but that's Tuesdays and Thursdays. I'd bet on lunch today, followed by a drinkie or three."

It sounded to Jessica like the old gal would be in no hurry to return home. "I don't suppose you know which restaurant she favors on a Monday?"

"That I do not, but she shouldn't be too hard to find. Just keep an eye out for her wheels. If you see a '63 Plymouth Valiant parked on the street, Glo won't be too far away."

Jessica finished the iced tea and gave Harry one of her new business cards. He offered a card of his own, in case she needed anything else or wanted to view one of the vacant apartments. As much as silence unnerved her, living next door to a construction site would seriously piss her off. Jessica took the card out of politeness.

Then she went in search of an old car and an old lady who liked to keep an eye on what was going on in the neighborhood.

6

PRYCE

Detective Vic Medina tossed a copy of the *Los Angeles Times* onto Pryce's desk. It landed on top of a blue plastic ring binder. Jordana Ford's murder book.

"Can you believe those hacks already have a story about the Ford murder? The woman's barely even cold yet."

Pryce nodded. "Jessica called. She said the news broke late last night."

"Jeez. At least they don't know shit about what happened. If they did, it'd be on the front page, not buried inside."

Medina handed Pryce a takeout coffee from a cardboard tray, dropped into the chair at his cubicle and propped his feet up on the desk. It wasn't even eleven a.m. yet and already ninety-five out, but Medina was dressed in his usual black leather jacket, white t-shirt, and blue Levi's jeans, Ray-Bans propped on top of his long dark hair. He rarely took the jacket off even in warm weather. Pryce suspected it was because his partner was trying to disguise the little middle-aged spread thing he had going on. While Pryce was out pounding the streets of Los Feliz every morning in a desperate bid to hold onto his youth and fitness and vitality, Medina's only exercise was prowling the bars of West Hollywood after dark in search of female company.

"How is Jessica anyway?" Medina asked. "Still hanging around with that PI?"

"They work together."

"And that's all?"

Pryce eyed his partner. "Why are you so interested?"

"No reason." Medina held up his hands. "He sounds kind of like an asshole is all. She deserves better."

"Yeah, she does. So, don't get any ideas."

Pryce had come to think of himself as something of a father figure where Jessica was concerned, now that her own dad was gone. Tony Shaw had been his best friend growing up and Pryce felt like it was his duty to look out for Jessica, the same way he would his own daughter. Maybe he was a little overprotective at times, but she did have a bad habit of finding trouble.

He picked up the newspaper and unfolded it. Quickly skimmed the article. Medina was right, the media clearly didn't know the key facts about Jordana Ford's death—namely, how she had died and what had been used to kill her. The LAPD's press office was preparing a statement, and there was talk of scheduling a media conference for later in the day, but the details would be kept to an absolute minimum—the main purpose of talking to the press to appeal for witnesses, rather than whip up a frenzy of speculation.

If the truth got out, it *would* lead to a feeding frenzy, no doubt about it.

"What do you think we're dealing with here, Jase?" Medina asked. "Revenge attack? Copycat killer?" His eyes widened. "Oh, jeez, you don't think they fried the wrong guy all those years ago and the real killer is back?"

Pryce took a sip of black coffee and shook his head. "For a start, Ford wasn't fried, he was executed by lethal injection. And there's no doubt he was the guy—the survivor's positive ID, his DNA on one of the victims, all that shit he had in the basement of his house."

Pryce had never worked the Valley Strangler case—he was still very much a rookie cop back then—but he knew all about it. Most LAPD cops of a certain vintage did. It was the stuff of legend. For five long years, Ford had terrorized the neighborhoods of Van Nuys and Chatsworth and Canoga Park and Reseda and Valley Village. Young women stopped going out alone and natural redheads started dyeing their hair blonde or brunette. A veil of fear and suspicion hung over an entire community. Folks would look at friends and neighbors and ask themselves—is he the guy?

Medina was younger than Pryce, would've been a teenager when Ford was active. "The Strangler liked redheads, didn't he?" he said. "Killed them with their own undergarments. What was it—ten, twelve victims?"

"Fifteen."

The youngest had been eighteen years old, just a year older than Pryce's own daughter was now. He shuddered, despite the clinging heat of the squad room. Dionne knew all about the dangers out there in the world, she was a cop's kid after all, but the fear still kept him awake at night.

Medina pulled an onion bagel from his jacket pocket and tore a piece off and popped it in his mouth. The squad room was busy. Monday morning meant weekend paperwork to catch up on. All around was the sound of telephones ringing and computer keyboards clattering and the low hum of conversation. Desktop fans recycled stale warm air and wafted the stink of onion bagel around an already unfragrant room.

"Remind me of the highlights," Medina said, between bites.

Pryce said, "The Valley Strangler was mostly meticulous—the only two mistakes he ever made were with his first and last victims.

A miniscule speck of semen was found on Teri Hodges's underwear when her body was discovered. She was his first kill. The first that we know of, anyway. There was no evidence to suggest that any of the women were sexually assaulted by Ford but . . ."

"He got off on the act of killing itself," Medina supplied.

"Right. This was back in the days when DNA was in its infancy, when most cops had never even heard of DNA. After Teri Hodges, he never slipped up, never left anything behind at the scene. He got smarter, more careful, more experienced. Then, one night in the spring of '93, he stopped to help a young woman by the name of Kristen Zoeller, whose car had broken down by the side of the road.

"Zoeller didn't have a cell phone, most people didn't in those days, so she'd been relying on a Good Samaritan to stop and offer some assistance. Ford was more than happy to oblige. The prosecution later claimed Ford had been stalking Zoeller for weeks. Her car had been tampered with; the breakdown was no accident. He offered to take her to a nearby auto shop but when he tried to drive out to Stoney Point Park instead, she realized something was up. Zoeller threw open the truck's door and rolled out of the moving vehicle onto the street."

Medina stopped chewing. "Fuck."

Pryce went on, "She suffered a broken arm and collarbone and some cracked ribs, but managed to make her way to a payphone and call the police. She gave them a good description of Ford and his truck, as well as the license plate number. His arrest led to his DNA being collected, which led to a match with the semen on Hodges's underwear. Ford claimed he must've had consensual sex with Hodges before she was murdered but denied any involvement in her death. The walls of his basement were covered with newspaper cuttings about the Strangler murders and photos of the victims. Again, Ford protested his innocence, said an interest in true crime wasn't a crime in itself. The jury didn't buy his lies—even if women like Jordana Ford did."

"Wasn't there a bunch of groupies at the courthouse for his trial?" Medina said.

"That's right. The public gallery was packed out every day. Lines around the block. It was like trying to get a ticket for the Super Bowl. Thousands of women supposedly wrote Ford in prison and some even tried to get into San Quentin to visit him."

Medina shook his head. "Man, I just don't get the attraction. Is it the danger? Those sexy orange scrubs? The guy was a psychopath. Or sociopath. Whatever the shrinks want to label him, he was a nut who murdered fifteen people."

"He always said he was innocent, right up until his last breath." Pryce shrugged. "And he was handsome and charming. Didn't look like your average psychopath. Or sociopath."

"Hey, I'm handsome and charming but I don't get that kind of attention."

"Don't forget modest too, bud."

Pryce moved the newspaper to one side and opened the murder book. Now Jordana Ford had been killed in much the same way as Ford's victims. A blow to the head to stun and incapacitate her, before the life had been choked out of her by a pair of pantyhose. Details the media didn't know about the homicide and *couldn't* know, to avoid the whole city asking the same questions that Medina had voiced earlier.

Revenge attack?

Copycat killer?

The original Valley Strangler hunting again after all these years?

Pryce thought back to the scene that had greeted him and Medina and the CSIs at the Morello Drive property Sunday morning.

As crime scenes went, it wasn't the worst any of them had attended, not even close. Jordana's next-door neighbor had noticed her front door was ajar when he went for his early-morning run. Thought it was a bit weird but didn't ponder on it too long. The door was still open an hour later when he returned. The man had called through the open doorway and gotten no response. There was an eerie stillness, he'd said, a feeling that something was off. It was a nice neighborhood but he didn't want to enter the property, thought it might not be safe if something *was* wrong, so he'd called the cops instead.

Pryce thought about the open door. The perp hadn't been confident enough to kill Jordana outdoors, like the Valley Strangler did with his victims. But he'd wanted her to be found; he'd wanted the world to know what he'd done to her.

Pryce turned the pages of the ring binder until he came to the clear plastic wallet holding the crime scene photos.

Jordana had died sometime Saturday evening. Her body was on the floor in the living room. She was lying face down. The carpet had absorbed most of the blood from the head wound, which had likely been inflicted by a hammer. The type you'd buy at Walmart and keep on the tool rack in the garage, for hanging a picture frame or building flat-pack furniture.

Jordana's dark hair was matted with blood and stuck to the back of her skull where she had been struck. The hammer wasn't found at the scene. There was no sign of a struggle, no upturned furniture, nothing broken or out of place, no sign of forced entry. It was as though she had opened the front door and invited the killer into her home. A glass of red wine had been poured and was on the kitchen counter next to Jordana's cell phone, which the tech guys were still trying to unlock.

It was the pantyhose, still around her neck, that had drawn a chorus of "Oh fuck" from everyone in the room. They all knew who she was; they all knew what the pantyhose meant.

The hosiery didn't belong to Jordana, as far as they could tell. She was wearing pants and a search of her closet suggested she rarely wore skirts or dresses. Her underwear drawer contained no pantyhose or stockings. The ones she had been strangled with—tan, forty-denier—had folds in the fabric like they were packet-fresh, just bought at the store. Forensics had since confirmed that they'd never been worn, that the killer had brought them to Jordana's home with the sole purpose of ending her life with them.

Which ruled out a random attack.

Which left Medina's questions hanging in the air as heavy as a thunderstorm about to break.

Pryce knew Ford was the Valley Strangler. Christ, his own boss had been a key part of the team that had put him away, and Lieutenant Sarah Grayling did not make mistakes—not even back then as a young detective. Pryce mentally ruled out that option.

The neighbor who'd alerted the cops hadn't heard anything suspicious on Saturday evening. No argument or fight or sounds of a struggle. Didn't see anyone enter or leave the Ford house. It was the same story with the rest of the neighbors during the door-to-door interviews.

Pryce turned to the clear pocket holding xerox copies of pages from Jordana Ford's daybook. On Saturday afternoon, hours before her death, she'd been interviewed for a true-crime podcast at a recording studio just off Sunset Strip. On Friday evening, she had attended a meet-and-greet signing event for her new book, at the Hidden Pages bookstore.

"We need to follow up on the podcast interview and the bookstore," Pryce said.

"Who's up first?"

Pryce considered for a moment. "The bookstore. Let's do it chronologically. And it's close by."

Medina said, "I watched some of her TV appearances on YouTube last night and she was feisty as hell. Didn't back down to anyone. Some of it was quite heated. She came across a little cray-cray, you ask me."

Pryce had watched the same videos. Jordana Ford had reminded him of a morning-show presenter—stiff hair, stiff smile, stiff pantsuits. He couldn't decide if the woman genuinely believed in her deceased husband's innocence or if Ford had been a meal ticket for her. Their marriage, their entire relationship, had been conducted behind bars. Pryce couldn't even begin to imagine what that must've been like; to not be able to touch and hold and talk to the person you loved most in the world whenever you wanted to. To know all about the terrible things they had been accused of.

Pryce got up and trashed his empty coffee cup. Picked up his car keys and Armani sunglasses. "Let's go."

Revenge attack or copycat killer?

The former was bad enough; the latter didn't even bear thinking about.

As he made his way through the squad room, with Medina following, Pryce thought about the phone call from Jessica, about Veronica Lowe and her own connection to Travis Dean Ford. He stopped by the desk of Silvia Rodriguez. The detective's dark hair was pulled back in a sleek ponytail, her head down, engrossed in paperwork. She had assisted with the interviews the previous day on Jordana Ford's street.

"Hey Silvia, can you do something for me?" Pryce asked. "It's about the Jordana Ford homicide."

Rodriguez looked up from the stack of interview statements. "Sure thing, boss."

"Find out everything you can about a prison pen-pal group called The Lonely Hearts Club."

7

JORDANA

Jordana Ford watched the rows of seats begin to fill up and felt the knot of anxiety tighten in her belly.

She wasn't nervous about the book launch. Jordana never suffered from nerves. She had appeared at dozens of these events over the years and had, mostly, enjoyed them. Even the ones that had gotten a little . . . lively. She especially loved the signings held here at Hidden Pages, her all-time favorite bookstore.

No, it definitely wasn't preshow nerves that dampened her skin beneath her J.Crew suit and kicked her heart rate up a notch. It was something else, something she couldn't quite put her finger on, a feeling of dread that had been hanging around like a bad smell for weeks now.

She told herself the apprehension was down to this being her final book tour. The big farewell to her true-crime career and the years of campaigning in Travis's name. The only life she had known for the past two decades. Soon, it would all be over. The books, the TV appearances, the notoriety and everything that came with it. She had given her best years to Travis—both while he was alive and after his death—and now it was time for Jordana Ford to reclaim her life for herself.

A thought popped into her head just then, unbidden and unwelcome. More of an image, really. One of those wizened old cops in the movies, the ones who have done their thirty and are a week away from retirement and have one last case to solve. But, this being the movies, you just know, with a sinking feeling in your gut, that the cop isn't going to make it through the week—that he's not going to live long enough to get that gold watch. Maybe Jordana would be like that cop. She shook her head and told herself she was being ridiculous. This was real life, not the movies.

The plan was to retire to Malibu and live quietly by the beach and write some novels under a different name. If things turned out the way she hoped, she might even have someone to share a dinner table and a bed and a real life with. Just as soon as this publicity tour was over and her bank balance had been bolstered by sales of what was set to be another *New York Times* bestseller.

Lockdown Love: A Death Row Romance was different from anything she had written before. Her previous works had been almost exclusively about Travis—his life and so-called crimes, his claims of innocence and the failed appeals, his controversial execution, Jordana's ongoing fight to clear his name, her campaign against capital punishment. This time, the story was about *them*, not *him*. For the first time, she would be sharing their private correspondence and intimate details of their relationship, as well as previously unseen photographs, including their wedding at San Quentin. This book would be a love letter to her husband, before finally letting him go.

That was the PR team's spin on it anyway.

It appeared to be working. Preorders indicated *Lockdown Love* would enter the bestseller list at number one.

Jordana sipped her Merlot and tried to zone back into the conversation with Drew, the store's assistant manager, who was talking through the format as though she were a debut novelist who had never done a book signing before. He was in charge tonight and painfully obviously excited by the extra responsibility in the absence of Graham, the owner, who was attending a family birthday party.

"I thought we'd kick things off with a few words from myself about the author—which would be you of course." He smiled, and then frowned when Jordana didn't return the smile. She stared at him and waited for him to finish his spiel. "Then a reading from yourself and some preapproved questions from the audience, before commencing with the signing session."

"Two readings," she said.

"Pardon me?"

"I always do two readings. Not one. Before and after the audience Q&A."

Drew nodded vigorously, visibly flustered. "Sure thing. Two readings. No problem at all. Let me just . . ." He pulled one of four pens from his breast pocket and made a handwritten amendment to the typed top sheet of paper on his clipboard. The other sheets included the names of all those in attendance tonight, the audience questions, and a "banned list" of people not permitted entry to the ticketed event. The latter was a mix of unscrupulous and unsympathetic journalists, and known hecklers from previous signings.

The store clerk, Chad something or other, who was posted at the front door to greet the guests, had the same information on his own clipboard.

Jordana finished her wine and sent Drew in search of another as she took her seat at a table piled high with hardcovers. She recognized some familiar faces in the front row and returned their smiles while absentmindedly twisting the platinum wedding band she still wore.

Hidden Pages was Jordana's happy place, had been since she was a kid, back when the Nancy Drew cardboard cutout was taller than she was. The store had barely changed in the decades since then. Fairy lights still blinked lazily in the big picture window, and dimly lit lamps gave the room a cozy, intimate feel, while over-stuffed armchairs and poufs in maroon and green leather practically begged customers to sit a while and flick through the pages of a book.

So, why didn't she feel happy tonight? Why the stirrings of unease?

It was here, among the polished, dark wooden shelves, that the eighteen-year-old Jordana Ferrer, as she was back then, had decided to become a writer. She remembered the day like it was yesterday. How she had settled down on one of those old Chesterfield chairs, in a quiet corner of the store, with a copy of *In Cold Blood* by Truman Capote.

She had only intended to read the first few pages. When she finally looked up from the book it was fully dark outside the window and she had devoured every word. She bought the paperback and reread it over and over again until the creased spine fell apart and the pages came loose from their sticky binding. Jordana told herself she would write a book just like it one day.

Her first two attempts—focusing on the unsolved Black Dahlia and Zodiac cases respectively—resulted in enough rejection letters between them to paper the entire wall of her college dorm. The editors who bothered to provide any feedback all said the same thing—Jordana was a gifted writer but she offered nothing new in the genre. They had read manuscripts just like hers a million times before. If she was serious about being published, she'd need to come up with something fresh and exciting, a manuscript that would set her apart from every other aspiring author.

Then came the game-changer. The Valley Strangler was finally caught by the police and Jordana knew she had her story. He was attractive and charismatic and funny and smart. Los Angeles's answer to Ted Bundy. She was a Valley girl herself, Canoga Park born and bred, a native of the killer's hunting ground, a young woman in the neighborhood at a time when that was the most dangerous thing you could be. She had even known one of the victims. But it wasn't enough. She needed something more. Jordana needed to get close to Travis Dean Ford.

At first, he had been as disinterested as those New York publishing houses. Except he didn't even bother to write her back with a polite "thanks, but no thanks." It took time and perseverance and, yes, doing things she didn't feel entirely comfortable with, in order to gain his trust. But Jordana Ferrer wanted a book deal, and she wanted Travis Dean Ford, and Jordana Ferrer always got what she wanted.

Even if that meant Veronica Lowe no longer being in the picture.

Veronica Lowe.

The bad feeling in Jordana's belly intensified.

What had happened back then had nothing to do with Jordana, she told herself for the millionth time. It was a coincidence, that was all. Nothing more than a tragic coincidence.

"Here you go! Sorry for the delay, bit of a struggle with the corkscrew."

Jordana started at the sound of Drew's voice in her ear and she accidently bumped his hand as he placed a full glass of wine on the table in front of her. Some of the Merlot sloshed over the rim, and trickled down the side of the glass, and soaked into the white linen. She watched the little red spot flower like a drop of blood, as Drew introduced her to the audience.

Once he was done, he handed a microphone to Jordana, who opened her copy of *Lockdown Love* to the first of two marked pages. She began to read. Occasionally, she lifted her eyes to make sure she had the full attention of everyone in the room. She did. They were rapt. The tension in her shoulders eased and she felt herself relax a little.

Then she became aware of movement at the back of the room. The store clerk had gotten up from his seat and made his way to the front door again. He returned a few seconds later and ushered a late arrival into the chair he had just vacated.

Jordana stopped reading.

Even in the half-light at the back of the room, she recognized the man immediately. It had been how long since she'd last seen him? A year? Eighteen months? But she'd know him anywhere. That determined gait, the poker-straight posture, the indignant tilt of his chain. She felt the weight of his stare on her, as uncomfortable as a hand around her throat.

Drew stepped forward and asked in a stage whisper if she was okay. Jordana noticed the concerned frowns and glances between the guests in the audience and she nodded, even though she was anything but okay.

She cleared her throat and smiled in what she hoped was a reassuring way. Found her place on the page again and resumed her reading. Tried not to look at the man in the back row, whose name had been top of the list of those who shouldn't be here under any circumstances. Not after what happened last time.

But here he was.

And Jordana knew she had been right to be worried.

8

JESSICA

Larchmont Village was a picturesque little neighborhood between Beverly and 3rd Street that had been a streetcar suburb of LA at one time. Now it was crammed with independent boutiques and quaint restaurants and lots of trees. A strange mix of charming and hip.

Jessica thought the place was familiar but she couldn't put her finger on why as she'd never visited before. Maybe a scene in a forgotten movie she'd watched once and it had stuck somewhere in her brain. There was a kind of intimate feel about the neighborhood and the search for a single car no longer seemed quite so daunting.

She drove her Chevy Silverado as slowly as she could get away with without annoying other drivers, eyes scanning both sides of Larchmont Boulevard. Before too long, she spotted a promising candidate—a classic convertible, nose facing the sidewalk in a diagonal parking space.

Jessica pulled into a vacant spot alongside and got out for a better look. The old car was black and sleek as a panther. Its top was down, showing off an immaculate lipstick-red leather interior. It had a big, silver grille and wide-spaced bug-eye headlamps on the front. Jessica didn't know a whole lot about cars but the chrome plate above the grille with the word "Plymouth" meant she didn't need an encyclopedic knowledge of vintage vehicles to figure it out.

It was languishing under a giant oak outside an Italian restaurant and a cheese and wine place. Both had sidewalk seating, and Jessica studied the al-fresco diners at those establishments. She quickly ruled out the café. Her gaze settled on two seniors at a table close to the entrance of Vernetti. They seemed to be doing a whole lot of drinking and not a lot of eating.

Jessica got closer and saw their pasta bowls were empty but the carafe of rosé wine between them appeared to be freshly loaded. She didn't feel so bad about interrupting seeing as they seemed to have finished their meal and had moved on to what Dorfman had referred to as "a drinkie or three."

The women were probably seventy-something but not prim or faded in any way. Quite the opposite. They were both stylishly dressed in silk blouses and well-cut slacks and chunky ceramic jewelry, no doubt purchased at one of the many trendy boutiques. They were wearing enough makeup between them to keep an entire Sephora store going single-handedly. One wore her hair bobbed in an alarming shade of red that was probably called Ruby Fusion or Sinful Scarlet. She was like a septuagenarian Travis Dean Ford groupie. The other had a silver pixie cut like Judi Dench, with tortoiseshell eyeglasses propped on top.

The scene could've been Veronica Lowe and Christine Ryan in thirty years' time if circumstances hadn't pulled them apart. Maybe there was still a chance of bringing them back together, Jessica thought hopefully.

The one with the silver hair was smoking a menthol cigarette, the filter stained glossy peach, and Jessica would bet her retainer on the woman being Glo Goldson. The two women eyed her with a mixture of curiosity and suspicion as she approached the table.

"Good afternoon, ladies," Jessica said. "Sorry to interrupt your lunch but would either of you happen to be Glo Goldson?"

The redhead's eyes widened, while the Judi Dench lookalike calmly took a draw of her cigarette. "Who wants to know?" she asked nonchalantly.

"My name is Jessica Shaw and I'm a private investigator."

That revelation prompted the pal's pencil-thin eyebrows to hike to her dyed hairline. Judi Dench sipped her wine.

Jessica went on, "I'm trying to track someone down and was hoping Mrs. Goldson might be able to help. Harry Dorfman, her building manager, told me where to find her." She gestured toward the Plymouth. "Or where to find her car at least."

"You found her. Well done. You'd be a pretty bad private eye if you didn't. I'm Glo. What's this all about?"

Up close, Jessica could see Glo Goldson was every bit as well preserved as the car. Both had plenty of miles on the clock, and both, Jessica suspected, had had some work done over the years to maintain appearances.

"I'm looking for Veronica Lowe. She had a rental in your building around 2003. I believe you and her were friends back then."

Glo Goldson shook her head. "I don't remember anyone by that name. It *was* quite some time ago, and I've seen plenty of neighbors come and go over the years, but I'm pretty sure I don't know any Veronicas. Sorry."

She threw an amused glance at the redhead, who shrugged and looked like she was enjoying herself.

Jessica found one of the copies she'd made of the photo Christine Ryan had given her in her bag and handed it to Glo. "This is Veronica. It was taken a few years before you'd have been neighbors."

Now it was Glo's turn for an eyebrow hike as surprise registered on her face.

"That's Roni," she said. "Sure, I know her. Or at least, I did. Haven't seen her in years. I never knew her as Veronica, though. I guess she preferred Roni in the same way I prefer Glo to Glory. Also, her hair was shorter when I knew her." Glo waved a hand just beneath her chin, her ceramic bangles clanking. "Around this length."

So, Veronica had started calling herself "Roni" and had made some effort to change her appearance after quitting Silver Lake. Jessica wondered just how bad the fallout from that prison photo had been.

"What did this Roni or Veronica do?" asked the pal. Dried mascara flakes stuck to her eyelids as she blinked at Jessica. "Why's a private eye trying to find her? Is she in trouble?"

Glo turned to the redhead. "Why don't you pop inside and say hello to Irene and Mae?"

The other woman frowned. "We already said hello when they first arrived." She craned her neck to look in the window. "And they're still eating."

Glo gave her a pointed look. "Go say hello again. They won't mind."

"Oh, sure. Okay." The redhead pulled a linen napkin from her lap and tossed it on the table. She stood up and made her way slowly toward the entrance to the restaurant like she was reluctant to leave.

"Take your time with Irene and Mae," Glo called after her, stubbing out the cigarette in an ashtray.

Jessica settled into the seat the redhead had just vacated and dropped her bag at her feet.

Glo said, "Cora is a sweetheart but she's a terrible gossip. Can I pour you a glass of wine or ask the waiter to bring some coffee?"

"I'm good but thanks for the offer. Tell me about Roni. You knew her well?"

Glo nodded. "Well enough that she trusted me to babysit her daughter. Mia was a gorgeous little thing. Had the most striking blue eyes I ever saw. Roni worked a lot, found a waitressing job not long after she moved into the building."

"Do you remember the name of the restaurant where she worked?"

"Sure. The Big Coffee Cup on Western. I wouldn't take any cash for babysitting so Roni would often bring me dinner from work as a thank you. Honestly? The food wasn't the best but it was free, and Mia was a joy to look after in any case. But that was Roni, didn't want anything for nothing. A nice, considerate girl. The first time I met her, in the lobby, she insisted on helping me upstairs with my groceries. That's how we got friendly. She was chatty but I always thought she was also kind of guarded too, in a way."

"How so?"

"We'd gossip about all sorts over coffee or a glass of wine. TV shows we enjoyed, what the other neighbors were up to, that kind of thing. She'd let me ramble on about my grandkids and show off their photos. But she never spoke much about her own life. One time, I asked about Mia's dad and she shut down the conversation so fast I didn't dare bring it up again. I wondered if he was dead or married to someone else."

The change of name. The haircut. The new job. The secrecy over her daughter's father. Veronica had clearly gone to some lengths to hide her connection to Travis Dean Ford—but had someone found out anyway?

"What about visitors?" Jessica asked. "Any friends or boyfriends that you were aware of?"

"Friends, sure. Boyfriend, no. Not that I know of anyway. Sometimes I looked after Mia when Roni wasn't working, when she was all dressed up for an evening out. I guess she could've been dating but she never said as much. I always assumed she was meeting girlfriends."

"I don't suppose you remember anything about these friends?"

Glo nodded as she opened a silver case and pulled out a fresh cigarette and lit it with a matching lighter. "I saw her with a woman a couple times. I'd say she was a little older than Roni. A tiny thing with big boobs and big hair. A brunette. I'm pretty sure she had a Southern accent, although I don't think we were ever properly introduced."

Bibi Durrant?

Again, Jessica made a mental note to speak to the woman.

"Then there was the one who showed up after Roni had moved on."

"Oh? Tell me about her."

"There's not a lot to tell I'm afraid. Another brunette, quite hard-faced. I found her hanging around outside Roni's old apartment. She said she was a family friend, asked if I'd seen her recently. I told her Roni had moved on and I didn't have a forwarding address. She seemed quite pissed about that. I never saw her again."

"Harry Dorfman says Roni wrote you a letter when she left?"

"That's right. I never did understand why she didn't tell me she was leaving, why she didn't say goodbye in person. Especially as I'd been babysitting Mia and Roni must've left the letter in my mailbox not long after picking her up. I was hurt at first, then I was worried. I remember Harry was mad because he didn't know they were gone until days later when he tried to collect the rent and Roni hadn't given notice or anything. That made me even more concerned. It was out of character. Roni didn't let folk down like that."

"You said you were worried before you even knew she'd skipped on the lease. Why?"

Glo took a long drink of wine before answering.

"I guess it was just the way she was acting in the days before-hand. For a while, she was happier than I'd ever seen her. Smiling all the time, a real spring in her step. Then her mood seemed to turn on a dime. A couple times, she looked like she'd been crying hard. She seemed distracted, as though her mind was somewhere else half the time. When I asked if she was okay, she fobbed me off. Said she was coming down with something, had been working too many hours at the restaurant. But that last night, when she came to collect Mia . . ."

Glo stopped talking and chewed on her bottom lip.

"What about that last night?" Jessica prompted.

"She was on edge. Jumpy. Scared, even. She was late picking up Mia too. I'd already put the child to bed in the spare room, assum-ing she'd be sleeping over a second night. When I asked Roni what was wrong, she told me she was fine. Then she lifted Mia from the bed and said she'd speak to me tomorrow. The next day, I found the letter in my mailbox. Roni and Mia were gone. I always hoped she'd get in touch. Drop me another letter or call or visit. But she never did."

Jessica tried to keep her expression blank but her brain was buzzing. "Sometimes it's just time to move on."

Glo gave her a hard stare. "Is Roni in trouble? Who's trying to find her?"

Jessica figured the old woman had spent long enough worrying about Veronica over the years without throwing Travis Dean Ford into the mix. "Just an old friend trying to track her down. They lost touch a long time ago. Just like you."

"The brunette with the big boobs?"

"No, a blonde. Her name is Christine."

Glo nodded. "Yes, I remember Roni mentioned a Christine once or twice. I hope you find her so they can reconnect. I'd like to see her again too. Would you ask her to call or write me if you do track her down? I'm in the book."

"Of course," Jessica said. "It's finding her that's the tricky part. Can you think of anything at all that might help me locate her? Someplace she'd been to in the past or wanted to visit one day?"

"I know she traveled to San Francisco a few times and stayed overnight. That's where she'd been that last time I babysat Mia. I have no idea what she was doing there. Like I said, she was very private. I assumed she was seeing family or friends."

Jessica knew the trips north were to visit Travis Dean Ford at San Quentin, which meant Veronica had met with the killer right before she'd disappeared with Mia.

"Anything else?" she asked.

"I don't think so," Glo said. "Other than the farmhouse."

"What farmhouse?"

"Roni and Mia had vacationed there maybe six months before they left Beverly Boulevard. And, no, I don't know where it was, before you ask. All she said was it was good to escape the city for a couple weeks and that Mia had had a ball playing in the big, wide-open spaces. I remember she showed me a photo of the two of them. They were sitting on a makeshift swing made from an old tire and a piece of rope hanging from a tree. Roni was hugging Mia and they were both laughing. They looked happy."

Jessica mentally bullet-pointed the key facts.

A farmhouse.

An old rope swing.

Somewhere outside the city.

And then the big question.

Who had taken the photo?

9

VERONICA—1999

Veronica had been stunned when Travis Dean Ford wrote her back.

Like, literally.

She had stood there, rooted to the spot, her outstretched hand hovering just inside the mailbox. Shaking a little, staring at the handwritten envelope tucked between the bills and the junk mail, too scared to touch it, as though it were a grenade that might explode.

Then her neighbor, Mrs. Brenner, had appeared at her shoulder and broken the spell by asking if she was "feeling all right dear," and Veronica had mumbled something about being lost in a daydream and had snatched up the mail and run upstairs to her apartment.

Once inside, she had torn hungrily at the envelope like a kid ripping open a Christmas present. The letter was written on cheap prison-issue paper. Travis's handwriting was small and neat and intense, as though he'd been leaning heavily on the ballpoint pen. She could feel the indentation of the words on the other side of the paper like Braille under her fingertips.

He thanked her for writing him and sending a photo, said he thought she was beautiful. He told her about himself, what life had been like before prison and what it was like now. He asked questions about Veronica and wanted them to write to each other regularly if that was okay with her? He ended the letter by saying he was innocent of the terrible crimes he had been accused of and hopefully, if given the chance, he would show her that he wasn't the monster everyone claimed he was.

In the four months since then, they had exchanged dozens of letters. Those envelopes, with the prison stamp on the front and the San Quentin return address in the top left corner, quickly became the highlight of her day whenever Travis wrote her.

Then she'd received a letter that left her just as surprised and shaken as that first one. Her stomach had flip-flopped like a dying fish on a deck. This one had included a visitation form. Veronica didn't know if she was ready for that step—thought it was too much, too fast.

Now, less than a month later, here she was, more than four hundred miles from home, outside the oldest prison in the state. Too scared to get out of the cab, that weird feeling back in the pit of her belly again. What the hell had she been thinking? Jumping on a plane to meet a complete stranger—someone who'd been convicted of murder, no less—and blowing her entire savings on the flight and motel room to boot. Christine had loaned her the rest of the cash she'd needed for the trip.

Chrissie had, predictably, lost interest in The Lonely Hearts Club very quickly. She hadn't been impressed by the letters she'd received from Clay. His handwriting was as messy as a child's and his spelling was really bad and he was a yoga-bore. She was back on again with Richard, her on-off-on-off boyfriend, and had trashed all the prison correspondence she'd received. She had agreed to attend one social event with Veronica "for the drama," and then declared most of the Lonely Hearts to be as "batshit crazy" as the men they were writing to.

Veronica suspected the "drama" was the reason Chrissie had agreed to give her the loan for the visit to San Quentin—that her best friend was enjoying the fledgling relationship between Veronica and Travis in the same way she lapped up trashy daytime soap operas. Travis Dean Ford was different from the likes of Clay, Chrissie had said, because he was a celebrity and that made him interesting, even if he was famous for killing women rather than making movies or writing chart-topping songs.

"Just don't wear pantyhose to the visit," she'd advised Veronica when handing over the cash.

Veronica stared out of the cab's window now. Beyond the high, steel gates, the chalk-colored buildings of the old prison loomed big and pale against the backdrop of an angry sky heavy with storm clouds that promised plenty of rainfall later on.

The place had been built by the hands of prisoners before opening in 1852 with sixty-eight inmates, according to the book on San Quentin she'd checked out of the library. Veronica had also spent an uncomfortable hour reading up on Travis and his alleged crimes and his trial, on the library's microfiche machine.

She unscrewed the cap from a plastic bottle of Coca-Cola she had stashed in her big purse and sniffed the contents. The smell of forty-percent-proof JD mixed with the soft drink was eye-wateringly reassuring and she tipped her head back and drank down half the bottle. Breathed out fumes that could strip wallpaper and smothered a gassy burp with a trembling hand.

The cab driver's eyes met her own in the rearview mirror. "Need a little Dutch courage, huh?"

Veronica's cheeks flamed with booze and embarrassment. "Sorry," she said, sheepishly screwing the lid back on.

The man laughed. "No need to apologize. I've been driving this cab to and from the prison for near-on thirty years. I see it all the time, and a lot more besides. Some folk don't even bother trying to hide it, just leave their liquor bottles right there in the back seat. Hell, some months I make more from the bottle-recycling plant than I do in tips."

Veronica offered him a shaky smile and waved an arm in the general direction of the visitors' gate. "All of this, it's a bit scary."

"This your first time, sweetheart?"

"Yes."

"It gets easier, trust me."

Veronica nodded, although she was pretty sure this would be her first and last visit to the prison. She handed over some bills for the fare and pushed open the door. Inhaled the salty scent of the bay carried on a stiff breeze, then got out of the cab and smoothed out the creases from an outfit that felt all wrong for the occasion.

The entire contents of her closet had been dumped onto her bed ahead of the visit, tops and jeans and dresses discarded as no good—and not just because of Chrissie's silly warning not to wear pantyhose. The biggest problem Veronica had when packing for the trip north was the pages and pages of rules and regulations for those visiting an inmate at San Quentin.

Attire should not resemble clothing worn by the prisoners, which didn't seem like too big a problem until you realized blue denim pants and chambray shirts were out, as well as orange tops and bottoms. Ditto anything too similar to the staff's uniforms, so no forest green pants or tan shirts or camouflage. Anything too sexy was a big no-no too, so forget halter tops, strapless tops, bare midriffs, miniskirts, and anything sheer or figure-hugging. God forbid a hint of cleavage or thigh was on show to corrupt and titillate the inmates! Oh, and forget about any items that wouldn't pass a metal detector, such as underwired bras and metal buttons, which pretty much ruled out her entire jeans collection.

In the end, Veronica had purchased a new pair of black pants and a cream blouse on sale at Banana Republic, and felt like she was attending a job interview rather than a first date. The thought gave her pause and she stopped walking. Was that what this was? A date? Could you even "date" someone in prison? Someone who was on Death Row?

Veronica became aware of the rumble of the cab's engine still running and realized the driver was waiting in case she changed her mind. No doubt he saw that plenty of times too. She knew it wasn't too late. She could get back in the cab and put as many miles as possible between herself and Travis Dean Ford. That would be the sensible thing to do. Write the weekend off as an expensive sightseeing tour. See the Golden Gate Bridge and Lombard Street and Pier 39. Ask for some extra shifts at the restaurant so she could pay back the cash she'd borrowed from Chrissie.

Instead, Veronica turned and raised a hand to the cab driver, perspiration dripping from her underarms down past her non-underwired bra. Her message to him was loud and clear: you can go now.

The driver leaned on the horn—two quick honks of acknowledgment—and then he was gone.

No going back now.

Once through visitor processing, she was taken to a room and directed to a secure booth with an orange, molded plastic seat screwed to the floor facing a thick Plexiglas partition smeared by dozens of damp fingertip touches. An old-fashioned telephone receiver hung on the wall off to the side.

The prison didn't smell as bad as Veronica had thought it would.

It reminded her of the boys' locker room at high school, that time she'd snuck in to make out with Bobby Luster when she was a sophomore and he was a senior. Sweat and old socks and testosterone and bravado. Boy smell, she'd thought at the time.

San Quentin was much the same but more pronounced. Man smell. Her own body odor was every bit as ripe and she was glad it wasn't a contact visit—that Travis wouldn't be able to catch the scent of her anxiety.

Then he was right there in front of her on the other side of the dirty, scarred glass.

Shackled by handcuffs, dressed in navy pants and a V-neck chambray shirt over a white tee that made his blue eyes pop. A hard body that couldn't be disguised by the prison garb, dark hair longer than in the photographs she'd seen, the beginnings of a beard shot through with bolts of silver.

Veronica figured it was just as well she was sitting down, because her limbs went slack and her heart rate shot through the ceiling and her tongue stuck hard to the roof of her mouth.

An intoxicating cocktail of nerves and lust and excitement pumped through her veins. She'd read about dark lightning in a magazine article once. It was a release of high energy that was completely invisible to the naked eye but completely devastating all the same. That's what it felt like seeing Travis Dean Ford for the first time. And all before he'd even picked up his receiver and said a word to her.

There was something else in the mix too, another emotion she couldn't quite put her finger on in the moment. It was only later, in the cab back to her motel, that Veronica realized what it was.

Fear.

10

PRYCE

Pryce cruised along Sunset with the windows of his midnight blue Dodge Charger buzzed all the way down.

He flipped the visor to block out a low-hanging sun. The heat in the air was heavy for so late in the season. His shirtsleeves were rolled up and the light cotton fabric stuck to his back. Next to him, in the passenger seat, Medina still wore the leather jacket. The man was a lunatic.

They passed by the Ace Budget Motel, which was Jessica's latest temporary home. It was right around the corner from the Hollywood station on De Longpre, and Pryce liked that she was so close by. He hoped she'd make a proper commitment to settling in LA one day. He just wished she didn't feel the need to have Matt Connor in her life.

The car radio was tuned to a station playing old-school rock tunes, which seemed like an apt soundtrack for the Strip. Or at least how the Strip used to be. Pryce could still remember those big, vivid, hand-painted billboards from when he was a kid growing up in the '70s. Diana Ross and Santana and Bowie looming over Mustangs and Chevelles and Datsuns. Shrines that were temporary but lived long in the memory. It was a bygone era, when celebrities carried out secret affairs at the Chateau Marmont, and The Doors and The Byrds performed booze-soaked sets at the Whisky a Go Go and the London Fog.

Now Pryce counted a half dozen billboards for reality TV shows and the latest series on Netflix and Amazon Prime and HBO. He didn't think he'd remember any of them next week, never mind in thirty years' time.

He parked outside the Hidden Pages bookstore. The place was well named. It wasn't hidden as such; it was right there on the Boulevard for all to see, jammed between a branch of Chase and a blow-dry bar. But it was a tiny shopfront, with a quaint canopy and fairy lights in the picture window, and it was easy to miss. Hidden in plain sight. Once inside, the store was more spacious than it seemed from the outside. Not quite the Tardis but the same idea.

The detectives made their way toward the counter, where a middle-aged man was serving a customer. He wore a crisp white dress-shirt tucked into black pants with creases as sharp as razor-blades. His too-black hair was neatly parted to the side. He had a small scab on his chin where he'd nicked the skin shaving that morning.

He finished up the sale and waited for the customer to leave. Then said, "Are you from the police department?"

"I'm Detective Pryce and this is my partner, Detective Medina." They both showed their LAPD badges. "Was it yourself who called the station this morning about Jordana Ford?"

"That's right. Graham Kaminsky. I'm the manager here."

He offered a hand and they all shook. Some customers were nearby, browsing the shelves. Pryce said, "Is there someplace we can talk, Mr. Kaminsky?"

"Of course." Kaminsky turned to a young woman who was stacking books on a shelf in the "True Crime" section. "Bianca? Can you take over the register please?"

"Sure thing, Mr. Kaminsky."

Bianca dumped the pile she was holding onto a trolley. Pryce noticed they were all hardcovers of Jordana Ford's new book.

Kaminsky followed his gaze. "*Lockdown Love* has been flying off the shelves today. We're one of the only places with signed copies. The stock we have won't last the day. I guess murder sells."

The comment could have been crass, but Pryce didn't think it was meant in a flippant way. Kaminsky's face was drawn, his expression grim. He didn't look like someone relishing an uptick in sales off the back of a tragic event.

They followed him up a Victorian spiral staircase to a mezzanine area where a small café was located. Groups of twos and threes occupied most of the tables, drinking coffee and chatting in low voices, as though they were in a library. A couple of lone patrons were leafing through *Lockdown Love* while sipping their lattes. A man wearing the same style of polo shirt as Bianca downstairs was sitting at a table for four at the back of the café on his own.

"Would either of you like a coffee or a soda?" Kaminsky asked.

Medina started to nod but Pryce said, "Thank you but we're good."

They weaved their way through the maze of tables toward the young man in the staff uniform. When they reached him, Kaminsky said, "This is Drew Tannen, my assistant manager. I was at my niece's twenty-first birthday party Friday night, so Drew was running Jordana's event in my absence."

Once the introductions were out of the way, and they were all seated, Pryce said, "We believe there was some kind of altercation at the launch, Mr. Kaminsky? That's what you told the desk officer?"

"I'm afraid so." Kaminsky turned to Tannen, solemn-faced. "Tell the detectives what happened, Drew."

A strong smell of body odor was coming off Tannen and dark patches had spread beneath the underarms of his purple polo shirt. Little clumps of acne, so bright they almost glowed, provided the only color on an otherwise pale face. He ran his tongue over chapped lips before speaking.

"The evening started off so well." Tannen's voice was shaky and high-pitched, as though it was about to break. "I was totally buzzed that Mr. Kaminsky had given me the extra responsibility, especially for such a well-known author. The event space was packed, every ticket sold, which isn't always the case for some of our other book launches. The staff on duty had a guest list, as well as a list of people who weren't allowed to attend."

He paused and darted a look at Kaminsky, who gave a small nod of encouragement.

Tannen went on, "Partway through the first reading, I noticed a late arrival slip into the back row. I guess Mrs. Ford noticed too because she stopped reading and appeared a little distracted. I asked if she was okay and she assured me she was and then she carried on with the reading. I figured she *was* fine—and the latecomer had simply disrupted her flow for a second—because everything appeared to run smoothly after the interruption. That is, until the audience Q&A. That's when things started to go wrong."

Tannen licked his lips again and picked up a glass of water on the table in front of him. He was trembling so badly, he needed both hands to steady the glass and lift it to his mouth and take a long drink.

Next to Pryce, Medina was breathing weird, and he realized his partner was trying to take in air through his mouth only so he wouldn't catch the smell of the kid's sweat.

"Carry on, Drew," Kaminsky urged.

Tannen said, "The audience questions were preapproved by Mrs. Ford. I called for the first guest on the list, who stood up. I think the question was going to be along the lines of why Mrs. Ford had decided now was the right time to publish personal correspondence between herself and her husband. I only know this because I already had the list of questions. The woman in the audience didn't get a chance to ask it. The man in the back row, the late arrival, stood up and shouted that he had some questions of his own.

"I told him, 'Sir, we have a list. If your question is on the list, you'll have to wait your turn.' But he wouldn't listen. He was very angry. He started yelling at Mrs. Ford. How was she able to sleep at night? What about the victims? What kind of person makes money from other people's grief? It was all quite distressing."

Tannen paused for another sip of water. Again, two-handed, like a toddler with a sippy cup. "God, I can't believe she's . . . That Mrs. Ford is . . ." He shook his head. The water glass was now empty.

"What happened next?" Pryce prompted gently.

The question was directed at Tannen, but it was Kaminsky who answered.

"Another staff member, Chad Coleman, escorted the man from the premises. Chad's a big guy. He works out five times a week and doubles up as our security at reader events. Not that security is usually required, of course, unless it's a celebrity author. I believe the incident was dealt with very quickly. Wasn't it, Drew?"

"That's right, Mr. Kaminsky," Tannen agreed. "I asked Mrs. Ford if she wanted to cut the launch short but she refused. We carried on with the audience questions, and another reading, and a signing too. Afterward, Chad made sure she got into a taxi safely. The heckler appeared to be long gone."

Kaminsky said, "I can confirm Jordana made it home okay without further incident. Drew called me at the party to tell me what had happened, and I phoned Jordana immediately to apologize and check on her. She seemed fine. Even joked about a little drama being good for sales."

Medina had been taking notes in a small black leather-bound notepad. He turned to a fresh page. "What can you tell us about the heckler? Do you have a name? Description?"

Kaminsky withdrew a sheet of paper from his breast pocket and unfolded it.

"The name given was Eddie Joiner," he said. "Chad remembers because it was the first name on the guest list. In other words, the guy had been the first person to book a ticket. But he was the last to arrive and be checked off the list. Tickets were five dollars, redeemable against the purchase of a book. I checked: Eddie Joiner's ticket was paid for by credit card and the confirmation email was sent to an address in Eddie Joiner's name. But the guy at the event wasn't Eddie Joiner."

"Someone used a fake name to access a book event?" Pryce asked.

"That's correct, Detective," Kaminsky said. "When Drew told me what happened, I had a pretty good idea who was responsible. I texted a photo from a newspaper article and Drew confirmed my suspicions. The man who showed up at our event on Friday was Lou Hardwick. Top of the banned list. Believe me when I say, if I had been managing the event myself, Mr. Hardwick would not have been allowed to set foot over the threshold of Hidden Pages."

Tannen flinched at the comment as though he'd been physically struck. The kid looked downright miserable.

Pryce's brain raced.

Hardwick.

The name was familiar but Pryce couldn't quite place it. Where did he recognize it from?

"There had been an unfortunate incident involving Hardwick at a previous Hidden Pages event," Kaminsky said. "This would have been around eighteen months ago. Before Drew and Chad joined us, for sure, which is why they didn't recognize Hardwick as a troublemaker.

"On that occasion, Hardwick didn't just heckle Jordana, he threw a glass of wine over her too. It was all very ugly. The police were called but I believe he escaped with nothing more than a rap on the knuckles. Jordana refused to take out a restraining order, despite admitting Hardwick had also harassed her at home. Don't get me wrong, I feel bad for the guy after what he's been through and all. But none of that was on Jordana. I just wish she had listened to me and taken her safety and security a little more seriously."

"Who is Lou Hardwick?" Pryce asked. The flicker of memory wasn't turning into a flame.

"He's the father of one of the victims," Kaminsky said. "Travis Dean Ford murdered Lou Hardwick's daughter."

11

PRYCE

Lou Hardwick lived in a one-and-a-half-story house in Thousand Oaks in Ventura County, around thirty miles from LA.

It had a red stucco roof and siding the color of a martini olive. A bland, single-family home on a street filled with other bland, single-family homes. A silver Volvo was parked in the drive next to a groomed front lawn with no flowers. The porch was empty of decor or clutter.

An elderly man—presumably Hardwick—was standing in the open doorway of the house.

"Detectives! What took you so long?" He held the door open wider as Pryce and Medina made their way up the porch steps. "Come on in."

They hadn't even had a chance to show their badges or introduce themselves yet. They exchanged a look as they passed him and entered a spacious hallway. Pryce and Medina had spent most of the forty-minute journey discussing how they would approach the conversation with Hardwick.

This wasn't the welcome they had been expecting.

"This is about Jordana Ford, right?" Hardwick closed the door behind them. "I thought you'd have been here first thing this morning. Maybe even last night. Better late than never though. Head on through the first door on the right and make yourselves comfortable while I go grab us some coffee. I just made a fresh pot."

"What a weirdo," Medina muttered, as they entered the living room and took a seat on either end of a beige chenille sofa big enough for three. "Although, at least he's offered us coffee. I was starting to have withdrawal symptoms. You know caffeine is my crack cocaine."

It was another dig at Pryce for refusing refreshments at Hidden Pages. Medina had mentioned it more than once on the way to Thousand Oaks.

Pryce took in the room. It was tidy and clean but drab and outdated, like the outside of the house. Pale yellow walls, dark mahogany furniture, heavy burgundy-and-cream patterned drapes, a glass chandelier ceiling fan's wooden blade whirring quietly on a low setting that provided a pleasant coolness. The TV was off. A thick word-search book lay open on the coffee table, next to a pen with a chewed lid.

There were no ornaments or knickknacks, no real personal touches, other than three framed photographs on one wall. Kodachrome shots of a fat baby in a lemon knit cardigan; a younger Hardwick with an awkward teen with wild red hair and braces; the same teenager, clearly blossoming into a pretty young woman, at her high-school prom, wearing a dazzling smile, a floral corsage on her wrist, and a blue dress in a shiny fabric that looked highly flammable.

Mary Ellen Hardwick.

Hardwick appeared carrying a tray holding three mugs of coffee, a carton of creamer, and a bowl filled with brown sugar cubes. He dumped the tray on the coffee table, picked up the word-search book and dropped it into a magazine rack next to an armchair. Then he settled into the chair with his mug.

Hardwick was in his seventies and as neat and tidy and non-descript as the house he lived in. His gray hair was clipped short at the sides and thinning on top. He wore brown corduroys and a light blue button-down shirt and tan loafers. His eyes were a watery green behind silver wire-rimmed glasses and his whole face appeared to be dragged down by age and gravity. Jowls and chins wobbled above the shirt collar. He was old but well-built.

Pryce wondered if the man was physically capable of bludgeoning someone with a hammer and then strangling them. He decided he was.

After the formal introductions were out of the way, Medina opened his notepad.

Hardwick eyed him in his Levi's and leather. "You remind me of that actor. Whatshisname? Was around years ago."

"James Dean? Yeah, I get that a lot."

"No, not James Dean." Hardwick clicked his fingers. "Henry Winkler. That's the one."

Pryce said, "He gets that a lot too."

Medina scowled. "Anyway. Back to why we're here—"

"Look, detectives," Hardwick said, cutting him off mid-sentence. "You're both very busy men, so why don't we just cut straight to the chase here. You want to know if I killed Jordana Ford, right? The answer is no, I didn't. I'm not a murderer. Not like the man who killed my daughter."

Pryce said, "But you *were* involved in an incident Friday night at the bookstore?"

Hardwick sat back and crossed his legs and cradled his coffee. "I think 'incident' is being a little dramatic. I attended Jordana's book launch and I asked some questions. So what? An audience Q&A was part of the evening's format."

"You were escorted from the premises."

A shrug. "I guess Jordana didn't like the questions I asked."

"You used a fake name and email address to purchase a ticket."

Hardwick laughed. "It wasn't a fake name. Eddie Joiner is very real. Lives right next door, in fact. He was happy to book the ticket for me after I told him my internet was down and I gave him the five dollars in cash. Just neighbors being neighborly."

"You know what, Mr. Hardwick?" Pryce said. "You're right. We are busy. We're trying to solve a homicide. So now *I'm* going to cut to the chase. You weren't supposed to be at the book launch. You were banned after throwing a glass of wine over Mrs. Ford at a previous event. You were warned by the police to stay away from her. You tricked your way onto the guest list and then drove all the way from Thousand Oaks to LA on a Friday night. So, what exactly were you doing there?"

Hardwick ignored the question. "Do either of you have kids?"

Medina shook his head. "God, no."

Pryce said, "Yes, one."

"Boy or girl?"

Pryce paused a beat. "A daughter."

"Same as me," Hardwick said. "How old is your daughter, Detective Pryce?"

"Seventeen."

"A young woman now but I bet it seems like only yesterday that you and Mrs. Pryce were picking out the crib and the stroller and the furniture for the nursery and those tiny little outfits." Hardwick locked eyes with Pryce. "Now imagine how it must feel to pick out your child's coffin, the flowers for her funeral, which outfit she should be laid to rest in."

Medina shifted uncomfortably on the couch. Pryce realized his fists were clenched. The coffee swirled dangerously in his gut.

Hardwick went on, "Mary Ellen had the world at her feet when she was murdered. She was beautiful and kind and smart and funny. Everybody loved her. I know that's what they always say about folk who die young—but it's true. And do you know what? It wouldn't have mattered if she'd been a selfish brat who'd been shallow and obnoxious. She was just a kid. She didn't deserve to die the way she did. No one does."

He pointed to the prom picture of Mary Ellen in the blue dress.

"She was around the same age as your daughter in that photo. If she had died as the result of illness or an accident, that would've been devastating enough. But to know someone took her from us deliberately . . . How is any parent supposed to live with something like that?"

Pryce didn't answer. Hardwick's words were hitting him like bullets. The thought of anyone hurting Dionne was enough to turn his insides to ice.

"Travis Dean Ford's execution was supposed to bring much-needed closure for the families," Hardwick said. "That's what the experts claimed anyway. I watched him take his last breath, along with the others. Do you know what his final words were? 'Thanks for coming, y'all. Hope you enjoyed the show!' How's that for closure? Even at the end, he was mocking us. I told you I wasn't a murderer. But if I'd gotten to Ford before the police did, I would've killed him. No doubt about it." He gestured to Medina. "Stick that in your notepad. That bastard got to breathe air and have a family and get married, while my daughter lay rotting in the ground."

No one spoke for a long moment. The only sound in the room was the soft *whoomph* of the ceiling fan.

Eventually, Pryce broke the silence. "Back to Jordana Ford. You heckled her at book launches. You showed up uninvited and unwanted at her house. You were harassing her."

"Jordana was Mary Ellen's friend for Chrissake!" Hardwick yelled. "She had sleepovers at our house in the Valley. We cooked her dinner, made her breakfast. Bought Girl Scout cookies from her and picked her up from soccer practice after school when her own parents were at work. And how did she repay us? By marrying the man who killed Mary Ellen. All for a fucking book deal. All I did was try to make her see that what she was doing was wrong. Try to make her understand how much her actions were hurting other people."

The revelation that Jordana and Mary Ellen had been friends surprised Pryce. He wondered what kind of person that made Jordana, for her to marry a man accused of murdering someone she'd apparently been close to as a young girl. But he had to remember that Jordana Ford was a victim now too, so he kept his expression, and his tone, neutral.

"Where were you Saturday evening between six p.m. and one a.m.?" Pryce asked.

"I already told you, I didn't kill Jordana. I hated the person she became, what she stood for. But I didn't want her dead."

"Where were you Saturday evening?" Pryce repeated.

Hardwick sighed and sipped his coffee. "I was at the Tipsy Goat early on. Walked home after some drinks. Ordered a pizza. Watched a movie. Typical exciting Saturday night."

"What time did you leave the bar?" Medina asked. "What time did you arrive home? What time did you call for the pizza delivery?"

Hardwick shrugged. "I left the bar, say, around eight-thirty. I don't remember exactly. That's the whole point of going to a bar. To drink and forget. I phoned for food not long after I got home. The walk is around twenty minutes."

"And the bar staff and pizza delivery place can verify this?"

Hardwick shrugged again. "Sure, I guess. I used my card to pay the bar tab. Cash for the pizza but they might still have a record of deliveries from the weekend."

He gave Medina the details of the pizza place and the route he'd walked from the bar to his house.

"What movie did you watch?" Pryce asked.

"A really old one."

"Can you be more specific?"

Hardwick leaned over the side of the chair and rifled through the magazine rack. Pulled out a TV guide and flicked through some pages.

"Here you go."

He leaned over the coffee table and handed it to Pryce. *The Bridge on the River Kwai* was circled in blue ink.

"You're right, it is old," said Pryce. "I'd ask about the plot but that's not really going to help us, is it? I must've seen that movie at least ten times and could tell you all the main plot points."

"What do you want me to say, Detective Pryce? If I'd known I'd need an alibi, I'd have made more of an effort to have some company Saturday night."

"You live alone?"

"That's right."

"What about Mrs. Hardwick? Mary Ellen's mom?"

"Mrs. Hardwick is now Mrs. Romero. Lives in San Luis Obispo with her forty-year-old husband, Matías. After Mary Ellen died, we had grief therapy, couples therapy, individual therapy. All kinds of therapy that cost a hundred dollars a session. I guess the 'Get over it and move on with your life' stuff resonated more with her than it did with me."

"So, after the bar and the takeout delivery, no one can vouch for you being here all night? That's what you're telling us?"

"Yep. That's what I'm telling you."

"Would you be willing to provide a voluntary DNA sample?" Pryce asked. "It'd be the quickest way to eliminate you from our inquiries."

Hardwick uncrossed his legs, placed the coffee mug next to his feet, and leaned forward. "You don't seriously think I did this, do you?"

Pryce glanced at Medina, who withdrew a DNA test kit from his inside pocket.

Hardwick looked between the two detectives, then nodded in resignation. "Okay, let's get this over with."

After the swab had been taken, Hardwick followed Pryce and Medina out onto the porch. He leaned on the railing and watched them as they made their way to Pryce's Charger.

"No one ever remembers the victims, do they?" he called. "Ford, Bundy, BTK, Gacy. You know *their* names, don't you? Name me one—just one—of their victims."

Pryce backed out of the driveway of the forgettable house and drove along the forgettable street in the direction of the 101.

Lou Hardwick was right.

Pryce couldn't recall the names of any of those killers' victims.

No one remembered Mary Ellen Hardwick other than her father.

12

JESSICA

The Big Coffee Cup, Veronica's former place of employment, was a bust.

The oldest waitress was younger than Jessica. Mid-twenties, twenty-seven tops. Looking around at the women—and almost all of them *were* women—wielding trays stacked with plates, it was as though the management believed anyone over thirty was no longer capable of writing down an order or delivering meals and drinks to tables. As well as being young, the waitstaff were all slim and attractive.

The Hooters of greasy spoons.

According to the twenty-seven-year-old, the only person old enough to remember coworkers from twenty years ago would be the owner, Ron. He showed up maybe once or twice a week to check on the takings and make sure everything was running smoothly. Jessica handed over one of her business cards to pass on to Ron the next time he stopped by. She had to grudgingly admit those cards were coming in handy.

Finding an address for Bibi Durrant was next on her list.

Jessica grabbed an empty table and pulled her laptop, notepad, and pen from her bag. Her belly growled but she resisted the temptation to order food. She remembered Glo Goldson's less-than-flattering review of the cuisine, and a quick survey of what was on the plates at the other tables suggested the standard hadn't improved any over the years. She ordered a black coffee and opened her laptop. When the drink arrived, she took a sip and tried not to wince. Even the coffee was bad.

Tracking down the founder of The Lonely Hearts Club proved to be harder than Jessica had anticipated. She couldn't find anyone with that exact name listed anywhere in Los Angeles. There were several B. Durrants who were maybes, but nothing definite. None of those listed were in Culver City, where TLHC's mailing address was located, although the woman could have moved home several times since purchasing the PO box a couple of decades ago.

Jessica began to wonder if Bibi was the woman's real name. She tapped her pen against the coffee mug while pondering her next move. She decided to try a different tactic, this time searching for information on Bibi's wedding to Denis "Doc" Durrant.

Doc wasn't famous enough to merit the kind of extensive coverage that Travis Dean Ford and Jordana Ferrer's big day had attracted, but Jessica eventually found a small side column about the Durrants' nuptials as part of a bigger feature. It had been a mass wedding day at San Quentin, with twelve couples getting hitched on a spring day on the first Tuesday of the month. Six brides were no-shows. Durrant's wife-to-be wasn't one of them. The three sentences devoted to the new Mr. and Mrs. Durrant told Jessica all she needed to know.

> *Convicted murderer Denis Durrant married high-school sweetheart, Barbara Burr, in a ceremony lasting four minutes. The bride wore white silk and lace, the*

*groom wore the blue denim garb of the California State
Department of Corrections. Afterwards, they dined on
candy and soda from the visiting room vending machine
in the absence of the traditional cake and champagne.*

Barbara Burr.

B.B.

Bibi.

Once Jessica had the name, it didn't take too long to find an address for a Barbara Burr Durrant in the northeast of the city. She packed up her stuff and left enough bills on the table to cover the cost of the bad coffee, as well as a good tip for the waitress. Being cheap would only result in the business card ending up in the trash.

◆　◆　◆

Jessica was still reasonably new to LA and she'd never been to Cypress Park before. It was a mostly affordable neighborhood surrounded by hills and the Los Angeles River.

The Silverado's GPS guided her to a tree-lined street and a house so tiny it had a "½" stuck on the end of the street number. It wasn't ramshackle as such but there was an air of neglect about the property. The once-white siding had faded to a dirty gray and the cornflower blue trim had blistered and flaked like a bad case of psoriasis. The small patch of lawn ringed by chicken-wire fencing was overgrown, and junk was stacked in one corner. The creaking porch steps announced Jessica's arrival before her knock at the door did.

Bibi was also tiny. At five-five Jessica had at least a few inches on her in her sneakered feet. Bibi wore cowboy boots, tight-fitting blue jeans, a brown leather belt with a big silver buckle, and a low-cut clingy tank top under an open plaid shirt. Her boobs and her hair were the only big things about her.

"Can I help you?"

"Mrs. Durrant?"

"That's right." Her expression was polite but wary.

"My name is Jessica Shaw. I'm a private investigator."

Bibi smiled apologetically. "If this is about Jordana Ford, I can't help you. I already spoke to the other lady detective—Rodriguez I think her name was—and told her the same thing. I haven't been in touch with Jordana for years. I'm sorry you've had a wasted journey. Have a nice day."

Bibi moved to close the door.

"I'm not here about Jordana," Jessica said. "I wanted to talk to you about Veronica Lowe."

Shock registered on Bibi's face. "Veronica? What about her?"

"An old friend hired me to find her. I was hoping you might be able to help."

Bibi quickly regained her composure. "I'm afraid not. I haven't seen Veronica in years either. Even longer than Jordana. I have no idea where she is."

Jessica could feel the afternoon rays start to burn through her thin tee and turn her arms pink as she stood there on the doorstep. She was wilting in the heat like the dead flowers in the yard.

"You and Veronica were friends though, right? Maybe she told you something back then that could help me find her now."

"Veronica and I weren't friends," Bibi said quickly. "Not really."

"Okay. But you did know her back then. It would be real helpful if we could have a chat." Jessica smiled. "And I wouldn't say no to a cold drink."

Bibi huffed out a delicate sigh. "I guess I could spare ten minutes. Come on in."

The inside of the house was nicer than the outside. All white walls and light laminate flooring to give the false impression of space. Sparsely furnished in cheap, but well-positioned, items from

Ikea. A rainbow-striped rug took up most of the living-room floor, and colorful blooms filled glass vases on the coffee table and window ledge. Most importantly, the AC was turned up high.

Bibi returned from the kitchen carrying two highballs filled with lemonade and ice. Jessica took one of the drinks and perched on the edge of the sofa and drank thirstily. The insides of her cheeks tingled almost painfully.

"Tell me about Veronica," she said. "You first got to know her through your prison pen-pal group?"

Bibi nodded. "Veronica joined The Lonely Hearts Club back in the late nineties, along with a friend of hers. Christine, I think. Anyway, the friend lost interest quite quickly but Veronica did attend a few of our socials. She seemed nice enough as far as I could tell."

"You said you and Veronica weren't friends, but isn't that the whole point of the socials? So that TLHC members can bond with each other and form friendships with other people with stuff in common?"

"Well, yes, we were all *friendly* but not best buddies, if you know what I mean. There can be twelve to fifteen attendees at our social events, sometimes more. It's not like Veronica and I were meeting up for cozy one-to-one chats."

"But you *were* friendly enough to visit her at her Beverly Boulevard apartment? Not long before she and Mia disappeared? A neighbor remembered seeing you there."

Bibi hesitated as though unsure whether to tell the truth or not. She opted for a lie. "I was never at Veronica's apartment. It was a long time ago. The neighbor must be mistaken."

Jessica didn't think so. The woman sitting facing her was fairly distinctive-looking—a brunette Dolly Parton but with a harder edge—and she was pretty sure Glo Goldson would still be able to pick her out of a lineup.

Jessica decided to let it go for now. "Tell me about Veronica's relationship with Travis Dean Ford."

Bibi shrugged. "There's not a lot to tell. Veronica started writing him and they hit it off and became exclusive very quickly. By that I mean, Veronica decided not to write any of our other prisoners and Ford pulled his profile from our booklet because he was only interested in Veronica."

"Until Jordana. After Veronica was gone."

Bibi frowned. "Right."

"What did you think of Veronica and Ford's relationship?"

"What do you mean?"

"Did you approve? Disapprove? He did kill fifteen women after all."

"What I think doesn't matter. They were two consenting adults."

"So, you didn't approve?"

Bibi gave a small laugh, a tinkly musical sound. "I didn't say that. I told Veronica what I tell all my members—be smart and don't be naive. What happens next is really up to them."

"Veronica moved apartments after a photograph of her and Mia with Ford appeared in the newspaper. Did she ever talk about it?"

Bibi paused a beat, as though considering her words carefully. "I think she had a little trouble at the time."

"What kind of trouble?"

"Oh, you know. Reporters showing up at her apartment, some hang-up calls, folks hanging around her workplace."

"What folks?"

"I have no idea."

"Did Veronica know how the newspaper got hold of the photograph?"

Bibi's cheeks turned pink. "Not that I know of."

Another lie, Jessica thought.

103

"Did Veronica have any similar 'trouble' after she moved from Silver Lake to Larchmont?"

"I really don't know. Like I said—"

"You weren't friends. Got it. What about the farmhouse?"

"Huh?"

"Did Veronica ever mention visiting a farmhouse with Mia?"

"No, I don't think so. Why?"

"Just a lead I'm looking into."

"Look, I really don't think I'm the right person to be asking all these questions."

"Tell me more about The Lonely Hearts Club. I'm intrigued. Why do so many women want to write prisoners?"

"For some it's about friendship, while others want to find a life partner. Just like any other dating website or app. TLHC has brought a lot of happiness to a lot of people."

"I'm sure it has, but isn't it hard being in a relationship with someone who's behind bars? I guess you would know, what with your own husband being in prison. That must be tough for you?"

An amused smile tugged at the edges of Bibi's mouth, as though Jessica had said something funny but wasn't in on the joke.

"My marriage is much the same as any in the outside world," she said. "We have our ups and downs but we love each other so we make it work. If anything, being apart has made us appreciate each other even more. I don't regret marrying Doc for a second, if that's what you're asking."

"Why's he known as 'Doc'? Does he have a medical background?" Jessica thought it was unlikely, unless he'd robbed liquor stores to pay his way through med school.

"No, not at all." That tinkly laugh again. "He mostly worked in bars as security. The nickname came about years ago, when we were both teenagers. There was a big summer cookout, half the town was there, and this kid, who was about seven or eight, started choking on a corn dog. Everyone panicked except Doc. He grabbed the kid around the chest and did that thing with the funny name—what do you call it?"

"The Heimlich maneuver?"

"That's the one. Doc says he learned it from one of those medical dramas on TV. Anyway, the corn dog came flying right on out and the kid was absolutely fine. Folks started calling him 'Doc' as a joke and I guess it kinda stuck."

Jessica finished up her drink and Bibi seemed relieved. But she wanted to know more about Jordana Ford before leaving. "You said outside you hadn't kept in touch with Jordana either. Why not?"

Bibi's face hardened. "Let's just say Jordana and I didn't get on. She said some horrible things about TLHC over the years. And that new book? Well, I knew from interviews she did recently that it was going to be full of lies."

"Such as?"

"For a start, Jordana never loved Travis Dean Ford. She loved the book deals and the TV appearances and the attention. That whole 'love letter to my dead husband' bullcrap? Give me a break. She also claimed in the book that I never passed on any of her letters to Ford when she first joined TLHC. That I lied to her when I told her he wasn't interested. Said if I hadn't sabotaged their relationship in the early days, they would've gotten together sooner and had more time as husband and wife before he was executed. None of it was true. Travis Dean Ford wasn't interested in her. Or at least he wasn't back then."

"Not until after Veronica disappeared."

"Right."

Jessica was about to wrap things up and be on her way when she heard the loud, throaty growl of a motorbike engine out front. Bibi's little amused smile returned. The engine cut out, followed by heavy footsteps on the porch and the sound of the front door opening and slamming shut again.

A man appeared in the doorway of the living room. He was huge. At least six-two and as broad as a barn, thick arms covered in a lot more tattoos than Jessica had. He filled the tiny space like an Action Man crammed into a dollhouse.

Jessica recognized him immediately from the photographs she'd seen online.

Doc Durrant.

13

VERONICA—1999

Veronica checked her watch as she fast-walked into the restaurant. Ten minutes late. Her hair was still damp from the shower and a trail of sweat snaked down her spine and past the waistband of her slacks.

Once again, she cursed her boss at the restaurant for keeping her late, clearing away brunch plates and setting tables for the lunch crowd, well after her morning shift was done.

She hated being late for anything but she particularly hated being late for lunch with the other Lonely Hearts. It wasn't so much missing out on the food she was worried about. She knew the others wouldn't have ordered yet, would still be perusing the drinks menu. Veronica's anxiety was more about the lack of choice when it came to the seating arrangements and the mortification of walking into a room on her own when everyone else was already there.

After she was done cursing her boss, Veronica began silently cursing Chrissie for leaving her at the mercy of these women, as she tapped her fingers impatiently against the empty hostess stand.

The maître d' finally appeared and led her through the busy restaurant, which was noisy with conversation and clinking glasses and the scrape of metal cutlery against plates. They carried on to the rear of the room and out through a set of open French doors, to a gorgeous courtyard framed by big palm trees and potted plants and hanging macramé decorations. Sure enough, Veronica was the last to arrive. There were eight of them sitting on plump cushioned wicker chairs, around two marble-topped tables that had been pushed together. Veronica's arrival knocked off the perfect symmetry.

The only available chair had been wedged awkwardly between two regular place settings at the corner of the table, meaning she would likely spend the entire lunch bumping her knee against the metal table leg. The good news was that Bibi would be directly to her left so she didn't have to worry about making excruciating small talk with members she barely knew. The bad news was that Jordana Ferrer would be seated to her right.

All eyes turned to face Veronica as she approached the table, full of apologies.

"Don't be silly, honey." Bibi cut her off with a wave of her hand. "Sit yourself down and relax and order up a drink." She stuck a hand in the air and waved to a waiter on the other side of the courtyard.

Veronica pulled out the vacant chair and plonked herself down onto the overstuffed cushion, and immediately banged her knee hard against the table leg.

Most of the other women offered small waves and hellos. Jordana nodded coolly in her direction. It was the woman's default demeanor around Veronica—never any warmer than the ice cubes in their drinks.

The copper tones in Jordana's professionally colored hair flashed like flames in the mid-afternoon sun, complementing her sleeveless dark blue all-in-one pantsuit. Another bottle redhead, whose own dye job was more drugstore than salon, straight up glowered at Veronica. The woman was thickset, with heavy-lidded eyes and a perpetually downturned mouth. Her name was Tara or Tanya or Tonya, Veronica couldn't remember which.

The waiter, young and handsome with too-long fair hair and a single gold stud in his ear, appeared with a pencil poised over a notepad.

Bibi gestured to Veronica. "My friend here needs a drink as fast as you can manage. Another lunch menu too."

"Of course." The waiter turned to Veronica. "What can I get for you?"

She glanced around for the wine list. Noticed it was in front of Jordana, her hands resting on it, no intention of offering it up. Veronica would be damned if she was going to ask for it. The rest of the Lonely Hearts were nursing martinis or G&Ts or wine. Jordana was drinking red, Bibi was on the white. Veronica always thought of red wine as a winter drink and it wasn't even close to Labor Day yet. Plus, she was wearing cream-colored slacks and her golden rule was "light-colored clothing = light-colored drinking," so she asked for a Chardonnay.

"Any particular kind?"

"Large," Veronica said. "Is there any other kind?"

"I meant what—"

"I know. I was teasing. House is fine."

The waiter grinned. "I knew that. Coming right up."

He scuttled off through the French doors into the restaurant.

The courtyard was busy, every other table occupied, diners indulging in light lunches and cool drinks. The palm leaves flapped gently in a soft breeze and provided just the right amount of shade from the sun. The delicious aroma of cooked salmon mingled with a hint of California rose and jasmine epitomized the scent of early summer. The place was a big improvement on the restaurant where

Veronica waitressed, that was for sure. She could still feel the grease on her skin and smell it in her hair, despite the quick shower after her shift.

She turned to face Bibi and they caught up with each other's news since they'd last spoken. They'd become good friends these last few months, often meeting for coffee, just the two of them. This was a development that pissed off Chrissie big-time. She was having nothing more to do with TLHC and wasn't keen on Veronica spending so much time with Bibi. Chrissie had only met Bibi once and had disliked her instantly. She claimed she wasn't trustworthy and the whole "sweet Southern gal" thing was an act. After all, Chrissie said, Bibi Durrant had chosen to marry a criminal—a murderer no less—and now she was encouraging other women down the same path.

Christine had, of course, conveniently forgotten she was the one who had encouraged Veronica to get involved with TLHC in the first place. Veronica figured her friend's take on Bibi was largely down to jealousy. Chrissie never had liked to share, even as a kid, whether it was dolls or clothes or makeup or friends. It was almost as though she expected her friendships to be just as monogamous as her romantic relationships. Her attitude to both was the same: "You have me, so why would you need anyone else?"

But Veronica liked Bibi a lot and she enjoyed spending time with her, so Chrissie would just have to suck it up.

The waiter returned with the menu tucked under his arm and the Chardonnay on a tray. It was nicely chilled, the glass already steamed with condensation in the warmth of the sun. He placed a paper napkin on the table with a flourish and the wine glass on top.

He handed Veronica the menu with a smile and a gaze that lingered a little too long. "I'll give you ladies a few more minutes to decide and then come take your orders."

He retreated to another table and Bibi nudged Veronica playfully in the ribs. "I think he wants more than just your order, honey."

Veronica could see Jordana bristle out of the corner of her eye. She took a sip of wine and was pleased to note it was delicious despite her having had no time to peruse the wine list. She suspected the waiter might have poured something a little better than the house option.

Jordana got up from her seat and announced she was going to pay a visit to the little girls' room, and asked if someone could order a salade niçoise in her absence. As she picked up her purse from the table it nudged her half-full Merlot, and the glass wobbled almost in slow motion before it tipped over and its contents flowed across the table.

Veronica scraped her chair back quickly and noisily on the patio paving amid little yelps of surprise from the other ladies. But she wasn't fast enough to prevent the wine splashing onto her lap.

"Oh God, I'm *so* sorry," said Jordana, who looked not the least bit sorry as she eyed the rapidly spreading burgundy stain on the cream fabric of Veronica's pants with barely disguised glee.

Bibi mopped up the spillage with the napkins that had been supplied with the drinks, then stood up and grabbed Veronica by the arm. "Let's go sort you out, honey."

Jordana was still standing, clutching her purse. Bibi glared at her. "I'd sit back down if I were you."

"Pardon me?" Jordana frowned in confusion.

"Three's a crowd. You can hold off on that bathroom visit until we get back."

"Oh, right." Jordana sat back down.

"What about the lunch order?" asked a plump-faced brunette. Her name also escaped Veronica but she remembered the woman's fiancé was in Men's Central for aggravated assault.

"For Christ's sake, Betsy," Bibi snapped. "Can we forget about the food for five minutes, please? We have a *situation* here, in case you hadn't noticed."

Bibi began steering Veronica in the direction of the French doors, pausing just long enough to call over her shoulder for someone to order up some fresh drinks while they were gone. Veronica noticed Tara/Tanya/Tonya smiling behind the rim of her G&T fishbowl.

Inside the restroom, Bibi kicked open all the stall doors to make sure they were alone and then turned to Veronica, little pink dots of anger on her cheeks. "You know that was deliberate, don't you?"

Veronica grabbed a handful of paper towels from the wall dispenser, wet them under the faucet and dabbed at the stain on her pants. "Yup. I don't think Jordana likes me very much. Same goes for that other woman with the bad dye job."

Bibi chewed on her bottom lip. "I think this is my fault. I had to go and shoot my big, fat mouth off, didn't I?"

Veronica stopped dabbing. "Why? What did you say?"

"I told Jordana about Travis, that he's only writing you now. We had a little chat, girl to girl, and I made it clear that it was time for her to move on, that she should try writing one of my other fellas."

"When was this chat?"

"Last week."

It didn't explain the other stuff that had been happening. Things she hadn't told Bibi about. That stuff had been going on for weeks now.

"How do you know he's only writing me? Not all the mail goes through TLHC."

"That's true, honey. Travis is no longer using our PO box to write anyone else but he also declined to renew his subscription.

When I asked why, he said he had no interest in corresponding with anyone other than you."

Veronica's heart punched against her rib cage. Did this mean she and Travis were exclusive now? She hadn't been on a single date since her first visit to San Quentin. It wasn't something Travis had requested or demanded of her, although, from his gentle questioning, she guessed he didn't much like the idea of other men in her life. In any case, she had lost all interest in the dating scene. She had been to see Travis two more times at the prison since her first visit, working her ass off at the restaurant and pulling double shifts to get the cash together.

Bibi said, "I met Jordana for a coffee and tried to let her down gently. Told her Travis had made his choice. Plus, it would save her a fortune on stationery and salon appointments. I didn't say that to her face but it's true. She's about as natural a redhead as Lucille Ball was."

"Wait, Lucille Ball wasn't a natural redhead?"

"Duh. Anyway, Lucille might've had you fooled but Jordana ain't fooling anyone, least of all Travis Dean Ford. It's the same with Tonya. She has, at least, started writing some other guys. But Jordana is stubborn."

Veronica was about to ask why Jordana was still bothering with TLHC and their social gatherings if she had so little interest in using the service to connect with other prisoners. She only stuck around herself because of her friendship with Bibi. But the answer was obvious: Jordana Ferrer was hell-bent on hanging around so she could make Veronica's life as miserable as possible.

"Can't you just eighty-six Jordana from TLHC?" Veronica pushed herself up onto the vanity counter and angled the hand dryer at the wet patch on her pants, which was now pink like a new bruise.

"Believe me, I would if I could," Bibi shouted over the roar of the dryer. "But she hasn't technically broken any of our rules. She's a sneaky bitch, for sure, as that little display outside proved, but I can't ban her because of an 'accident.'"

Veronica considered telling Bibi about the hang-up calls in the middle of the night and the pizza deliveries she hadn't ordered, but she had no proof Jordana was behind those pranks. She hit the dryer's off button and slid off the counter.

"These slacks are only good for the trash now, so I think it's best if I quit while I'm behind and head on home. Pass on my apologies to the other girls."

"You'll do no such thing." Bibi pulled the silk scarf from around her neck and tied it around Veronica's waist like a sarong over the ruined pants. "There, that doesn't look too bad. Let's get back out there and show Jordana she's not going to win."

Veronica smiled. "You're right. Why let her ruin my day, as well as my pants?"

Bibi winked. "That's my girl." Then she turned serious. "Just be careful, huh?"

"Don't worry, I can handle those bitches."

"I wasn't talking about Jordana and Tonya."

Veronica frowned. "Who, then? Travis?"

Bibi looked uncomfortable. "Look, it's great that you two have hit it off and all, it's just . . ."

"Just what?" Veronica demanded.

"Maybe don't tie yourself to a guy you have no future with."

"What does that mean?"

"He's on Death Row, honey. He ain't ever getting out. There's not gonna be a happy ending there. Just keep your options open, that's all I'm saying. Check out some of our other profiles. Have fun with guys in the outside world. That waiter's very cute and totally crushing on you."

114

"I don't want to date the waiter!"

"Okay, okay." Bibi held her hands up in mock surrender. "Just remember TLHC's advice, okay? Be smart and don't be naive. I say the same to all my girls who start getting serious about one of my boys."

"And that's it?"

Bibi hesitated, then nodded. "That's it."

Veronica felt like there was something else Bibi wasn't telling her. "You really don't have to worry about me, Bibi. I'm a big girl. I can look after myself."

Bibi gave her arm a little squeeze. "Sure you can, honey. Forget I said anything. Let's get back to the others."

14

JESSICA

"Who's your friend?" Doc Durrant asked. "I don't think we've met before."

The question was aimed at Bibi but his eyes were on Jessica. His amiable tone didn't match the coldness of his stare.

"She ain't no friend," Bibi said. "She's a private investigator."

"We don't know anything about what happened to Jordana Ford. Bibi already spoke to the cops." This time Durrant's words were aimed at Jessica.

"She's not here about Jordana, she's been asking questions about Veronica Lowe," Bibi said. "I told her I don't know nothing about Veronica either."

"I think it's time for you to leave," Durrant told Jessica.

"I was just about to."

She pushed past the big man into the hallway, and out the front door, and down the creaking porch steps. Felt like eyes were boring into her back as she headed toward her truck. Jessica climbed into the Silverado and jammed the key into the ignition.

Sure enough, a shadowy outline watched her from behind the thin curtain in the front window of the house. The dark shadow was tall and wide.

Doc Durrant.

She started the truck and drove off. She was still reeling from the unexpected appearance of the convicted murderer. She'd been more than happy to make a hasty exit at his invitation.

After circling the block, Jessica parked at the curb at the far end of Bibi's street, tucking the truck between two other vehicles. She just about had a view of the house, while being obscured from sight herself.

She pulled up Google on her cell phone, her eyes flicking between the screen and the Durrant residence. Found nothing about Doc Durrant's release online. Again, he was nowhere near as newsworthy as someone like Travis Dean Ford. But unlike for Durrant's wedding, Jessica couldn't even find a small side column this time.

Sudden movement from the Durrant place caught her attention. The front door swung open and Bibi emerged, slipping on big shades and glancing both ways along the street. Jessica slid down in her seat and watched as Bibi got into a tomato red pickup parked next to a motorcycle propped on its stand.

Jessica stuck her cell into the charger on the dash and put the truck into drive, and followed Bibi as she made her way toward San Fernando Road. She called Connor, while hanging three cars back from the tomato red pickup.

His voice boomed out over the speaker system. "Hey, Shaw. What's happening?"

Jessica suppressed a sigh. Enough with the Shaw already. Then she immediately contradicted herself by saying, "Connor, are you at the office?"

"Sure am. Why? What's up?"

"I'm on the road. Can you look something up for me real quick?"

"Shoot."

"Denis Durrant." She spelled out his full name. "He was in San Quentin on a murder rap. Got busted back in the nineties. He's out now. Can you get me some info on his release?"

"Will do. Call you back."

Jessica stayed with Bibi as her truck joined Highway 110 heading south. Adrenalin pumped through her veins and she tapped her fingers against the hard leather of the steering wheel. Jessica was convinced her visit had prompted Bibi to make this outing, wherever she was headed.

The woman had seemed determined to play down her friendship with Veronica Lowe. No doubt about it. But why? Could Bibi be about to lead Jessica directly to Veronica right now? Could it really be that simple?

Jessica glanced at the cell phone screen. Still no word from Connor. She turned her focus back to the road and kept the rear end of Bibi's red truck in her sights. Concentrated on hanging back just enough that she wouldn't be looming in the woman's rearview. Her black truck blended in with all the other anonymous dark-colored vehicles on the highway. It was the first rule of being a PI: don't drive a vehicle that stands out.

The shadowy outline of downtown appeared up ahead, like a mirage in the distance.

Jessica's cell phone ringer burst through the speaker system. She swiped to answer. "Connor, what have you got for me?"

"Okay, Denis Durrant. Two failed parole hearings over the last decade. Didn't get enough votes from the parole board on each occasion. He was up for parole again earlier this year. This time he lucked out. Got out six months ago."

"Six months ago? Damn. Thanks, Connor."

"Where you at?"

"I'm either following a potential lead in the Veronica Lowe case or I'm following a woman heading out for some retail therapy."

Connor chuckled. "Good luck. Catch you later, Shaw."

Jessica swore under her breath and ended the call.

Up ahead, Bibi kept on driving and ignored exits for Chinatown and Dodger Stadium and North Hollywood. After a while, the glittering tower blocks of downtown loomed over the free-moving traffic. Bibi's blinker flashed and she moved into the lane for the 10 heading west.

Jessica buzzed down the window and lit a cigarette and turned on the radio. She listened to several chart hits, none of which she recognized, before Bibi finally hit the blinker again and eased onto a ramp that led onto Crenshaw Boulevard. After a while on the main thoroughfare, Bibi slowed down as she approached the intersection with Pico Boulevard and Jessica's heart rate ramped up a notch. Bibi pulled into the lot behind Gus's World Famous Fried Chicken restaurant.

Jessica carried on farther down the street and parked up curbside. She slammed her hands hard against the steering wheel in frustration.

"Fuck!"

Had she seriously just spent a half hour following a woman with a craving for fried chicken? Then another thought occurred to her. What if the restaurant was the meet place with Veronica?

Jessica rifled through an overnight bag on the floorboard of the passenger seat and pulled out an old Guns N' Roses tee and a Dodgers ball cap. She was a Yankees fan but figured the local team was less conspicuous. She pulled on the band tee over her striped t-shirt and tucked her hair under the hat. Popped the glovebox and pulled out a pair of Ray-Bans and stuck those on too.

Then she grabbed her big leather shoulder bag and got out of the truck and hurried along the street. She slowed her pace, as she spotted Bibi emerging from the parking lot on foot. Jessica expected the woman to head straight inside the restaurant.

She didn't.

Instead, Bibi made her way to a payphone by the front door. It was located next to a big picture window and under the shade of a striped canopy. Jessica figured it must be one of the few payphones in the city that still actually worked. And the only reason she could think of for driving all the way across town to make a call that could've been made on a cell or home phone was a conversation you didn't want to risk being traced.

She took advantage of a break in the traffic and jogged across the street. Then took up position behind the thick trunk of a giant tree outside a Western Union on the shaded side of the street. Found her Nikon camera in her bag, and peered through the viewfinder and adjusted the telephoto lens until Bibi came into sharp focus.

Jessica was too far away to have seen what digits Bibi punched into the payphone even if the woman hadn't angled her body just so to block the view. What Jessica could see was how often the woman was feeding the coin slot—which was a lot. It was a short call. Less than a minute. Jessica figured the person she was calling was out of state.

Bibi hung up and headed back in the direction of the restaurant's parking lot. Apparently, she wasn't tempted by the world-famous fried chicken while in the neighborhood. Jessica rushed back to her own truck. She tailed Bibi all the way back to the entrance for the 10. Assuming Bibi was heading on home again, Jessica ditched the tail and headed back to Gus's. She was starving. Fried chicken sounded just the ticket.

After being seated at a table for two with a good view of the "specials" board and a TV on the exposed brick wall, Jessica ordered three pieces of chicken with sides of baked beans and slaw, washed down with a pint of Angel City IPA. As she waited for the food to be delivered, she spotted Pryce on the widescreen. She couldn't hear what he was saying but she guessed it was an update on the Jordana Ford murder and an appeal for information from the public.

The food arrived, and Jessica decided it was definitely worth the drive out to Crenshaw, regardless of the importance of Bibi's phone call. She was just debating whether or not to order a slice of chess pie when her cell phone vibrated across the blue and white checkered tablecloth. Jessica swallowed the last bite of chicken and wiped her hands on a paper napkin from the chrome dispenser. Accepted the call despite not recognizing the caller's number.

"Jessica Shaw?" a gruff voice asked.

"Yep, that's me."

"It's Ron."

"Ron . . . ?"

"Ron Casey. From the Big Coffee Cup. You left your card for me."

"Oh, hi Ron. Thanks for getting back to me. I didn't expect to hear from you quite so soon."

"Dana called to let me know you'd stopped by the restaurant. Seemed to think it was important I got back to you ASAP."

"I'm glad that she did."

"She's my best waitress, very conscientious. This is about Roni Lowe, right?"

"That's right."

Ron sounded concerned. "She's not in any trouble, is she?"

"Not that I know of. Just an old friend trying to reconnect with her."

"Good, I'm glad. I liked Roni a lot."

"So, you remember her, then?"

"Sure I do."

"We're definitely talking about the same person? I appreciate it's a big ask to keep track of all the staff who have come and gone over the years."

"Pretty sure. Red hair, good body, gorgeous, single mom."

"Sounds about right. You have a good memory, Ron."

"Truth be told, I remember Roni because I had the hots for her big-time. Ron and Roni. I thought we'd make a cute couple."

"Okay."

"Not in a 'Me Too' kind of way," Ron added hastily. "I asked her out to dinner once and she said no and that was the end of it. There was no sexual harassment in the workplace or anything like that. No siree. Not in my restaurant."

"Of course."

"Roni and me, we got on great. Honestly, if it wasn't for the boyfriend, I reckon we might've really hit it off."

"Boyfriend?"

Had Veronica's boss found out about her relationship with Travis Dean Ford?

Interesting.

"Yeah, he'd been in the restaurant a bunch of times before they started dating."

Not Travis Dean Ford. Even more interesting.

"Tell me about the boyfriend, Ron."

"Um, lemme think. Early thirties, black, clean-cut, kind of preppy."

"He was definitely her boyfriend?"

"No doubt about it."

"You're sure? He wasn't just a friend or a casual acquaintance or a regular at the restaurant who she got friendly with?"

"Uh-uh. Like I said, I was used to seeing him at the restaurant, especially when Roni was on shift. Then, one time, he came to meet her after she clocked off for the night. The way he greeted her—well, let's just say I don't kiss my friends like that."

"I don't suppose she ever mentioned the guy's name?"

"Nope. Roni was a private person. That's why she was embarrassed by the PDA."

"That's what she told you?"

"No. But, after that night, I never saw the guy at the restaurant again. I don't think she liked mixing business with pleasure. Liked to keep the two separate, know what I mean? It's probably the real reason she turned me down."

"I don't doubt it for a minute, Ron. Tell me what you remember about Roni quitting her job. Did she give a reason? Did she have something else lined up? Was she planning on moving on someplace new?"

"She didn't quit," Ron said. "At least, not in the usual way. She never gave me notice, never told me she was leaving. Just didn't show up for a shift one day. Don't get me wrong, I have waitresses quit on me all the time. But they're flaky. Roni wasn't like that. She was just like Dana. Conscientious. Reliable. Didn't let folks down. Until she did. You want me to tell you what I think?"

"Please do."

"I think the boyfriend was the reason why Roni left me in the lurch the way she did."

Jessica found herself nodding. She thought Ron might be right. But which boyfriend?

15

PRYCE

Lieutenant Sarah Grayling did not look happy.

She welcomed Pryce and Medina into her office with a grim expression and a sweep of the hand in the general direction of the two chairs in front of her desk.

"Sit," she said.

It wasn't an invitation. There was no choice in the matter. Pryce and Medina did as they were told.

Grayling was five years older than Pryce and still a handsome woman. Slim but muscular in her starched white uniform shirt and black pants. She spent an hour in the gym every morning, even on the weekends. She always wore her pale blonde hair swept up in a tight bun and she never smiled. There were reports of a smile once, over a decade ago when the Grim Sleeper had been apprehended, but Pryce was pretty sure it was an urban myth. Only the small, framed photos on her desk of her husband and med student son reminded him that the woman really was human and not some kind of android.

Grayling seemed even more pissed than usual this afternoon. "Give me an update on where we're at with the Jordana Ford homicide," she said, without bothering with any pleasantries.

Pryce told Grayling about Lou Hardwick and the altercation at the bookstore event, and their subsequent visit to his home in Thousand Oaks and his agreeing to provide a voluntary DNA sample.

Prints had been taken from the house and possible DNA had been found under Jordana's fingernails and on the pantyhose.

Grayling nodded. "I've already told the lab we need a rush on both the DNA and prints from the scene. This case is top priority. I do not want the Valley Strangler Mark II running around Los Angeles. What do you plan to do next?"

"Jordana Ford recorded an interview for a podcast on the day she died," Pryce said. "We're just about to go speak to the podcast producer. See if we can also get hold of a recording of the interview."

"Good. Keep me informed. Anything else?"

"There is one thing," Pryce said. "A friend of mine, Jessica Shaw—"

"The private investigator—yes, what about her?"

"She's just been hired to find a missing person."

"And?"

"And the missing person is Travis Dean Ford's ex-girlfriend and the mother of his child. The daughter is also missing."

Grayling closed her eyes and rubbed her temples. "Missing for how long?"

"Fifteen or sixteen years, I believe."

"Okay, that's not so bad. No reason to assume her disappearance is connected to Jordana Ford's homicide. Do we have a missing-person report on file? Is there any reason to believe this woman or her daughter are in imminent danger?"

Pryce shook his head. "No missing-person report for either the mother or the daughter. Jessica thinks they may have chosen to go off-grid to avoid the heat from the press."

"Makes sense."

"Jessica will keep me up to speed on her investigation."

Grayling nodded, apparently satisfied.

Pryce and Medina got up to leave.

"Not so fast." Grayling pointed to two big cartons filled with folders on the floor next to her desk. "Some light reading for you both."

"What is it?" Medina asked.

"The Travis Dean Ford file. If Jordana Ford's murder was the work of a hero-worshipper or a revenge killing, the connection could be in those pages. Read up and get familiar with the cases. You can go now."

They took a carton each and found Rodriguez hovering outside Grayling's office waiting for them.

"What's up, Sylvia?" Pryce asked.

"There's someone here you should speak to. One of Jordana Ford's neighbors. She showed up at the station twenty minutes ago. Says she's remembered something that might be important."

Emma Alves was a small woman with huge dark eyes.

She sprung halfway out of her seat when Pryce and Medina entered the interview room before flopping back down again, like a broken jack-in-the-box. She'd drunk the coffee Rodriguez had provided and all that was left was a tiny mountain of Styrofoam pieces on the table in front of her. She clasped her hands tightly on her lap.

Alves was clearly as nervous as a kitten and Pryce tried to put her at ease.

"Would you like another coffee or some water, Mrs. Alves?" he asked. "I don't know about you, but I sure could do with some caffeine myself."

Her eyes darted from Pryce to Medina. "Some water would be good, thanks."

Medina left the room to fetch the drinks and Pryce took a seat and used a remote control to start recording on the camera positioned high on the wall. He picked up his pen and wrote the date and witness's name on a notepad.

"Detective Rodriguez says you've remembered something about the night Jordana Ford was murdered?"

Alves shook her head. "No, not about . . . the murder. I didn't see or hear anything Saturday night, which I guess makes me a bad neighbor, huh?" She shook her head sadly. "The thought of Jordana in that house, desperately needing help . . ."

Pryce gently urged Alves to continue, asking again what she remembered.

"It happened months ago," she said. "I'd forgotten all about it until after the officer interviewed me yesterday about Jordana's murder. Then I started thinking it might be important. I've been up most of the night worrying about it. My husband told me to come down here and make a statement or whatever, so he can get some goddamn sleep tonight. That's his words, not mine. I just hope I'm not wasting your time. Folk can be arrested for wasting police time, can't they?"

Pryce smiled. "I don't think that's going to be the case here, Mrs. Alves. Now, why don't you tell me what you remember, and I'll decide if it's important or not? How does that sound?"

Alves nodded. "Okay. Like I said, this was some time ago. I'd say maybe five months, as it was springtime. It was late afternoon. I was in the living room when I heard raised voices on the street outside. Well, when I say voices, what I mean is one raised voice. There was a man outside Jordana's front door yelling at her. She wasn't yelling back but she was clearly embarrassed because she grabbed him by the arm and pulled him inside. She seemed furious, which is no surprise because Jordana was a very private person."

"Did you get a good look at this man?"

"Our house is right across the street from Jordana's place so I only saw him from behind."

"What did he look like?"

The door opened and Medina entered the room balancing two coffees and a plastic cup of water. Alves stared at Medina as he placed all three cups on the table.

"He looked like him," she said.

"Huh?" Medina asked. "What did I miss?"

Pryce frowned. "You're saying the man outside Jordana Ford's house was Detective Medina?"

"No, no," Alves said, flustered. "I mean they were very similar in appearance. Long dark hair. Jeans, leather jacket, big boots. But this man was taller and broader in the shoulders than the detective."

"What about a vehicle? Did you see him get out of a car or park in Mrs. Ford's driveway?"

Alves's brow furrowed. "No, I'm pretty sure only Jordana's car was in her drive. That's not to say he didn't park on the street. I only saw him at the door."

"Did you see him leave?"

"I didn't. I watched the house for a while. Then my husband came home from work and told me to get away from the window and stop snooping on the neighbors and start making dinner."

"Did you ask Mrs. Ford about the altercation?"

"Not directly. I should've said right at the start that Jordana and I weren't friends. When she first moved to Morello Drive, I was so excited to have another woman of a similar age to myself on the street. I hoped we would become friends and I did make a real effort at first. You know, welcome basket with some wine, cookies, and flowers. Then a home-baked pie. But she didn't seem interested in making friends and there are only so many times you can pop over with pie without being invited in for coffee before you take the hint. She pretty much kept to herself and didn't seem close with any of the other neighbors either.

"The morning after what happened with the gentleman on her doorstep, I made an excuse to go over there—I can't remember what exactly—just to check she was okay. She seemed fine and it quickly became apparent she wasn't going to mention the angry guy, and I didn't feel we were close enough for me to come right out and ask her."

"Did you ever see this guy at Mrs. Ford's place again?"

"Not at her house, no. I did see someone one other time, maybe a month or so later, that could've been the same man, but I couldn't say for sure."

"But not at the Ford home?"

"No, he was walking along the street. I'd just come out of the house, and was about to get into my car, when I saw him. He turned the corner before I could get a proper look at him. By the time I drove to the end of the street, in the direction he'd headed, he was gone. Like he'd never been there."

"Did you ever witness any other, similar, altercations between Mrs. Ford and anyone else? Ever see anyone else suspicious hanging around the property?"

"No, I don't think so. Just the angry guy."

Pryce put down his pen and shared a look with Medina. His partner had missed the beginning of the interview but had been in the room long enough to get the gist of what Alves was saying.

The angry guy wasn't Lou Hardwick, not from the description Alves had provided. Pryce had checked and the incident with Mary Ellen's father at Jordana Ford's home had occurred at her previous residence, not at the Morello Drive property.

"You think I've wasted your time coming down here, don't you?" Alves said.

Pryce shook his head. "No, I don't think you've wasted our time at all."

Just the opposite, he thought. Another public altercation. Another man who had a problem with Jordana Ford.

Another suspect in the woman's homicide.

16

JORDANA

The taxi driver waited at the curb until Jordana was safely inside the house, just like Chad, the bookstore clerk, had told him to. Part of her was pissed at the humiliation of it all; the other part was grateful as she made her way up a front path cloaked in shadow. She double-locked the front door and slid the deadbolt into place.

When Jordana had first moved to Morello Drive, she'd had all the locks changed so that no one, other than her, had access to the house. There was no reason to believe the previous owners had kept a spare set of keys, or that the realtor had had a copy made—but she wasn't willing to take any chances. Not after what happened with Lou Hardwick at her previous home.

The night he had shown up, drunk and yelling and cussing her out on the street outside, had embarrassed her, more than anything. The way curtains had twitched, and blinds had been prized apart; the pretend concern from those brazen enough to open their front doors and ask what was going on. All of them secretly enjoying the show. She could've had him charged, but she didn't, because he was Mary Ellen's dad. As a kid, he had been more of a father to Jordana than her own dad had been. She'd often fantasized that the

Hardwicks were her parents, instead of her real mom and dad, who had never seemed to have time for her, who were always too busy with their own important lives.

Had Jordana been envious of Mary Ellen, with her peaches and cream complexion and her slim figure and red hair, and her perfect family? No doubt about it. Had she been glad when the girl had died at the hands of a monster? Absolutely not. Did she believe Travis was responsible for her friend's death? That one was trickier to answer. All she knew was that he'd looked her straight in the eye and told her he was innocent, that he was not the Valley Strangler, that he was simply a man who'd had an interest in the case, like half the Valley did back then.

Jordana could understand Lou Hardwick's anger toward her, his sense of betrayal. Of course she could. But the way she saw it, she wasn't the one who'd murdered Mary Ellen. And turning her back on Travis—on the opportunities that had opened up to her as a result of her relationship with him—wasn't going to bring back his daughter.

Hardwick didn't see it that way. She thought of the last book launch he'd ruined for her. How he'd grabbed her glass of Merlot and thrown it in her face. The burn of humiliation as the audience gaped at her, red wine stinging her eyes and dripping from her face.

That memory segued into another, this one from many years ago. A lunch with the Lonely Hearts where Jordana had deliberately knocked a glass of red over Veronica Lowe. She'd been jealous of Veronica too. The beautiful face and pale skin and fiery hair, just like Mary Ellen's. The way she had Travis Dean Ford under her spell. Even the waiter had tried to hit on her that day. As always, whenever she thought of Veronica, a knot of guilt tightened in Jordana's belly. She thought of the hang-up calls and the pizzas she'd had delivered to the woman's apartment back then and was embarrassed. But that was kid's stuff—harmless, really—compared to what had happened later.

Jordana made her way to the kitchen to check the deadbolt was in place on the back door and to pour herself a drink. Lou Hardwick showing up tonight had shaken her more than she'd realized. As she fumbled for the light switch, she heard the muffled ring tone of her cell phone in her purse where she'd dumped it on the couch. She went back into the living room and found the phone. It was Graham Kaminsky, the manager at Hidden Pages. Jordana sighed and accepted the call. If she didn't, he'd only keep on trying. There was the muted sound of thumping music in the background, as though Graham had stepped out of a club or a bar. It seemed out of character for a man who was as square as a crossword puzzle. Then she remembered he was at his niece's birthday party, which was why he had missed the book launch.

He spent the next ten minutes apologizing and asking if she was okay. Jordana eventually cut him off, having assured him several times that she was absolutely fine. "Hey, a little drama is good for sales, right?" she said. "I'll speak to you soon, Graham. Go back to your party and have some fun."

Jordana ended the call before he could bore her with any more apologies. She switched the cell phone to silent mode and left it on the coffee table as she went back into the kitchen. A bottle of red was already open, but she decided to pour herself a large brandy instead. She took it upstairs to the bedroom, where she undressed and hung the J.Crew suit in the closet. She pulled on a pair of satin pajamas, then sat at her dressing table and removed her makeup and smoothed cold cream onto her skin and brushed the styling products out of her hair.

The sensor light outside came on.

Jordana crossed the room quickly to the window. The back-yard was flooded with brilliant light. She caught sight of a figure dressed in black darting toward the back door. Someone tall and well built. Lou Hardwick? Jordana realized she'd forgotten to check if the deadbolt on the back door was secured after being distracted by the call from Graham Kaminsky.

Fear prickled her scalp as she made her way out into the hallway. She listened at the top of the stairs. Over the thumping of her heart, she heard a distinct click. The sound of the back door closing. Then footsteps on the tiled floor of the kitchen.

Someone was inside her house.

Whoever he was, he was making no attempt to be quiet. Did he think there was no one home? Or did he know Jordana was upstairs? Did he want her to be scared?

It was working.

She ran through her options in her head, as she edged away from the top of the stairs. There weren't that many. Jordana could either lock herself in the bathroom and call 911 and hope the flimsy door held out until the cops arrived, or she could return to the bedroom and get the gun she kept in the top drawer of the nightstand. Then she remembered she'd left her cell phone downstairs and had no way of phoning for help.

The gun it was then.

She tiptoed, barefoot, across the hallway to the master bedroom, trying not to alert the intruder to her movements. As she removed the gun from the drawer, Jordana heard heavy footsteps climbing the staircase. Her mind was a jumble of thoughts. Had Lou Hardwick broken into her house? Would he go that far? What else was he capable of? Or was it someone else? Would she be able to pull the trigger? She'd never fired a gun before, other than at the shooting range.

Jordana retreated to the far corner of the room. The last time her heart had beat this hard and fast was the first time she'd visited Travis at San Quentin. She raised the gun in front of her, using both hands to steady the small Smith & Wesson as best she could. It still trembled dangerously.

A shadow fell across the hallway right outside the bedroom. Then a large figure filled the doorway.

Jordana recognized him immediately.

17

JESSICA

Dusk was beginning to claim the day when Jessica arrived back at the motel.

The bright blue sky bled into navy and then the pink of a cosmopolitan cocktail. Backlit billboards on the Strip aggressively suggested this evening's TV viewing or choice of beer. Yellow rectangles blinked on one by one at the Ace Budget Motel as residents settled in for the night.

Jessica flicked the light switch as she entered her room, and was drawing the curtains when her cell phone rang. It was Connor.

"Don't keep me in suspense any longer," he said by way of greeting. "Hot lead or shopping trip?"

"Huh?"

"Your bird-dogging expedition earlier."

"Lead. I think. This woman drove all the way across town to use a payphone. Right after I paid a visit to ask about Veronica Lowe."

"You ask me, the only people who use payphones these days are loonballs who think the government is tapping their home and cell phones, and those with something to hide."

"Hard agree," Jessica said.

"So, what does this woman have to hide?"

"That's what I intend to find out."

"She anything to do with this Doc Durrant guy who just got out of the can?"

"She's his wife."

There was silence for a beat, before Connor said softly, "Be careful, Jessica. I'd hate to think I've got you involved in something dangerous here."

His use of her first name for a change threw her for a second. Then she was distracted by the flashing light on the landline on the nightstand.

"I have another call," she said. "I'd better go."

"You're not just trying to get rid of me, are you?"

"If I was, I'd tell you."

Connor laughed. "I don't doubt it for a minute."

Jessica disconnected, then strode across the room and picked up the motel phone receiver before it rang off.

"Hello?"

She plopped down on top of the mustard and navy bedcover.

"Jessica? It's Tyler on the front desk. Sorry to bother you."

Tyler was a cute college kid who worked reception at the Ace Budget Motel when he wasn't in class at UCLA.

"Hey, Tyler. That's okay. What's up?"

"I saw your truck pull up a few minutes ago. You have a visitor."

"A visitor? Who?"

"He didn't want to leave his name. Said you'd want to speak to him though."

"Where is he now?"

"In the bar. I didn't want to give out your room number."

"I appreciate it, Tyler. Who's on shift tonight?"

"It's Regan."

"Great. I'll be over just shortly."

Jessica replaced the receiver in the cradle and sat on the bed for moment, racking her brain, trying to think who her mysterious visitor might be. She knew it wasn't Connor because she'd just spoken to him. In any case, he knew her room number, and wouldn't have to go through the front desk.

She got up and pulled off her t-shirt. Spritzed some body spray under her arms and picked out a black and white polka-dot blouse from the closet. Ran her fingers through her hair and applied a slick of red lipstick. She grabbed her bag, cell phone, and room key, and headed out into the warm evening.

The Happy Hour Lounge was small and intimate, and lit by lamps with low-wattage bulbs that cast a deep amber glow over the room. It was no-frills and old-fashioned, and Jessica loved it. The glass shelving in front of the decorative mirror behind the bar was crammed full of Scotch, bourbon, gin, and vodka bottles. Five swivel leather stools faced the polished wood bar. One of them was occupied by a large man hunched over a whisky tumbler.

Doc Durrant watched Jessica in the mirror as she climbed onto the stool next to him.

The bartender put down her paperback—it would be a James Patterson thriller, she only ever read James Patterson—and sauntered over to where they were sitting.

"Hey, Jessica. Your usual?"

"Thanks, Regan. Make it a double, would you?" Jessica turned to Durrant. "You want another?"

He nodded. The ice in his glass clinked as he pushed it toward the bartender. "I'll have a double too, if that's okay?"

"Fine by me," Jessica said.

Regan poured a generous measure of Talisker for Jessica, before switching to Knob Creek for Durrant. The woman had cheerfully described herself as "forty and fabulous" after celebrating a milestone birthday not so long ago and Jessica couldn't disagree. She had honey-highlighted hair and green eyes and more curves than Lombard Street in 'Frisco. Durrant's eyes probed her like an airport metal detector.

Regan eyed the tattoos on both Jessica's and Durrant's arms. "Is this a meeting of the *LA Ink* fan club or what?" She laughed at her own joke. "Holler if you need anything else."

Regan returned to the other end of the bar and picked up the paperback. Jessica could just about read the title on the cover. It was one of Patterson's novels that had been made into a movie starring Morgan Freeman.

She swallowed some Scotch, let the burn warm her chest and bones, before addressing Durrant. "How'd you find me?"

He drank from his own glass before answering. "I followed you."

"What do you want?"

"I want you to stop following my wife."

Heat touched Jessica's cheeks that had nothing to do with the whisky. "I guess you're better at bird-dogging than I am."

"Looks like it. Why'd you tail her?"

"She lied to me."

"About what?"

"Being friends with Veronica Lowe."

"You should drop it."

"Why?"

"You just should. Trust me."

Jessica turned on the stool to face Durrant. "Why should I trust you?"

He smiled and raised the bourbon to his lips again. Didn't answer her. The neon Budweiser sign washed his skin in red and blue. There were deep lines around his eyes and mouth. His nose was wide and spread across his face as though it'd been smashed against a concrete wall more than once. But there was something strangely attractive about Doc Durrant.

Jessica resisted the urge to drop her gaze, kept her eyes locked firmly on his own. "Who did Bibi make the call to?"

He shrugged. "Who knows? That's her business. And it's none of yours."

"The call was out of state, right? Did she speak to Veronica Lowe? Warn her a PI was looking for her?"

Durrant smirked. "You really don't have a clue, do you?"

"No? Why's that?"

He fixed Jessica with an intense stare as heavy as the burden of a broken promise, and she felt her underarms grow damp.

Durrant nodded. "Okay. Let me tell you a story."

"Sure. I don't have anyplace else to be."

Durrant took another slug of bourbon, before he started talking. "When you do a long stretch in prison, like I did, you come across all sorts. Good guys, bad guys, stone-cold psychopaths. Some are innocent. Some are guilty and ashamed of their crimes. Others are guilty and make sure everyone knows it so they can rule with fear. Then you have the guys who tell the outside world they're innocent but can't help boasting about what they did inside. Travis Dean Ford was one of those guys. He was a murderer, plain and simple, despite what his groupies wanted to believe."

"Just like you."

"No, not like me. I took a life to save a life. That liquor store owner had already shot one friend. I did what I had to do to stop him turning the gun on another one. Travis Dean Ford? He killed because he wanted to. Because he got a kick out of it. When he first tried to get involved with Bibi's pen-pal thing, I told her to shut him down fast."

"But she didn't take your advice?"

140

"The thing about Bibi is, she always wants to see the good in people, give them the benefit of the doubt. And, believe me, there are a lot of good guys in prison, who deserved the opportunities she put their way over the years. Ford wasn't one of them. But Bibi figured he was on Death Row so where was the harm? It's not like he could pose a threat to her girls from behind bars, right? Wrong. Veronica Lowe made the same mistake."

He finished his drink, and Jessica did likewise, and Durrant signaled for Regan to refill their glasses. She poured two more doubles and Jessica didn't stop her. She had a feeling she might need it.

Durrant went on, "When Bibi told me about Ford and Veronica writing each other, I told her to warn Veronica off. Bibi tried but Veronica wouldn't listen. Ford had cast his spell over her by then and she was too far gone. According to Bibi, the lifers and Death Row inmates are the most popular among her members."

"Really? That surprises me."

"It shouldn't. For most of these women, writing someone in prison is a fantasy. Like reading those *Fifty Shades* books. If the guy is never getting out of prison, it remains a fantasy. They don't ever have to deal with the reality. At least, that's what they think anyways."

"But that's not always the case?"

"No. And it definitely wasn't the case with a guy like Travis Dean Ford. He got off on being in control. Didn't matter if he was picking up women in bars and taking them out to the middle of nowhere or if he was pulling the strings from a prison cell. Read any article about Ford and it'll state, as fact, there were fifteen victims. I'm here to tell you that's wrong."

The baby hairs on Jessica's arms stood on end and she felt cold all of a sudden despite the liquor. "What are you saying?"

"I'm saying Veronica Lowe was number sixteen."

Jessica was finding it hard to breathe. She threw back some whisky. It didn't help. "Says who?"

"The San Quentin grapevine at the time."

"What did you hear exactly?"

"Ford put the word out that he was looking for a gun for hire. Plenty of guys willing to help him out. This would've been around sixteen years ago. You're the private dick, I'm sure you can work it out."

"Around the same time Veronica disappeared."

"Bingo."

"You really think Ford had her killed? Why?"

"Sounds like the sexy redhead was losing interest. The visits were becoming less frequent. She was barely writing him. Was even making noises about wanting to move on with her life. Ford didn't like that. Especially not with his kid being involved."

"What happened to Mia?"

"No idea."

"You don't think he had her killed too?"

"I'd hope not, what with her being his own flesh and blood and all. But who knows? Sure, Ford could turn on the charm when it suited him, but he wasn't like normal people. To do what he did to those women, there was something wired wrong in his brain. I know all those shrinks tried to make out like he ended up the way he did because of his daddy but I don't buy that BS for a minute. My own daddy walked out on me and my mom when I was a baby. Didn't turn me into a psychopath."

Jessica figured it probably wasn't the best time to point out that Durrant had spent decades in prison himself. She said, "I already searched for murder victims that could've been Veronica Lowe and I didn't find anything."

Durrant shrugged. "Maybe you didn't look hard enough."

Before Jessica could respond, a text flashed up on his cell phone. He drained his glass and slid off the stool, picked up a black leather jacket, and leaned in close to her. She could smell the bourbon on his breath, and his sweat, and a hint of cologne.

"Veronica Lowe is dead," he said in her ear. "Drop the investigation. And stay away from my wife."

18

VERONICA—2002

Veronica felt like her life was in ruins.

She'd had to quit her job, move out of her apartment, even change her name. Her life had become fodder for the tabloid press. Even worse, the whole city seemed to be obsessed with her little girl, after the photograph of herself and Mia with Travis had appeared in the newspaper.

The daughter of a serial killer, who, himself, was the son of a murderer.

What was the name of the Valley Strangler's secret daughter? Had she inherited her daddy's evil genes as well as his blue eyes? How had Travis Dean Ford been able to father a child on Death Row? What kind of woman had a baby with a serial killer?

All those questions and more were being asked and debated every single day. In the newspapers and the trashy magazines. On daytime talk shows.

Yet, sitting across from her now, Travis was the one who was pissed—and all because Veronica had changed her appearance.

"You look different," he said. "You've changed your hair."

Before, Veronica's long, center-parted hair had almost reached her elbows. Now it fell just below her chin. She'd also had thick bangs cut above eyes that were brown instead of pale blue thanks to colored contact lenses. She'd considered going brunette or blonde but had stopped short of buying a hair-dye kit.

She nodded. "I had to after the photo appeared in the newspaper. People were recognizing me in the street."

"I don't like it."

"And I don't like reporters showing up at my home and my workplace," she snapped, then immediately regretted her tone. He was angry enough with her.

Travis frowned. "Have you put on weight?"

"A few pounds."

It was closer to ten pounds. The weight gain had been deliberate too.

"I don't like fat women."

Veronica ignored the comment. "I've had to move to a new apartment. Quit my job. Even change my name."

"You moved apartment?" Travis's bright blue eyes bored into her. "When did this happen?"

Veronica swallowed hard. The palms of her hands were damp. "Around a month ago. Soon after the newspaper article was published."

"You didn't tell me you'd moved."

"I'm telling you now."

"What if I'd tried to write you?"

"I guess the letters would have been returned here. It's not a big deal."

"Not a big deal? Do you realize how stupid that would have made me look? Not knowing where my girlfriend—and my own daughter—are living?"

Travis's voice was low but his hands were clenched, as though he wanted to punch her. But he wouldn't. He was too smart for that. He didn't shout when he got mad, didn't bang his fists on the table, or lash out. Instead, quiet fury oozed out of him like pus from a sore.

Veronica knew she was safe here in the visitation room, surrounded by other prisoners' family members and watchful guards. Travis had managed to convince the prison authorities a long time ago that a thick, plastic partition between himself and his visitors was no longer necessary. He was the model Death Row prisoner. Charming, humorous, intelligent, obliging.

Travis wouldn't hurt her—no matter how badly he wanted to.

Not like Leon had.

Christine was the only person who knew what Veronica had endured at the hands of her college boyfriend. Even then, it'd taken her best friend the best part of a year to figure it out. Veronica's major was philosophy, and her minor had been lying about the bruises.

She'd tripped over her own feet on the sidewalk.

She'd had a little too much to drink and had fallen over.

She'd walked into a cupboard door she'd left open.

And so on.

If the black eyes and split lips were really bad, she'd hide herself away in her room and miss class until her injuries had healed enough to be concealed by makeup.

Christine wasn't stupid. She knew Veronica. She knew she wasn't that clumsy, didn't get sick that often, wasn't so unhappy and withdrawn all the time without good reason.

Veronica had finally broken down and told Chrissie everything after two bottles of cheap white wine. They'd packed up her stuff that very same night and she'd spent the next six weeks on her best friend's sofa. Her time at college was over but she was free of

146

Leon Geffen and his cruel punches and cutting remarks and quick temper.

Leon had found her, but he'd also found the hard fist of Chrissie's boyfriend, Richard, and the promise of a police complaint for domestic abuse and battery if he ever came anywhere near Veronica again. Like most bullies, Leon was also a coward. She never heard from him again.

For a long time, Veronica didn't date at all. When she finally did, she chose men who were a million miles away from her usual type. No alpha males or big personalities or imposing physiques. Chrissie was a big fan of therapy—"Is there anything better than a whole hour just talking about yourself?"—but Veronica didn't need a shrink to figure out what was going on. She didn't need a professional to explain why she was choosing the men she was.

Had she loved Gray Allan? No. Had she felt safe with him? Yes.

Then she'd seen the photo of Travis Dean Ford in The Lonely Hearts Club's brochure and he'd been the perfect compromise. Strong, handsome, sexy—and safely locked away behind bars. She hadn't realized it at the time. Now it was glaringly obvious. Travis Dean Ford had been accused of unspeakable crimes but he didn't pose the same threat to her that Leon Geffen had.

Travis was another safe option. The difference this time was that she loved him too. Of course she did. Maybe just not so much when he was being like this; when he was looking at her the way he was right now.

"I think Jordana Ferrer leaked the photo to the newspaper," she said.

Veronica had shared the photograph with Bibi, who had then, quite innocently, posted it on The Lonely Hearts Club's members-only forum. Veronica had been horrified and demanded it be taken down immediately, which Bibi had done. But Veronica guessed Jordana had spotted the post before it was deleted and had gone to the press with the photo. Who else would be so mean?

"Would you quit going on about that damn photo?" Travis said. "Why does it even matter?"

Veronica stared at him. "Did you not hear what I just said about having to move home and find another job? Do you know what they're saying about me? They're accusing me of having hybristophilia. It means you get turned on by men who commit violent crimes."

Travis smirked. "Do you?"

"I'm being serious. That photo has ruined my life."

"Are you ashamed of me, is that it?" Travis demanded. His voice was still low, his eyes as hard as pebbles. "Because plenty women would love to be in your place, who wouldn't treat our family like it's a dirty secret."

Veronica said nothing. Maybe Jordana Ferrer wasn't the one who'd gone to the newspaper after all.

"Give me your new address," Travis said.

Veronica shifted uncomfortably in the chair. Her sweat was an adhesive pasting her cotton pants to the orange plastic. "Maybe that's not such a good idea."

"What did you just say? What exactly are you accusing me of, Veronica?"

"I'm not accusing you of anything. I don't know how the press got hold of that photo, is all. Maybe it was Jordana or another member of The Lonely Hearts Club. Or maybe it was someone in here. Maybe one of the guards 'borrowed' it and made a copy while you were out in the yard or something. It was taped to the wall of your cell, right? Look, I'm just trying to protect Mia."

Travis stood up.

"Where are you going?" Veronica asked.

"Visit's over."

"They haven't called time yet."

"This visit is over. You'd better write me with that new address. And you'd better look like you again next time I see you."

Her relationship with Travis was something Veronica had been thinking about for a while—busy thoughts keeping her awake at night, her brain fizzing with questions when she should have been fast asleep. Did she still love him? Did she want to continue seeing him? Was she scared of him?

The words were out of her mouth before she even realized what she was saying.

"Maybe it's best if we cool things between us for a while," she said to his back. "Just until all this interest in me and Mia dies down."

Travis froze and Veronica wished she could shove the words back into her mouth.

He turned to face her again. "You remember I told you about my daddy that time? How he had to leave me when I was a kid?"

Veronica's voice was a hoarse whisper. "Yes."

"No one gets to leave me anymore," Ford said. "Especially not you."

19

JESSICA

Jessica raced over to the window and watched as Doc Durrant climbed into the passenger side of a dark-colored truck at the far end of the lot. She could just about make out a large silhouette behind the wheel in the wash of blue neon from the bar's sign, as the pickup drove past and turned onto Sunset.

One thing was for sure: Bibi wasn't Durrant's ride.

Jessica paid the tab and made her way back to her room. Whisky shots from her own bottle were a hell of a lot cheaper than the bar prices at the Happy Hour Lounge. She climbed up the metal staircase and leaned on the walkway railing. Smoked a cigarette and thought about the conversation with Durrant. It was full dark now but not cold. The warm evening breeze ruffled her hair and her mind raced with unanswered questions. Did Ford really pay someone to kill Veronica? Where was her body? What happened to Mia?

Once inside, Jessica kicked off her Converse sneakers and poured herself a single from the bottle of Scotch, then added another finger's worth of liquor. She'd already had enough booze for a weeknight, but she needed another hit to soothe her nerves.

Sure, Durrant's claims about Veronica's untimely death were upsetting but, in her line of work, Jessica had delivered bad news to clients before. She knew what was really bothering her was Mia. If what Durrant said was true, the parallels with Jessica's own life were eerily similar.

A murdered mom.

A missing child.

A life filled with lies?

Jessica stood in the middle of the room and raised the stubby motel tumbler to her lips. She noticed a crimson smudge left behind on the glass and remembered the lipstick. A wave of embarrassment hit her. She wondered who the hell she'd been trying to impress. If a part of her had hoped it would be Connor waiting for her in the bar.

She set the drink down on the nightstand. Went into the bathroom and wiped her mouth roughly with a Kleenex from the metal dispenser by the washbasin and then scrubbed off the rest of her makeup. She undressed and threw the fancy blouse and jeans onto her laundry pile and pulled on an oversized tee.

She took the drink over to the table and chair by the window, which doubled as her desk, and opened her laptop. As she waited for it to boot up and connect to the motel's Wi-Fi, Jessica eyed her evidence board. It would need to be updated but, right now, Jessica wasn't sure what was fact, what was speculation, and what were downright lies.

The next hour was spent going through her databases again, looking for a Jane Doe that could be Veronica Lowe—this time focusing on unidentified female shooting victims around the time of her disappearance. Maybe Jessica had missed something first time around. She came across a handful of promising leads that were quickly snuffed out. Too old, too young, or later identified by family members.

Then Jessica searched for *all* women who had been shot in Los Angeles around sixteen years ago, in case Veronica had been carrying a fake ID and had been misidentified. There was nothing to pique Jessica's interest. If Veronica wasn't a Jane Doe or registered as deceased under a different name, it left the possibility she was buried in a shallow grave someplace or her body had been disposed of some other way.

If Doc Durrant was telling the truth, that is.

Jessica figured a laborious trawl through old newspaper articles could yield some answers, possibly turn up something to back up claims of a hit orchestrated by Travis Dean Ford. She knew the Los Angeles Public Library had archival back editions of the *Los Angeles Times*, so she decided she'd pay a visit in the morning. Hoped she wouldn't need to be a member to access their services seeing as they'd be unlikely to give out a library card to someone whose current address was a budget motel on the Strip.

She logged out of the databases she'd just searched and pulled up FaceTime. Clicked to connect with her old boss, Larry Lutz.

Everything about Larry was big—his build, his personality, his heart, and especially his smile. Jessica found herself grinning back as his face appeared onscreen.

"Well, if it isn't LA's hottest PI," he said. "How you doing, kid?"

"I'm doing good, Larry. You?"

"Can't complain. But, you know me, I usually do anyway."

Jessica noticed he was in his home office, even though it was almost midnight in New York. "You still working at this time of night?"

"Popped upstairs for an hour to finish the paperwork on a case. Marjorie is watching one of those horrible reality shows. The Real Housewives of God Knows Where. All the bitching and shouting was driving me crazy. And that was just Marjorie."

Jessica laughed. "What's the case?"

"Infidelity surveillance. In Manhattan!"

Jessica raised an eyebrow. "Manhattan, huh? Fancy."

"I know! Client is cheap as hell, that's why he came out to Blissville looking for a PI."

Larry was cheap too, which was why his office space was in Blissville rather than his native Brooklyn, where he lived. A mostly commercial neighborhood in Queens, there wasn't a whole lot in Blissville other than a cemetery and an expressway and, of course, Lutz Investigations. Hardly anyone lived there—but Jessica had, right up until her dad passed a few years ago. It was while working for Larry that she'd spotted one of the few residential properties for sale at a good price. Tony had bought the place and it was the first time they'd been able to afford a small house rather than a cramped apartment.

Larry went on, "This guy—we'll call him Len Snyder because that's his name—suspected his wife was cheating on him with another man. Wanted me to tail her on the nights she claimed she was working late at the office—you know the drill. I'll tell you something for nothing, Mrs. Snyder sure knew how to splash the cash even if her husband didn't. Turns out, she wasn't at the office, and I got to hang around outside some very nice bars and restaurants and hotels."

"Hotels? So she did have another man?"

"Nope. I only ever saw her out with the same gal pal every time. Snyder was relieved there was no other man but he was furious that his wife was blowing all his cash on friends while pretending she was working overtime."

"What happened?"

Jessica knew there was some kind of punchline coming, judging from the grin on Larry's face.

"Turns out she *was* cheating! With the gal pal! She's told Snyder she's leaving him and the marriage is over. I guess my fee will be another blow for the poor bastard but, hey ho, I gotta pay the bills and keep Marjorie in the life she has become accustomed to."

"You certainly do."

"What about you?" Larry asked. "Working on anything exciting?"

Jessica quickly filled him in on the Veronica Lowe case, finishing with the unexpected visit she'd just had from Doc Durrant.

Larry was suddenly serious. "You believe what this guy is telling you?"

"Honestly? I don't know what to believe. I've been trying to check it out, but I've found nothing so far to back up what he says."

"I wouldn't trust an ex-con. And, from what you've told me, the wife has a pretty loose relationship with the truth too."

"She was definitely downplaying her friendship with Veronica."

"Now the hubby is claiming the woman is dead. Why? What's it to him? Why go to the trouble of following you all the way across town to talk to you about someone he doesn't even know? Someone the wife claims she wasn't even friends with?"

"I don't know." Jessica bit her lip.

"What is it, Jessica?"

"I guess he kind of threatened me too." She frowned. "Although not really."

All of Larry's joviality was gone now. "What'd this asshole say to you?"

"He told me to drop the investigation and stay away from his wife."

"This was in a public place? Anyone else around? Anyone hear?"

"No, only the bartender was there. She was out of earshot. He kinda leaned in and whispered to me."

"I don't like the sound of this, Jessica. Not one little bit."

"I'm pretty sure he was just trying to spook me. I don't think he'd actually do anything."

"The guy is a criminal! And I'll say it again: what's his interest in this Veronica woman? Why is he warning you off?"

"I don't know," Jessica said. "But I'm going to find out."

"I still don't like it. You still got the Glock?"

"Yes. I sleep with it on the nightstand; I carry it in my purse." She raised an eyebrow. "Good enough for you?"

"I'm just worried about you is all."

Jessica smiled. "I know you are. You sound like Connor."

"Ah, how are things with the big guy?"

"Fine. He does his stuff, I do mine. We tag-team when necessary. Have the occasional beer. We don't see each other that often."

"That's not what I meant, and you know it. Is the stripper still on the scene?"

"Larry!"

"Sorry, 'exotic dancer.'" He made air quotation marks by waggling his fingers. "You do know it's you he wants, right? One word from you and Gypsy Rose Lee is history."

Jessica laughed. "Larry, you don't even know him. Or Rae-Lynn."

A memory of her recent conversation with Rae-Lynn flashed into her mind just then, and the laughter died in her throat.

Do I have to be worried, Jessica?

Not about me, you don't.

She pushed the thought away.

Larry said, "No, but I know you and he'd be crazy to let you slip through his fingers."

"It's not that simple."

"Sure it is."

"He's engaged."

"You ask me, he's fair game until there's a ring on her finger."

"There is. Tiffany, I believe."

"I meant a wedding ring. Paperwork involved. Everything official. Do you think I let Marjorie's boyfriends put me off? Not a chance. Not even half a chance."

"Oh, so Marjorie had 'boyfriends' when you two first met? More than one?"

"Well, no. She was single. But if she had been with someone, I would've fought tooth and nail for her. That's all I'm saying."

"You're nuts, Larry. But if you want to talk about folks with a loose relationship with the truth, Bibi Durrant has nothing on Matt Connor. He should have a diploma in lying."

"Sure, he's a schmuck." Larry winked. "But you like him, I can tell."

Jessica rolled her eyes. "Sure, Larry. Whatever."

"Actually," he said. "Forget everything I just said. If you do end up shacked up with the schmuck, I'll never convince you to come home."

It was a recurring theme in their conversations, Larry trying to convince Jessica to return to New York.

She laughed. "Bye, Larry."

"Bye, sweetheart. And remember what I said: be careful."

Jessica disconnected the call and sat back and drank some whisky. She thought about what Larry had said. Why would Bibi feel the need to lie about Veronica? Why was Doc Durrant interested enough in Jessica's investigation to warn her off?

She opened up a browser window and searched for The Lonely Hearts Club's website. This time, she ignored the prisoner profiles and navigated to other parts of the site. She clicked on a link for the "Members Only" section. A pop-up appeared, encouraging the user to log in or register for membership.

Jessica had a bunch of fake social media accounts and matching email addresses. It was a trick some PIs employed to gain information about people. There was "Jacob Matthews" (a history major at Cal State LA) and "Rachael Wilson" (twenty-something retail assistant from Pasadena) and "Thom Maddox" (hot single dad living in Rancho Park) and "Lorelei Givens" (single professional in her forties from Glendale).

Jessica didn't have any real social media profiles, and only the bare minimum of information about herself on her own website—not much more than a photo, short bio, and contact form. But a lot of people seemed determined to live out their lives online, and that was a gold mine of information for PIs.

She used the Lorelei Givens alias to fill out TLHC's membership request form. If Bibi, or anyone else, checked out the new applicant's credentials, an internet search would lead them to a public social media page that matched the name, city, and age provided by "Lorelei." The photos would show a middle-aged woman with average looks and a pretty home. Bibi would no doubt decide Lorelei was a perfect fit for the group.

Jessica hit send. If she wanted to know more about Bibi Durrant and what really went on at TLHC, she figured the best way to do it was by becoming a Lonely Heart herself.

20

PRYCE

Tuesday morning. Pryce and Medina were finally on their way to speak to the podcast producer who'd been with Jordana Ford just hours before her death.

They'd planned on interviewing him yesterday but, by the time they'd finished up with Emma Alves, Jared MacFarlane had a recording session about to get underway and had asked to raincheck until today.

Sunset Podcasts was located in West Hollywood, not far from the Chateau Marmont. Tall, skinny palms stood sentry on either side of the bubblegum pink three-story building. A billboard advertising the latest album by a band Pryce had never heard of was propped on top of the roof underneath a cerulean sky. The recording studio shared building space with a small modern art gallery, a fashionable hair salon, a juice bar, and a vegan food-truck hire place—all of which seemed intimidatingly young and trendy to Pryce.

Even Medina, who still liked to think of himself as youthful, partly because he was single and mostly because he was vain, looked like he felt just as out of place.

"You think the folks who work here will make us as cops or assume we're a couple old guys who got lost in the hip part of town?" Pryce asked.

"The kids don't use words like 'hip' anymore, grandad. It's seriously uncool."

"So is saying 'uncool.'"

They consulted a company directory in the lobby and climbed the cool, shaded stairwell to the top floor, where they found the recording studio. A young woman with a pierced nose, an intricate tattoo sleeve on each arm, and hair the same color as the building was behind the reception desk. She reminded Pryce of Jessica, apart from the pink dye job.

"Hi, I'm Boo." She offered them a dazzling Wite-Out smile. "Are you the detectives?"

Pryce returned the smile. "That obvious, huh?"

"Better than a couple lost old guys," Medina mumbled.

Boo said, "Jared is just finishing up in the studio. He shouldn't be too much longer if you want to head on through to his office. Can I bring you something to drink while you wait? Mineral water? Green juice? Chai latte?"

"Water would be good," Pryce said.

"Anything with caffeine?" Medina asked.

"Sure, I think we have a jar of instant somewhere."

"Better than nothing, I suppose," Medina muttered, as they headed through the doorway to MacFarlane's office.

They both sat on an oxblood Chesterfield leather sofa that was dented and cracked and showing the white foam stuffing where it had ripped. It was just like the ones in the coffee places Dionne liked to go to and Pryce guessed it was probably cool, like everything else in the building, even though Angie would be horrified at the thought of it in their condo.

He suppressed a yawn and wished he'd opted for the caffeine hit too. It had been almost two a.m. when he'd finally crawled into bed beside his wife, trying not to wake her. After a late dinner, he'd started reading the Valley Strangler murder books Grayling had given them and had found himself engrossed in the pages—not least because he still had Lou Hardwick's accusation ringing in his ears about how the victims in high-profile serial murders were often forgotten.

He read about Mary Ellen and how her body had been found in Stoney Point Park after she'd last been seen leaving a bar with a handsome man. And Devin Palmer, who wasn't much older than Dionne when she turned up dead in the same park just days later. And Molly Hagan, who was the last woman to be murdered by Ford. And Pryce read about the twelve others too. He agreed with Grayling that Jordana Ford's homicide could be connected to her late husband's killing spree but if the answers were in those case files, they weren't jumping out at him.

Boo returned with a chilled bottle of water for Pryce and a chipped mug for Medina, before retreating from the room and closing the door behind her.

MacFarlane's office was small and, apart from the battered old sofa, comprised a cluttered desk and lots of expensive-looking editing equipment. A large window in the west wall provided a view of a soundproofed room dominated by a table with two mikes and headphone sets, and a camera set up on a tripod. One of the two chairs was occupied by a slender guy in his thirties with light brown floppy hair. He wore thick black plastic eyeglasses and the skinniest jeans Pryce had ever seen on a man.

Medina said, "Those jeans look painful. How can he even sit down in them?"

Pryce said, "You're just jealous because you don't have a twenty-eight-inch waist."

"Thirty-two-inch," Medina said proudly, tucking a thumb into his waistband with some difficulty.

"Yeah, maybe back in 1995," Pryce said.

The hipster guy pulled off the earphones and switched off the camera and joined them in the office.

"Hi, I'm Jared," he said, shaking their hands. "Oh good, Boo got you some refreshments already. Are you all set? Is there anything else I can get for you before we start?"

"All set, thanks," Pryce said.

"Excellent."

Up close, Pryce could see that MacFarlane's eyes were red and raw-looking behind the big specs and floppy bangs.

"Neat place you got here," Medina said.

"Thanks, we like it." MacFarlane settled into the chair at his desk.

"Been set up here long?" Pryce asked.

"I've had the studio for five years now and my own true-crime podcast for way longer than that—before the likes of Serial and Dirty John came along. I guess they helped blow the whole thing up. Lots of folks want to start up their own podcast these days, so we do really well with the studio hire. Teen Detective and Finding Jane Doe are both recorded here."

MacFarlane said it proudly like they should be impressed, but Pryce had never heard of either of them. Then again, he didn't listen to podcasts. He'd ask Dionne about them later.

Pryce said, "Tell us about Jordana."

MacFarlane shook his head. "I still can't believe she's gone. She was sitting right where you are now, just a few days ago." His eyes were wide behind the thick lenses. "How can she be gone?"

"We appreciate this is really tough, Jared," Medina said, taking out his notepad and pen. "Take your time. We just want to know a bit about your relationship? What Jordana was like as a person?"

"We'd known each other for a few years and had become quite friendly in that time. Well, as friendly as Jordana gets—sorry, *got*—with anyone. We'd occasionally meet for coffee or a glass of wine. But she was quite a private person. Always seemed to be holding stuff back, you know? It's probably because of all the shit she'd had to deal with over her marriage to Ford."

Pryce said, "She was here Saturday to record an interview. What did you talk about?"

"The interview was all about plugging the new book. It was being marketed as a 'love letter' to Travis Dean Ford. You wouldn't believe the number of people who are into that kind of stuff, despite what he was accused of doing to those women. There were also a few hints for listeners that *Lockdown Love* could be Jordana's final book. That was on the record. Off the record, I knew for definite it was the last book about Ford. I also knew Jordana was planning on moving away once all the publicity was done and the cash was in the bank."

"Moving away where?" Pryce asked.

"I have no idea. Sorry."

"Why would she give it all up?" said Medina.

"I think she just got tired of it all," MacFarlane said. "It certainly wasn't a case of not being in demand anymore. Quite the opposite. She'd met with a TV producer very recently about a true-crime series. It sounded like quite a big deal."

Pryce frowned. "There wasn't anything about a meeting with a TV producer in Jordana's daybook."

"It wasn't planned," MacFarlane explained. "Jordana was having coffee in a local café and—as she put it—was accosted by this TV executive, who recognized her and had apparently been trying to set up a meet through Jordana's agent. I guess they had coffee and Jordana was impressed by the spiel—we're talking about a good network with an excellent track record in true-crime shows. I know she was tempted but she ultimately decided it was time to walk away from all the Ford stuff."

"Do you know the name of the producer and which network they worked for?" Pryce asked.

MacFarlane gave him the name of a well-known network, but he didn't know any other details about the TV executive.

"How did Jordana seem recently?" Pryce said. "Was she worried about anything?"

MacFarlane nodded. "There had been some . . . incidents. Hang-up calls and a feeling of being watched. A couple times, she thought someone was prowling around outside her home. You know, the sensor lights in the backyard would come on in the middle of the night or the neighbor's dog would start barking for no reason. Stuff like that. Then there was the incident with Lou Hardwick at the book launch Friday night. You know about that, right?"

"We do," Pryce said. "You were there?"

MacFarlane shook his head. "I couldn't make it. Date night with my husband. I've been so busy at the studio recently, I've barely seen him. I was worried Jordana would be pissed at me for missing the launch, but she was absolutely fine about it. She told me what happened with Hardwick when she came in for the recording on Saturday."

MacFarlane gave a secondhand account of the altercation at the bookstore that seemed to match up with Drew Tannen and Graham Kaminsky's version of events.

"How did she seem on Saturday?" Pryce asked. "Was she upset about the incident?"

"I think she was a little shaken at the time, but by the time she showed up here she was mostly just pissed. She's had problems with Hardwick in the past and thought that had all settled down

163

until his little performance at the bookstore. Mostly she was in good spirits, though."

"Oh yeah?" Medina asked.

MacFarlane smiled sadly. "When I said earlier that it always felt like she was holding stuff back? Well, I think she was seeing someone. Don't get me wrong, she'd had quite a few romantic liaisons in the past. She was no Doris Day, and Ford had been gone a long time. This seemed different somehow. Not just a fling. I think she was quite smitten."

Pryce leaned forward on the sofa. "Did she tell you anything about this man—or woman—she was dating? Anything at all?"

"A man, for sure. Jordana wasn't interested in other women— for friendship or anything else. She didn't trust them. As for any details about her new man, I don't think so. Just little hints here and there. Like I said, she was very private. And, sometimes, I think she enjoyed creating a bit of mystery around her private life."

"What about Saturday night?" Pryce asked. "Did she mention any plans she had for later in the evening, after the recording was finished?"

"She said she was looking forward to relaxing at home with a glass or two of wine ahead of a busy schedule promoting the book. She didn't mention anything about expecting company."

Pryce and Medina asked a few more questions before winding up the interview. They both got up and thanked MacFarlane for his time. Medina handed over a business card in case the producer thought of anything else.

Once outside on the street, Pryce said, "I can't believe you described the guy's studio as 'neat.' That's seriously uncool, Vic."

"I tell you what else is uncool. That coffee. I'm guessing the jar was older than the receptionist who served it up."

"What do we think about Jordana dating someone?" Pryce asked. "Tannen and Kaminsky didn't mention anything about a boyfriend being at the launch and there's nothing in her daybook to suggest any hot dates. She also seemed pretty coy about giving MacFarlane any details even though he seems to be one of the few friends she had. What does that tell us?"

"That she was screwing someone she shouldn't have been." Medina held up his cell phone. "And if she was, with a bit of luck, we might just be about to find out who. Missed call from Bobby Chung at the Latent Unit."

Medina returned the call as they walked to Pryce's car. There were a lot of "uh-huhs" and some nodding. They both climbed into the Charger and Medina hung up and turned to Pryce with a grin.

"Well?" Pryce asked.

"Bobby's going to email over the report with all the boring stuff. But the headline news is we have a name and we have an address."

Pryce started the car. "Where are we headed?"

Medina said, "Cypress Park."

21

JESSICA

Jessica woke with a mouth as dry as the Mojave and the familiar dull headache of a mild hangover. A slice of sunlight fell across the carpeted floor through the gap in the curtains, and the heat from the morning sun through the window made the room uncomfortably warm.

She fumbled for the glass of water on the nightstand, her fingers brushing the cold steel of the Glock. The gun reminded her of Larry's warning about Doc Durrant. Jessica still didn't think Bibi's husband was a threat, but she did want to know whether his claims about Veronica Lowe's death were true.

She found a blister pack of painkillers in the nightstand's top drawer, popped two out and chased them down with the lukewarm contents of the tumbler, then kicked off the bed sheets. After a quick shower on the cool setting, Jessica picked out black capri pants, a Breton tee, and white tennis shoes. She carefully applied some makeup, paying particular attention to concealing the purple smudges under her eyes.

Then she sat at the table by the window and opened her laptop. Drank some instant coffee while she accessed the Los Angeles

Public Library's website. They had branches all over the city, but it seemed like the Central Library downtown would be her best bet.

She grabbed a donut and a cold bottle of water to go from Dustin's for the fifteen-minute drive. Once on the road, Jessica buzzed the Silverado's windows all the way down, enjoying the breeze on her skin, as she shook out a Marlboro from the pack and lit it. She drove east along Sunset before joining the 101 at the big Home Depot and dropping south toward downtown. The traffic was free-moving to start with but soon became tangled, and she'd finished the water and donut and another cigarette by the time she'd reached the DTLA tower blocks, which always reminded her of home in New York. There was an added sense of déjà vu this time, after tailing Bibi less than twenty-four hours earlier to the fried chicken place.

The Los Angeles Central Library was located on West 5th Street, between Grand Avenue and Flower Street, in the heart of the Financial District. The building itself was something of a cultural landmark, the pale 1920s Art Deco construction nestled among the shiny sky-high office blocks like a vintage jeweled brooch in a pile of cheap costume jewelry.

Once inside, the place was a fascinating mix of old and new. Jessica knew nothing about art, but she couldn't help but feel a little awed by the impressive interior. On another day, she might've taken the time to wander around, check out the murals depicting Californian history and the Zodiac Chandelier in the Rotunda, which was widely regarded as the focal point of the older part of the library.

But the only history Jessica was interested in today was more recent. Sixteen years ago, to be precise. She found an information point in the main lobby which directed her to the Tom Bradley wing, where a set of escalators took her down four levels to the subterranean History and Genealogy Department.

The place smelled comfortingly old, like sniffing the yellowed pages of a well-thumbed novel. Among a wealth of history books, maps, and photograph collections were microfilm reader machines where she would be able to access old copies of the *Los Angeles Times*. She requested the microfilm reels from the year she was interested in and, once set up by a helpful member of staff, who thankfully didn't ask to see a library card, Jessica settled in for the task of trawling through newspaper pages from around the time Veronica was last seen.

Doc Durrant had used the phrase "gun for hire" so she focused her search on shootings and quickly established the vast majority involved male victims and a lot of those were gang-related. It seemed to Jessica that on the few occasions where women were the victims of gun violence, the details were particularly distressing.

There was a black female who survived after being shot in the face, while her male companion died of a gunshot wound to the head.

A Latina woman who was found dead in a car with a man in what appeared to be a murder-suicide.

A heavily pregnant woman whose own life, and that of her unborn baby, were ended by a bullet.

The descriptions of the women ruled out any chance of Veronica Lowe being the victim in any of those cases.

There was also another story about a white female who had been shot by her ex-boyfriend, before he turned the gun on himself. The age range was right but neither the name nor the photo were a match.

Jessica's eyesight began to blur, and a headache worse than the one she'd had courtesy of this morning's hangover was starting to bloom behind her eyes, as a result of fast-scrolling through the images onscreen and skim-reading so much text.

She was just about to give up when a photograph caught her attention. It showed an attractive black man with a great smile, wearing a striped shirt with a V-neck wool vest on top and a bowtie. The word that popped into Jessica's head was "preppy"—exactly how Ron Casey had described Veronica's new boyfriend.

The headline alongside the photo read: "Teacher Killed in Unprovoked Sidewalk Shooting; Cops Want to Speak to Female Witness."

Jessica read the article, her heart rate ramping up the further she read.

Maurice Wayland, a popular high-school English teacher, had been gunned down on the sidewalk early one July evening. He'd died instantly from shots to the heart and head. He was thirty-six years old. Eyewitnesses told how the two rounds of gunfire appeared to come from the partially open passenger window of a black SUV, before the vehicle drove away at high speed. Maurice was divorced, with one child, and had no known gang connections.

It was a horrific story, but that wasn't what got the blood pumping through Jessica's veins.

Witnesses also said a woman appeared to be with Wayland at the time of the shooting but she had left the scene by the time the first responders arrived. She was described as being in her late twenties or early thirties, of slim build, with shoulder-length red hair. Police wanted to speak to her urgently.

Jessica frantically scrolled through later editions of the *Times* for any updates on the Wayland homicide. There was only one, around a month later. The ex-wife and her new husband had both been ruled out of the investigation, as had gang-related violence, despite the execution-style nature of the shooting. Police, at that point, were looking at the possibility of a former student with a grudge against Wayland as a potential motive for his murder.

There was no mention of the cops tracking down the mysterious redhead.

Jessica paid fifty cents to print off both articles, then gathered her stuff together. Once outside, she switched on her cell phone as she made her way to where her truck was parked. She had two text messages from Connor.

Need to speak to you. Are you around later? Best to speak face to face. I can meet you in Hollywood.

Then: Jessica, did you get my message? It's important. Call me back.

She also had a new email in her inbox. Or rather, "Lorelei Givens" had an email. A notification from The Lonely Hearts Club confirming her application for membership had been approved.

Jessica was in.

22

VERONICA—2003

The journey from San Francisco to Los Angeles usually took Veronica around six hours. Today it felt like forever. Her mind didn't even register the sights of Half Moon Bay and Big Sur and Santa Barbara, never mind marvel at their beauty like she usually did on the coastal drive.

She'd been later than usual getting on the road back home after a visit to the prison. She'd made a stop at a payphone, then visited the bank and withdrawn every cent she had, before closing down the account.

This was after she'd fallen to her knees outside the gates of San Quentin, warm vomit hitting hot concrete, the contents of her purse spilled around her. After she'd stopped shaking long enough to start the car engine.

Travis had killed someone.

Veronica laughed and the sound bordered on hysteria. No, Travis had killed sixteen people. Fifteen women before she'd even met him. She just hadn't wanted to believe it. Not after he'd written her that first letter and told her he was innocent. Especially not after he'd looked her in the eye the first time they'd met and told her the same thing. The lies rebounded around her brain like shrapnel.

Circumstantial evidence.

Junk science.

An interest in the Strangler murders that was no different to everyone else who lived in the Valley at that time.

Now Veronica knew exactly what Travis Dean Ford was capable of.

She hadn't returned to San Quentin after that last visit, when he'd quietly fumed about her appearance and moving to a new apartment without telling him. She never did write him with the address in Larchmont. But he'd found her anyway. He'd known about Maurice. And he'd had him killed.

Meeting Maurice Wayland had been one of the best things that had ever happened to Veronica. She'd been happier than she had been in a long time. Maybe ever. She'd gotten to know him as a customer at the Big Coffee Cup first, then as a friend, then as a lover. He'd later admitted he thought the food at the restaurant was terrible but he'd kept on coming back until he'd plucked up enough courage to ask Veronica out on a date.

Maurice was kind and compassionate and gentle and thoughtful. Everything Leon Geffen and Travis Dean Ford were not. He cared about his students, he loved his little boy, he'd even managed to remain friends with his ex-wife and her new husband. Veronica hadn't told Maurice about Travis—not yet—but her prison romance was over for good as far as she was concerned.

That would mean Travis not seeing Mia. Something she should probably feel more guilty about than she actually did. But, really, prison was no place for a little girl. She'd figure something out when Mia was a little older—if Travis lived that long. He was fast running out of appeals.

It was early days with Maurice but, already, Veronica was starting to think, to hope, that what they had was the real deal. She was considering introducing him to Mia. He wanted Veronica to meet his son. Now he was dead. One moment they'd been walking along the street, laughing about how he wouldn't have to pretend to like the food at the restaurant they were headed to. The next, Maurice was dying on the sidewalk.

Veronica knew she shouldn't have run. She'd also known in that split second what it would mean for her and Mia if she stuck around until the police showed up. How their lives would be held up to public scrutiny once again. How they'd never be free of Travis Dean Ford.

She'd walked around in a fog of grief and despair those first couple of days. Then the fear had set in. The newspapers had mentioned a witness. A redhead. What if the cops figured out it was her? She hadn't met Maurice's friends or family yet. Her boss at the Big Coffee Cup, Ron Casey, had seen them together one night after work, but would he recognize Maurice in the papers? She'd only ever seen Ron read the sports section.

Then, after the grief and despair and fear, came the clarity of thought. The cops' theories about a jealous ex or gang violence or a student grudge didn't stack up. Not the Maurice she knew. What if the shooting hadn't been about him? What if it had been about *her*? What if Travis Dean Ford had been behind Maurice's murder?

The only way to find out was to visit him.

He didn't admit it with words. He didn't have to. One look at his face confirmed Veronica's suspicions. She'd asked him anyway.

"Did you do it?"

He'd smiled at her. "It's good to see you, Veronica. It's been a while. I guess you remembered what I told you last time we spoke?"

She did.

No one gets to leave me anymore. Especially not you.

"Did you do it?" she asked again.

"I have no idea what you're talking about." His brow furrowed in mock concern. "Is everything okay? You're not having the same problems in Larchmont that you had in Silver Lake, are you? You really should be more careful who you choose to spend time with."

There it was. Travis letting her know that he knew where she lived. That he knew about Maurice. Realization was a hard punch to the face. Travis had killed her boyfriend—and he'd murdered all those women too.

Once she'd pulled herself together in the car outside the prison, Veronica knew what she had to do—but she needed help.

There was no way she could drag Christine into this mess. Her best friend had saved her from Leon but this was a whole different level. She'd be way out of her depth.

Veronica had stopped at a payphone and made a call to the only other person she trusted.

Back at Beverly Boulevard, she picked up Mia from her neighbor, Glo Goldson. She felt sad knowing it was the last time she'd see her friend and there would be no proper goodbye. While Mia slept on the sofa, Veronica silently moved around her apartment, packing up the few things they'd need for the trip. The rest, she could buy once they arrived at the new place. She worked quickly by the glow of the streetlight outside, not daring to switch on a light. Not knowing if she was being watched.

She shrugged the rucksack onto her back and lifted Mia and locked up behind her. Jogged downstairs and slipped the letter she'd written Glo into the woman's mailbox, along with her apartment keys. Then she headed out the rear exit to the gated parking lot.

The car was waiting with the engine running.

As she buckled Mia into the back seat, Veronica leaned over and kissed her on the cheek, inhaling the scent of the "wacky watermelon" shampoo Glo kept for the little girl's bath time.

"Where're we going, Mommy?" Mia asked, sleepily.

"Somewhere no one will find us."

23

JESSICA

Jessica was itching to floor the gas pedal and return to the motel as quickly as possible now that she had full, unrestricted access to The Lonely Hearts Club's website. But this was Los Angeles, and the city's notorious traffic had other ideas. She endured a stop-start journey, fingers drumming impatiently on the steering wheel, staring at blinking taillights and rear fenders for what felt like forever, before finally arriving back on the Strip.

Once in her room, she fired up the laptop and logged on to her new member's account. A pop-up box immediately appeared with a cheerful welcome message from Bibi addressed to Lorelei Givens. Jessica heart thudded, a mixture of a guilty conscience and a weird feeling of being watched by TLHC's founder. Then she realized the pop-up was a generic, automated message when new members logged on for the first time. Bibi wasn't literally at her computer trying to engage with Lorelei. Jessica clicked the little "X" in the top corner to shut down the welcome greeting, then she opened the members-only forum.

As well as general chat, there were a whole bunch of threads dedicated to specific topics: advice for those writing a prisoner on

Death Row; what to expect when visiting a pen pal for the first time; whether to meet up IRL after release; how to deal with negative responses from friends and family; updates on scheduled executions and last-minute stays; what to do if your pen pal suddenly stopped writing you; requests from journalists, podcast hosts, and college students writing dissertations who were all looking to interview women who write men in prison.

Most of the OPs—original posters—had tiny profile pics alongside their usernames and Jessica was surprised to note that many seemed to be women in their early twenties, with the kind of pouting, over-filtered selfies more commonly found on the Instagram feeds of wannabe "influencers."

She had assumed most of the Lonely Hearts were middle-aged or older women who, for whatever reason, had found themselves on their own in their later years and who had turned to an unusual source in an attempt to fill a hole left by loneliness. With a flicker of shame, Jessica realized she'd been guilty of jumping to conclusions that weren't necessarily true. Based on what she was seeing on the screen in front of her, her Rachael Wilson alias would have been a better fit for the group than the forty-something Lorelei Givens.

Even so, Jessica couldn't help but wonder what exactly a twenty-three-year-old got out of writing someone who was incarcerated. Was it the excitement? A sense of rebellion? Or was it simply fashionable to champion a prisoner's cause these days in the wake of celebs, such as Kim Kardashian, lending their high-profile support to possible wrongful conviction cases?

Bibi was a frequent commenter on all of the threads, offering support and advice as a veteran prison bride, but Jessica saw nothing that gave her a better insight into the woman or her relationship with Veronica Lowe.

She exited the forum and turned her attention to a link titled "Local Meets." Here, she found details of upcoming social events, as well as photos from previous get-togethers. A "wine and whine" night was scheduled for West Hollywood for a week's time, hosted by Bibi Durrant. The description read: "Missing your man? Fed up with CDCR regulations? Family and friends don't get your prison friendship? Get it all off your chest with the gals—wine included! RSVP below." Twenty-one Lonely Hearts had confirmed their attendance so far. There were other meets taking place all over the country, with the San Francisco area, in particular, a hotbed of membership activity—perhaps unsurprisingly, given its proximity to San Quentin.

The final section that was also only open to members was "Our Stories." There were hundreds of photos, each captioned with a brief explanation of what was going on in the snapshot. The posts were chronological—most recent first—rather than by member name, meaning Jessica had no option but to sift through them all in order to find posts by Bibi. There were pics of women—made up, hair coiffed, nice outfits—posing with unshaven men wearing orange scrubs. There were prison weddings, pre-incarceration pics, post-incarceration pics, selfies outside the prison gates.

The most recent photo posted by Bibi was from six months ago and fell into the latter category. It showed Bibi and Doc Durrant, arms around each other, squinting in the winter sun, with San Quentin looming large and intimidating in the background.

The caption read:

> BEST DAY EVER! I finally get to take my man home. Thanks soooo much for all your support, gals. Here's to me and Doc enjoying the rest of our lives TOGETHER. Let's just say tonight is going to be . . . FUN! ;-) Hotel in 'Frisco tonight and then HOME. So, so happy xx.

It had hundreds of responses.

Jessica fast-scrolled through the huge gallery of images, searching for more posts by the big-haired, petite brunette. She also paused for a better look every time she came across a redhead, but none of them were Veronica Lowe. She didn't find a single shot of Travis Dean Ford's ex or his daughter.

In contrast, there were lots of Bibi. In some, she was dressed up to the nines, her ample cleavage just about covered by low-cut tops or dresses. Those were selfies she had shared with the group, before sending on to Doc while he was still behind bars. Then there were older photos, ones Bibi liked to call "Blasts from the Past," which showed much younger versions of Bibi and Doc, back in the days when they both still resided in Arizona and before he wound up with a serious rap sheet. Jessica had to admit they made a cute couple. Bibi, tiny and pretty and slim and soft with youth. Doc, ruggedly handsome and already showing some rough edges but none of the prison-honed menace he now exuded.

Jessica scrutinized those photographs for any clues, little details, anything at all that might shed some light on the Durrants' relationship with Veronica Lowe. She found nothing, but hooked up her printer to the laptop and made a copy of them all anyway. Scotch-taped the printouts to her evidence board.

Jessica continued her trawl back in time. Fashions and hairstyles changed the further back she went; the now familiar faces of long-term members grew younger in a strange sort of age-progression reversal.

The Durrants' nuptials were shared with the group on a milestone anniversary, the ceremony itself having taken place long before TLHC went online. Just as the newspaper sidebar had described, Bibi wore white silk and lace and looked incredible, while her groom was less appropriately attired in his regulation blue denim prison garb.

Jessica spotted a couple of posts by a young Jordana Ferrer, captured outside San Quentin, the time stamp confirming they'd been taken after Veronica and Mia disappeared and shortly before Jordana married Ford. There were no photos of the wedding itself; the woman savvy enough to keep those private until the publication of the book that now looked set to be a posthumous chart-topper.

There was a post that had been removed by the moderator, presumably Bibi, that gave Jessica pause. She had skimmed past others that had been taken down for violating member guidelines but what caught her attention about this one was the date it had originally been posted: just days before the photo exclusive of Veronica and Mia with Ford had appeared in the press.

Was there a connection?

Was it a coincidence?

Jessica didn't believe in coincidences.

She kept on scrolling and was almost at the end of the gallery when she finally hit pay dirt. Jessica's breathing got faster; adrenalin buzzed through her body.

Finally, a possible connection between Veronica and the Durrants that went beyond simply being friendly with Bibi back when Veronica was a member of TLHC.

The photo was another one of Bibi's "Blasts from the Past." Another cute snap of Bibi and Doc as loved-up teens.

The young couple were sitting side by side on an old rubber tire, their shoulders and thighs pressed together in the cramped space. The tire was attached to a sturdy tree branch by three lengths of thick, frayed rope. Bibi and Doc were both holding onto a rope each, their legs dangling above the dry packed dirt of a yard in summertime. She had the Dolly Parton thing going on with the big, white smile; he was offering up his best James Dean impression, a cigarette hanging from his lips.

Behind the tire swing, a farmhouse was just visible in the background.

24

PRYCE

"You're too late. He's gone."

The woman standing on the doorstep of the small house with the "½" street number was around a foot smaller than Pryce. She was very tan and barefoot with red painted toenails and, despite it being almost eleven a.m., was dressed in a midnight blue satin negligee and matching dressing gown.

She had one hand on her hip and the other high on the door-frame in a defiant, provocative pose. A kid of about twelve, who'd been practicing wheelies on his bike in the street outside when they'd arrived, had stopped to gape at her.

"Mrs. Durrant?" Pryce asked.

"Yep, that's me. For the time being, anyways."

Her Southern accent was soft, but her eyes were cold and her jaw set harder than concrete.

"We need to speak to Denis Durrant. It's important."

Durrant's prints had shown up all over Jordana Ford's house, meaning the ex-con had a hell of a lot of explaining to do.

"I already told you, my husband ain't here." The wife stepped aside and threw her hand out in a dramatic gesture. "But feel free to come on in and have a look for yourself."

Pryce took the inside of the house while Medina headed around the back to inspect the yard and any outbuildings. The search was done in under five minutes—closets, bathroom, under the bed. The woman sat on an armchair in the compact living room with her legs crossed, smoking a long menthol cigarette, watching as Pryce worked.

"Doc is over six feet tall," she said, as Pryce opened the door to what turned out to be a linen closet. "Not a whole lot of hiding places."

Medina returned from his inspection of the backyard with a shake of the head.

"What wheels does your husband drive?" Pryce asked.

The woman provided the make and model of a motorcycle, as well as the license plate number.

"What about a car?"

"He doesn't have one. The red pickup in the drive is mine."

Medina went into the hallway to make some calls in order to confirm the motorcycle was the only vehicle registered to Denis Durrant, as well as having a BOLO put out on it. He returned and stood in the doorway, while Pryce took a seat on the sofa facing Mrs. Durrant. Her eyes were bloodshot, and dark eye makeup was smudged underneath. It didn't look as though her hair had been brushed today. The satin slip wasn't leaving much to the imagination.

"Would you like to go put some clothes on, Mrs. Durrant?" Pryce offered.

"Not really. I'd rather get this over with if you don't mind. And, for God's sake, call me Bibi. All this Mrs. Durrant stuff is making me feel old." She blew out smoke and Pryce felt his eyes start to sting. "This is about Jordana, right? She always was trouble, that one."

"We really need to know where your husband is, Bibi."

She studied the cigarette. "Like I said, he's long gone."

"Gone where?" Medina asked.

She shrugged. "He didn't say. Didn't speak to me at all." She laughed bitterly. "Couldn't face telling me what he'd done to my face."

A look passed between the two detectives, which she caught.

"It's not what you're thinking," she said.

"What did he do?" Pryce asked.

"He didn't kill Jordana. He was screwing her."

Bibi pushed a handwritten note across the coffee table toward Pryce. He picked it up by the corner and read it. Showed it to Medina, then dropped it in a clear evidence bag that his partner produced from his inside pocket. It read:

Bibi, by the time you read this, I'll be in the wind. They'll be coming for me soon and I can't face going back inside. They'll tell you I did it, that I murdered Jordana. I didn't. But I did betray you and that's worse. I hope you can forgive me. You deserve better. Doc.

"When did you last see Denis?" Pryce asked.

"Doc," she corrected. "No one calls him Denis. He told me he had to go out yesterday evening to take care of some business, then he'd be working late at the bar."

"Which bar? What's he do there?"

"He works security at Rosco's on Pico. The bar, not the chicken and waffle place. And 'security' is just a fancy way of saying he's the doorman. He IDs the pretty, young girls, and throws the drunks out onto the street. An old buddy lined up the job for him after he got out of prison around six months ago. When I woke up this morning, he wasn't in bed beside me so I checked my cell. There were no messages. I was worried. I called his cell and it went straight to voicemail. I was even more worried. Then I got out of bed and made my way into the living room and that's when I found the letter."

"He wasn't at work last night?" Medina said.

"No, he wasn't. And he wasn't there plenty of other times either when he told me he was working. I checked. For months, I believed he was at the bar every Friday and Saturday night. He lied. He only worked Saturdays on the weekends. Friday nights, he was with her."

"You had no idea he was having an affair with Jordana?" Pryce asked.

"Of course I didn't. Sure, things haven't been great between us since he got out but I figured that was normal. We've been married a long time, but we don't really know each other, not anymore. We haven't lived with each other our whole married lives. I put the lack of sex down to issues he had readjusting to the outside world. I had no idea it was because he was screwing someone else. And Jordana of all people."

"You two didn't get on?" Pryce asked.

"I didn't like her, if that's what you mean. The feeling was mutual. We hadn't seen each other in years. Didn't stop her talking trash about my business, though."

"Your business?"

"I run a prisoner pen-pal service. It's how Jordana and I first met years ago. She was one of my members."

"The pen-pal service—is it The Lonely Hearts Club?"

"That's right," Bibi said. "I've worked real hard at building it up over the years and Jordana did her level best to knock it down. All those lies in her books and interviews, claiming I tried to stop her having a relationship with Travis Dean Ford by trashing the letters they wrote to each other and refusing to pass them on. The allegations of bullying and favoritism. It was all lies."

"How did your husband know Jordana?" Medina asked.

"As far as I knew, he didn't. Not really. But I can guess exactly when it all began. Not long after he got out, I was real upset over some interview Jordana had done teasing the new book. She'd trashed The Lonely Hearts Club yet again. Doc said he was going to go around to her place and sort things out once and for all. Let's just say he took his time coming home."

"When was this?" Pryce said.

"Around five months ago."

The timeline fit with the visit from the "angry guy" which was witnessed by Jordana's neighbor, Emma Alves.

Medina said, "So, your husband went around to Mrs. Ford's home to challenge her about her behavior toward you and your business, and what? He ended up in bed with her? Seriously?"

"That's about the size of it," Bibi said. "Doc is a very passionate man. He was all fired up, and Jordana was a very manipulative woman. I can see how it happened."

Pryce fixed Bibi with a firm look. "And you had no idea at all about the affair? Not until the letter?"

She held his gaze. "No, I did not, Detective. Believe me, Doc would not have been living under my roof if I had known."

Bibi crushed the butt of her cigarette in a glass ashtray on the coffee table and lit another from an almost-full pack.

She went on, "You know, I gave up years ago because Doc doesn't like me smoking, even though he's a twenty-a-day guy himself. But I always kept a spare pack hidden in the kitchen cupboard for emergencies. I guess this counts."

Medina nodded at the ashtray overflowing with dead butts. "Looks like more than one pack to me."

She shrugged. "I got the kid next door to cycle to the store and pick me up some more. It's not a crime, is it?"

"Technically, it is a crime to ask a minor to purchase tobacco for you," Medina said. "But let's get back to Doc . . ."

"Maybe I should've guessed," Bibi said. "All those nights he came home stinking of perfume and explained it away as women in the bar spraying themselves with scent after being outside for a smoke. Other times, he'd be late and crawl into bed reeking of booze and claiming his boss made him stay after closing time for drinks with the staff. It seems obvious now that he'd been with another woman. I guess I just didn't want to believe it. All those years waiting for him to get out of prison so we could be together properly . . . I didn't want to admit to myself that things weren't working out."

"Where was Doc Saturday night?" Pryce asked.

"He was at the bar. I know, that's what he always said. But this time it was true. I told you, he always works Saturdays. The bar manager said he was there all night. They have cameras. I'm sure they can confirm it."

"So, why did he run?" Pryce asked.

"He was scared, wasn't he? I bet you found his prints and DNA all over her house. In her bedroom." Bibi looked away. "Doc isn't stupid. He's fresh out of prison. Alibi or not, he figured you'd pin it on him somehow. Whatever Doc did to hurt me, I know he isn't capable of killing anyone."

"He was in prison for killing a man," Medina pointed out.

Bibi gave him a sharp look. "That was different. He was trying to save a friend from being shot. He saved his friend's life. You know he also saved a kid's life once, when he was a teenager? That makes it two to one in his favor in my book. I don't think Doc's going to hell for how he's lived his life and I know for sure he didn't hurt Jordana Ford."

"You said he split last night," Pryce said. "He had help?"

"I'd say so. Doc found out about Jordana Monday morning, like everyone else. He would've known you'd be coming for him as soon as you ran your tests, so I'm guessing he got in touch with some old contacts of his to make the necessary arrangements. Our joint bank account has been cleaned out so we're talking a car, fake papers, probably a passport. He could be anywhere by now. Mexico. Canada. Hawaii. The Bahamas. Probably on a beach some-place, sipping a cocktail and smoking cigars, while I'm stuck here being interrogated by you."

"What about you?" Pryce asked.

"What about me?"

"Where were you Saturday night?"

"I was here, at home. All night."

"Alone?"

"Yes, that's right."

"So, your husband has an alibi for Saturday night—but you don't?"

"What are you saying?"

"I'm saying, you have no alibi for the night Jordana Ford was murdered. But you had plenty reason to want her dead."

25

JORDANA

"Doc." Jordana breathed the word more than said it.

Doc Durrant's eyes widened, and he slowly held up his hands. "Why are you pointing that thing at me, Jordana? Put the gun down, honey."

She lowered the weapon and placed it on top of the nightstand. Her relief turned to anger. "I thought you were an intruder. What were you thinking, sneaking around my house at this time of night? It's past midnight."

The tension had visibly left Doc's body now he no longer had a Smith & Wesson pointed at him.

"I wasn't sneaking around," he said. "I wanted to see you tonight, find out how the book launch went. I sent you a text to say I was on my way and that I'd let myself in."

About a month after they'd first gotten together, Jordana had given Doc a key for the back door. She'd already known by then that what they had was the real deal, that it wasn't just sex like the others. But she didn't want the neighbors knowing she had a new man in her life. It was none of their damn business for a start, and would have been disastrous for the promotion of *Lockdown Love* if the affair had been leaked to the press ahead of publication. She'd given Doc the key so he wouldn't have to bang on the door at all times of night. He always parked his motorcycle a couple of streets away, and she left the deadbolt off on the nights they planned to spend together.

"The bedroom light was on, so I knew you weren't asleep," he said. "And the deadbolt was off. When you didn't answer, I assumed you were, um, changing into something sexy. I texted again to say I was making my way upstairs. I thought you'd be waiting for me in the bedroom; I just didn't think you'd be waiting for me with a gun."

"My cell phone is downstairs," she said. "I turned off the ringer after Graham from the bookstore called about what happened at the event."

Doc frowned. "What happened at the event?"

Jordana was still breathing heavily, adrenalin fizzing, every inch of her covered in goosebumps. "Forget about the launch. Get yourself over here right now."

After they'd finished making love, Doc whispered in her ear, "Wow, what just happened there?"

"I guess I was happy to see you."

It was the best sex they'd had, even better than the first time. On that occasion, Doc had appeared on her doorstep, furiously defending Bibi and the Lonely Hearts. One minute they were screaming at each other, the next they were screwing on the living-room floor. Forget booze or pills or even a cute ass in tight jeans; pure rage had been a far more powerful aphrodisiac that day. Tonight, it was fear that turned her on. It had always been part of her attraction to Travis too.

"What are you thinking?" Doc asked, softly.

Jordana smiled. Anyone else and that kind of question would really piss her off. But she knew it was Doc's way of showing her that he cared; that their relationship was about much more than the time they spent in bed. Or on the living-room floor.

"Malibu," she lied.

"I can't wait, honey. No more sneaking around. No more lies."

"What do you think Bibi will do when you tell her?"

"Probably kill us both."

The smile slipped from Jordana's face.

"What happened at the launch?" Doc asked.

"Just a heckler. No big deal."

"Are you okay?"

"Sure. We sold a ton of books. That's the main thing."

His eyes were filled with concern. "Are you sure you're okay? You could've blown my head off."

Jordana laughed, tried to lighten the mood. "I'm a terrible shot. I'd probably have missed."

Doc smiled, then groaned. "I'd better go take a shower and then hit the road. I told Bibi I was having a couple drinks at the bar." He kissed Jordana hard and deep. "I wish I could stay all night."

"I do too." And she meant it. She'd feel a lot safer with Doc in bed beside her.

After he was gone, Jordana dressed in her pajamas and went downstairs. She slid the deadbolt into place on the back door and retrieved her cell phone from the living room. She'd missed a call from a withheld number around an hour ago. Jordana frowned. It was almost two a.m. She thought about Lou Hardwick and his anger at the bookstore. Then she thought about Doc's words when they'd spoken about Bibi.

Probably kill us both.

Jordana shuddered. It wasn't the first time she'd had late-night calls. Again, her thoughts turned to Veronica Lowe. Jordana had done the exact same thing to her. Hanging around phone booths in the dead of night. Relishing the frustration and exhaustion in Veronica's voice. Annoying, for sure, but Jordana knew now, also terrifying for a woman living on her own.

She turned off the downstairs lights and wearily climbed the stairs. Got into bed and started to set the alarm on the cell phone—she had chores to do in the morning before the podcast interview with Jared MacFarlane—when it vibrated in her hand. Jordana almost dropped the phone.

A withheld number.

Now past two a.m.

Jordana hesitated a beat, then answered. "Who is this?" she demanded.

The caller said nothing. There was only the sound of their breathing on the line. Not the heavy breathing of perverts in old movies, just regular breathing. Someone letting Jordana know they were there, listening to her.

"What do you want?" she said.

Still there was no answer.

She was about to end the call when she thought she heard a car in the background. Whoever was calling her was outside, on a street someplace.

Her street?

She switched off the lamp and went to the window. The backyard was hidden in darkness. The sensor light stayed off. She moved through to the guest room at the front of the house. Pulled back the curtain and looked out onto the street, the phone still pressed tight against her ear.

She could still hear the steady breathing.

Streetlights softly illuminated the sidewalk beyond the front lawn. All the neighbors' lights were off, apart from the pale glow of a night light in the little kid's room in the house facing her own. The street was empty, but Jordana couldn't shake the feeling someone was out there, standing in the shadows, watching her at the window.

"I see you," she lied.

The line went dead.

26

JESSICA

Jessica stared at the photo of Bibi and Doc Durrant.

She knew there were thousands of farmhouses with old tire swings in yards just like this one, throughout the country. The logical part of her brain told her there was nothing to suggest the swing holding two lovestruck teenagers from almost forty years ago was the same one as in the photo Veronica Lowe had shown her neighbor, Glo Goldson, when she'd spoken about a vacation she'd taken once with Mia.

But Jessica's gut was telling her something else entirely. It was telling her it was the same rope swing. The same farmhouse.

She thought of the phone call Bibi had made outside the fried chicken restaurant. How the woman had kept on feeding the coin slot, even though it'd been a relatively short conversation with whoever was on the other end of the line. Jessica had suspected at the time that the call had been out of state. Now, she was thinking Arizona, where the old snapshot of Bibi and Doc had likely been captured.

She read the caption Bibi had attached to the image: "Halfway to heaven—another 'Blast from the Past' with my soul mate, Doc. Young love!!"

Jessica frowned. *Halfway to heaven.* What the hell did that mean? It made no sense. The only place Doc Durrant was halfway to back then was a murder charge and decades spent behind bars. She expanded the photo as much as possible without it pixelating, and got up close to the laptop screen to study it for any clues as to where exactly in Arizona it had been taken. She didn't find any. There were no visible landmarks or school letter jackets or hometown tees to narrow it down. Just a single-story farmhouse, with a wraparound porch and a red brick roof and dirty white siding, like a million other farmhouses.

Jessica then searched property records in Arizona for anything registered in the names of Barbara Burr or Denis Durrant—and drew a blank. She wasn't surprised. They'd upped and left for California at different times, but both were still young enough that it was unlikely they'd have owned property before their respective moves to the Golden State.

She tried googling the incident with the choking kid at the summer barbecue in the hope that Doc Durrant's heroics might've made the local press at the time. Another blank. Again, hardly a surprise. It wasn't exactly up there with the assassination of JFK or the Watergate scandal in terms of newsworthiness.

Next, she threw a selection of words, names, and phrases into the search engine—halfway to heaven, Barbara Burr, Denis Durrant, Bibi Durrant, Arizona—and finally found a result that appeared promising.

A small town in Arizona by the name of Halfway.

It had a hot desert climate and a large amount of sunshine all year round. There was a golf course, two elementary schools, one middle school, and one high school. It probably had some farmhouses too. And it just might have been the hometown of Barbara Burr and Denis Durrant.

Jessica tapped the office number for Halfway High School into her cell phone and waited for the call to connect. Asked to be transferred to the school librarian, and listened for thirty seconds to the kind of bad Muzak usually found in hotel elevators, before a cheerful voice answered.

"Hello, this is the library. Sabrina speaking."

"Hi, Sabrina," Jessica said. "My name is, uh, Lorelei Givens. I was hoping you might be able to help with a request I have."

"Sure. If I can, I will."

"My neighbor has a birthday coming up and I'm organizing a surprise party. She's a good friend, as well as being a great neighbor, and I want it to be really special."

"Uh-huh . . ."

"So, I'm trying to track down some photos of Barbara when she was younger. I thought it would be fun to have them blown up into posters that we could hang on the walls of the venue. It would be so cool to find her old yearbook picture from her senior year at high school. That's where you come in."

"Barbara was a student at Halfway High?"

"She certainly was." Jessica hoped she sounded more confident than she felt. "Do you happen to keep back copies of the school's yearbooks in the library?"

"We sure do," said Sabrina. "What's Barbara's full name and the year she would have been a senior here?"

"Barbara Burr. She would have been a senior in 1982."

"Okay, let me go have a look and I'll call you back in about ten minutes."

Jessica gave Sabrina her cell number and thanked her. Then spent the next fourteen minutes impatiently drumming her fingers on the tabletop. When the phone screen finally lit up with an incoming call from an out-of-state number, she snatched up the device and tried not to sound like someone who had been counting down the seconds waiting for the call back.

"Lorelei? This is Sabrina from Halfway High School."

"Hi, Sabrina. Were you able to find the photo of Barbara?" Jessica held her breath and crossed her fingers.

"I sure was," Sabrina said triumphantly. "Class of '82, just like you said. She was very pretty."

Jessica breathed out slowly, as her heartbeat accelerated. "Amazing work, Sabrina. I'm sure Barbara will be beyond delighted—not to mention totally surprised—that we were able to find her old yearbook picture. I can't wait to see it."

"Are you nearby? Do you want to stop by the school and make a copy?"

"I'm actually in California. Barbara lives in Los Angeles now."

"Oh, right. Well, why don't I take a photo on my cell and email it over? Would that work?"

"That would be perfect. Thanks, Sabrina."

Jessica gave the librarian the Lorelei Givens email address and disconnected the call. She didn't need to see the email or how pretty Bibi had been back in the early '80s. She already had what she wanted: confirmation of Bibi and Doc's hometown.

Halfway, Arizona.

The likely location of the farmhouse with the old tire swing.

The possible location of the call Bibi had made on the payphone outside Gus's World Famous Fried Chicken.

The town where Veronica Lowe and Mia Ford had been living under the radar for close on twenty years?

There was only one way to find out.

Jessica picked up the cell phone again, and started as it began to ring in her hand. Connor. She had completely forgotten about the messages he'd sent earlier while she'd been inside the library.

She rejected the call and pulled up the number she had stored for Christine Ryan instead. The woman answered almost immediately.

"Jessica." She sounded slightly out of breath, like she'd just raced across the room to pick up. "Do you have news? Have you found Veronica?"

"I'm sorry, Christine. I haven't found Veronica. Not yet anyway."

"Oh, okay."

"I may have a lead, though. I wanted to let you know I'll be out of town for a day or two, checking it out."

"A lead? What kind of lead? Where are you going? I'm coming with you."

Jessica sighed. "No, Christine. You're not."

"Why not?" Her tone was sharper than a supermodel's cheekbones. "I'm paying you, remember? I have a right to know where she is."

"Listen to me," Jessica snapped. "I don't know for sure where Veronica is. I'm following a lead is all. You have to let me do my job."

"But—"

"The answer is no, Christine. We've been through this already. Even if I do find Veronica, she may not want to be found. If that's the case, you have to respect her decision. You don't like the way I work? I'm happy to return the retainer and we drop the whole thing right now. Is that what you want?"

There was a long pause. Finally, Christine said, "No, it's not what I want. I'm sorry, Jessica. You're right. I'm just worried about her."

"I know you are, but I don't allow clients to tag along while I'm working, under any circumstances. No exceptions."

"Will you at least keep me informed of any developments?"

"That I can do. Speak soon."

Jessica killed the connection before Christine could say anything else.

She ran downstairs to the Silverado, the rubber soles of her tennis shoes banging noisily on the metal staircase, grabbed the overnight duffel, and jogged back upstairs to her room. The temperature felt like it was in the triple figures, and sweat beaded her forehead and pooled beneath her underarms. Jessica left the door open to allow stagnant air into the room, and bent over and tried to catch her breath. Then she went into the bathroom and gathered up her toiletries, and dumped them onto the bed along with a small mountain of underwear and clean clothing.

"What? You don't answer your phone anymore?"

Jessica spun around to find Connor standing in the doorway.

"Fuck," she breathed, grabbing her chest. "You could've given me a heart attack, Connor. You do know that shit runs in my family, right?"

He didn't smile. "You shouldn't leave your door wide open. And you shouldn't ignore important calls and messages."

"I wasn't ignoring you. I've been busy. Possible lead in the Veronica Lowe case."

Connor stepped into the room and closed the door. He wore light blue jeans and a navy t-shirt and impossibly white Adidas sneakers. He hadn't shaved in a day or two and she noticed for the first time just how much his hair had grown over the summer, back to the curling-at-the-collar length it had been the first time they'd met. Despite the heat, he looked so fresh he could've stepped straight out of the shower. He smelled good too.

"We need to talk," he said.

"Sounds serious."

Jessica turned away and wiped a slick of perspiration from her upper lip, acutely aware she neither felt nor looked as fresh as Connor did. The room was a mess too. Last night's whisky glass smeared with red lipstick was still on the table. Tangled bedsheets were bunched on the floor. A damp towel tossed over a chair. Dirty clothes and underwear strewn everywhere. It was like that Tracey Emin art installation.

"I'm getting married," Connor said.

Jessica stuffed a blouse into the bag. The small motel room felt even hotter all of a sudden. "That's usually what happens after folks get engaged."

"I mean I'm getting married soon. Real soon. This weekend in Vegas. I thought I should tell you in person."

Jessica bit down hard on her bottom lip. She felt like she'd taken a punch to the gut and the wind had been knocked clean out of her. She had to fight hard to hold back tears and swallow down the sob that was threatening to escape from her mouth. A physical reaction to the emotions she'd been trying to deny for months. No denying them now, at least not to herself.

Jessica kept on adding items to the duffel, even though she no longer had any idea what she was packing. Her hands were trembling and she balled them into little fists. "Wow. I guess congratulations are in order."

"Jessica, look at me."

She threw shampoo and conditioner and deodorant on top of the clothing and pulled the drawstring cord on the bag tight. "It's not a shotgun wedding, is it?" She laughed, sounding like a crazy person.

When Connor didn't answer, Jessica finally turned around and met his gaze.

He nodded once. "Something like that. Rae-Lynn is pregnant."

27

JESSICA

Jessica slung the duffel bag over her shoulder, slid on a pair of sunglasses, and picked up the keys for the motel room and her truck.

A baby? A Vegas wedding was one thing, but the news that Connor was going to be a father? That had completely blindsided her. Jessica realized now that she'd never really expected his relationship with Rae-Lynn to go the distance despite their engagement; that a part of her had even hoped there might be a chance for her and Connor one day. That wasn't going to happen, not now that Rae-Lynn was pregnant and would soon be his wife.

There was no way Jessica could be around Connor right now. No way she could risk him seeing everything she was thinking, everything she was feeling, written all over her face.

"Congrats again," she said. She was relieved to hear that her voice sounded calm and steady, didn't betray the storm of emotions raging through her. "That's going to be one cute kid. But now you have to leave."

"I'm not going anywhere," he said. "We need to talk about this, Jessica."

"I guess you'll have to talk to an empty room because I'm outta here. Make sure the door is locked behind you when you leave."

Jessica pushed past him onto the walkway and made her way quickly to the staircase. The door slammed hard behind her, followed by the squeak of rubber soles as Connor tried to catch her up.

"Slow down, will you?" he yelled.

"Sorry, no can do. Stuff to do."

"Jessica, we need to talk."

"No, we don't."

She darted down the stairs and strode across the parking lot to the Silverado, hitting the unlock button on the key fob on the way. Opened the driver's-side door and threw the duffel bag onto the passenger seat and climbed in. Connor reached the truck and grabbed a hold of the door before she could shut it.

"What?" he said. "We can't deal with this like adults?"

Jessica peered at him over the top of the shades. She told herself to breathe, play it cool, not let him see how rattled she was. "There's nothing to deal with, Connor. I already offered my congratulations on the wedding and the baby news but, honestly, your personal life is really nothing to do with me. I am your employee and, right now, I'm trying to do my job. So, could you please let go of the door so I can do it?"

"If I let go of the door, you'll drive off."

"That's kind of the point."

"At least tell me where you're going?"

"Arizona."

Connor gaped at her. "*Arizona?* Why? Because I'm getting married?"

Jessica shook her head. "You really are incredible, do you know that? Get over yourself, Matt Connor. Not everything is about you.

I'm trying to follow a lead and you need to let go of the goddamn door right now."

Connor did as he was told and stepped back from the truck. "You're coming back, right?"

Jessica leaned over and pulled the door shut, hit the automatic locks, and started the engine. Then she drove off with Connor standing there in her rearview mirror, where she should've left him months ago.

She headed east along Sunset and, once out of sight of both Connor and the motel, pulled into the lot of a strip mall and parked outside a 7-Eleven situated way at the back. She gripped the knotted leather of the steering wheel tight enough to drain all the blood from her hands, until she'd stopped shaking. Then she gulped some big lungfuls of air until she no longer felt like she needed the help of a paper bag to breathe properly.

The 7-Eleven proved to be a good option to stop in front of in order to compose herself. After stocking up on snacks, soda, cigarettes, and a takeout coffee, Jessica programmed her destination into the truck's GPS system. The journey to Halfway, Arizona, would take around five and a half hours. More than three hundred and seventy miles of driving. Nowhere near enough distance between herself and Connor, but it would have to do for now.

For the first hour, the cloudless blue sky stretching endlessly ahead of her was at odds with her foul mood, which wasn't helped by Connor phoning her cell phone every ten minutes. He finally gave up after a half-dozen attempts were rejected and directed to voicemail. As she hit the 10 and floored the gas, and buzzed down the windows to savor the feel of the wind on her face, Jessica finally began to settle in and enjoy the ride. It had been too long since she'd last been on the road.

The city and its smog and skyscrapers and tangled traffic gradually gave way to the arid yellow sands of the Mojave. It reminded her of the time she'd spent living out of an old Airstream trailer in the desert town of Hundred Acres, and a recent case a few months back, out by Twentynine Palms. She buzzed up the windows to prevent dust getting into the truck's cab and bumped up the AC enough for goosebumps to pop out on her bare arms.

By the time she'd reached Thousand Palms, Jessica needed to pee and fuel up on junk food. She spotted an In-N-Out Burger on the other side of the highway and, after a few false turns, finally found her way into the parking lot. The signs must also have been confusing for the driver of the cream Volvo behind her, who seemed equally as lost.

The restaurant was busy so she used the restroom, then ordered a Double-Double with a thick chocolate shake to go. Headed back outside and climbed on top of the Silverado's hard tonneau cover and ate the meal with the afternoon sun warming her face as a light wind whipped at fat palm trees. She smoked a cigarette, then trashed the burger wrapper and go-cup. The truck's GPS guided her back to the 10 and deeper into the desert.

Two hundred and fifty miles to go.

There wasn't a whole lot to look at out here in Nowhere, USA, other than bumper stickers on pickups, and "Please drive carefully" signs on the backs of eighteen-wheelers, and sun-faded desert billboards declaring "Sobriety is a Priority" and "Read the Bible!" and "Really Good Fresh Jerky—110 Miles Ahead."

Jessica was starting to think the folks around here must be real clean-living types, who were willing to travel a long way for dehydrated strips of meat, when she spotted a huge advert for a new strip club in the Coachella Valley. Above the silhouette of a curvy woman wrapped around a pole were the words "Girls! Girls! Girls!" in a brilliant white font against a hot pink backdrop.

Jessica had done a good job of not thinking about Connor or Rae-Lynn or the wedding or the baby for a few dozen miles, but the billboard forced an unwanted memory from a couple of weeks ago to the front of her brain.

◆　◆　◆

The first time she'd visited the Tahiti Club—a topless bar in Hollywood—Jessica had thought the place was dated and rough around the edges. This time, having sunk a few whiskies, it didn't seem so bad, its rough edges softened by the booze. The green and yellow neon palm-tree sign blinking above the front door was a little blurry as she made her way past the doormen.

It was Friday night and she'd spent the day working a surveillance job with Connor, before they'd decided to have a couple of drinks in a bar on Highland. He had stuck to light beer before making the drive back to Venice. She'd declined his offer of a ride back to the motel, saying she'd grab another drink and then call a cab. But Jessica didn't call a cab. She walked the six blocks to the Tahiti Club instead, knowing Rae-Lynn would be dancing that night.

Once inside, she took a seat at the bar and ordered a double Scotch on the rocks. Even as she handed over the cash, Jessica knew it'd been a dumb idea coming to the strip bar. She didn't think Rae-Lynn would recognize her—they'd met only once before and it'd been brief—but she had no idea what she hoped to achieve by coming here.

The Tahiti Club's more mature clientele was reflected in the DJ's song choices, which were usually older than the women dancing and stripping to them. The slow, atmospheric part of "In the Air Tonight" was playing through unseen speakers and the club was in near darkness, conveniently disguising the imperfections of the tatty interior and of any of the dancers—not that many of them needed it. Most of the twenty-something employees probably thought cellulite was a phone company.

The girl on stage had small breasts covered in glitter, and jet black hair, and was dressed only in a gold thong and matching platform heels. She moved languidly and teasingly around the silver pole to the music as the single spotlight followed her.

Jessica lifted the drink to her lips and discreetly gazed around the room for Rae-Lynn. She thought she spotted the familiar silver hair and matching mustache of Johnny Blue at a table close to the stage. He was a club regular she'd interviewed a while back, when Jessica had decided to investigate her mother's murder after finding out about her own secret, tragic past. Like Rae-Lynn, Eleanor Lavelle had been an exotic dancer at the Tahiti Club, and Johnny Blue had known Jessica's mother when she'd worked both the strip club and its clients back then. Jessica didn't see Rae-Lynn in the smoky gloom.

Then the song reached the iconic drum fill and the dancer on stage threw herself at the pole, her long legs kicking, hips jutting, muscles straining, hair flicking, as strobe lights flashed all around, and Jessica saw Connor's fiancée in a booth gyrating on the lap of a man old enough to be her grandfather.

He had a sparkly pink Stetson on his head at a jaunty angle and stupid grin on his face, and he was trying to feed her champagne straight from the bottle. She was wearing a denim bra and tiny matching panties, a belt with a star-shaped buckle slung low over her hips, and red high-heeled cowboy boots. Every part of her tanned body was toned and tight and pert. Jessica wasn't a whole lot older but, even though she was naturally slim, she figured she'd never look half as good because she'd always be devoted to In-N-Out Burger in the same way Rae-Lynn was clearly devoted to the gym.

She turned away from the stage and the booths and stared into her glass. Decided as soon as she'd finished the drink, she'd get the hell out of here. Phil Collins was replaced by "Love to Love You

Baby" by Donna Summer as someone slid onto the stool next to Jessica and the bartender walked over to the newcomer.

"Two mini Moëts, thanks."

The voice had an unmistakable Texas twang and Jessica's heart dropped as her eyes fell on the red cowboy boots.

"Shit," she muttered.

"Here to check out the competition, huh?" Rae-Lynn said.

Jessica turned to face the other woman. "Excuse me?"

Rae-Lynn had baby pink clip-on extensions entwined in her blonde hair which were a perfect match for the gloss slicked across plump lips. The Stetson was on the bar top. Jessica noticed she wasn't wearing the Tiffany diamond. Then again, an engagement ring didn't fit with the fantasy offered up by these types of establishments.

"I know who you are, Jessica. And I know the Tahiti isn't exactly your regular drinking haunt. Except that one time you were here with my fiancé when you were both . . . *working*." The bartender placed two little champagne bottles with silver sippers on the counter and Rae-Lynn pushed one toward Jessica. "Here you go."

"I already have a drink."

"Scotch is for old men. Take the fizz. We're celebrating."

Jessica raised an eyebrow. "We are? What are we celebrating?"

"You showing up here tonight. Me finally having the opportunity to tell you to your face to stay away from my man."

Jessica was glad it was dark in the club and Rae-Lynn couldn't see her cheeks turn the same color as the Stetson. "We work together. It's kind of hard not to see him."

Rae-Lynn tipped her head back and drank half the mini bottle of Moët.

"I know you're hot for him," she said. "And I know the two of you meet up to watch sports and sink a few beers when I'm working my ass off in this dump. It stops now, d'you hear me?"

"There's nothing going on between me and Connor. We're friends, is all. If you don't like his choice of friends, then I think you should be having that conversation with him."

Rae-Lynn finished the rest of the champagne and stared at her for a long, uncomfortable moment. Eventually, she said, "Do I have to be worried, Jessica?"

Jessica held her gaze. "Not about me, you don't."

Rae-Lynn nodded and snatched up the untouched bottle sitting in front of Jessica. "Just stay the fuck away from him, okay?"

Then she slid off the stool and disappeared into the darkness of the club.

◆ ◆ ◆

Jessica had expected Connor to confront her about her visit to the Tahiti Club but he never did.

Thinking back on the conversation with Rae-Lynn, Jessica might've wondered if the woman's sudden rush to get hitched had anything to do with her—had it not been for the baby.

She shook her head and laughed. She was as bad as Connor. She had to get over herself. The wedding was about the baby; not her. Although, the way Rae-Lynn was throwing champagne down her neck a couple of weeks ago, clearly being knocked up had come as a surprise very recently.

Jessica was someplace outside of Blythe when her cell phone rang in the holder on the dash. She glanced at the screen, expecting to see Connor's name. It wasn't. The incoming call was from Pryce.

"Pryce."

"Hey Jessica. How's things? Any progress on finding your misper?"

"Maybe. Hopefully. I'm on my way to Arizona to find out for sure."

"Let me know how it goes."

"Of course. What's up?"

"There's been a development in the Jordana Ford homicide investigation and I think you should know because it involves The Lonely Hearts Club. I know you've been looking at them."

"What's the development?"

"A positive hit on prints found at the scene. They belong to Denis Durrant. Fresh out of jail and married to the founder of the prison pen-pal group."

"You're kidding. Have you arrested him?"

"Nope. He's in the wind already. Looks like he ran last night."

"I was with him last night."

Pryce was incredulous. "What? Where? What were you doing with Durrant?"

Jessica told Pryce about the unexpected meeting with Doc Durrant in the motel bar; how he'd claimed Veronica Lowe was dead, courtesy of a hitman's bullet, then warned her to stay away from Bibi Durrant, before being picked up by someone in a dark-colored pickup.

Pryce sounded excited. "I'll get Vic to check out cameras around the Strip, see if we can find a lead on the vehicle. This is good, Jessica."

"Happy to help."

"Just be careful, okay? This guy's made contact with you once already. Now he's out there, having probably killed someone, desperate and dangerous. There's no telling what he might do next."

"I'll be fine. No one knows where I'm headed other than Connor. And I have the Glock."

"Okay, good. Stay safe."

Jessica disconnected the call, Pryce's warning echoing in her head. Despite her bravado of just a few seconds ago, she shivered with unease. The land all around was completely barren, save for dirt and rocks and some electricity pylons. A lone hawk squawked somewhere high in the pale sky. The stretch of road was so empty, she could have been driving on some uninhabited planet.

Jessica glanced in the rearview, half expecting to see Durrant's ride from the night before looming in the mirror. But there was no dark-colored pickup behind her.

The only other vehicle on the road was a cream Volvo, just like the one that had followed her into the In-N-Out Burger lot a hundred miles back.

28

PRYCE

There were a lot of decent options on Pico Boulevard for those seeking to enjoy a refreshment or two.

Rosco's Bar wasn't one of them.

It was the place you staggered along the street to after the doormen at the Arsenal, and neat., and Sorry Not Sorry had all uttered the dreaded words "Not tonight." The security at Rosco's wasn't there to prevent folks from getting inside; its sole purpose was to remove the troublemakers later on when things got a little too lively.

Early afternoon on a Tuesday, there was no need for anyone to man the entrance. The only patrons at this time of day were the dedicated alcoholics and the old men sipping beers and reading the sports pages. One old boy was slumped in the corner with his eyes closed and mouth hanging open. He was either asleep or dead.

The decor could be summed up in one word: "mahogany." The bar top, stools, low tables, high tables, walls, and flooring were all made of the same dark, polished wood. A boxy TV set mounted behind the bar showed only sports games. Two dartboards hung on another wall, next to a foosball table. The thought of drunk folks in possession of darts brought Pryce out in a cold sweat, his anxiety backed up by the smattering of pinpricks surrounding the boards. Thankfully, no one was showing an interest in throwing any darts right now.

He made his way over to the bar, where a heavyset woman with short blonde spiky hair was cleaning a glass with a dirty towel.

"Is Rosco around?" Pryce asked, showing his badge.

The woman raised untamed eyebrows at him. "I thought you lot were like socks, gloves, and balls."

"Huh?"

"Always come in pairs."

Pryce smiled. "That's funny. Is he here?"

"Whatever you think he did, he didn't do it."

"Who? Rosco?"

"No, Doc. He's the reason you're here, right? Lovely man. A real gent." She winked at Pryce. "Now, if it's Rosco we're talking about, he definitely did it. Let me go find him."

She disappeared through a door—mahogany of course—that had a chipped white pearlescent sign screwed on the front bearing the word "PRIVATE" in big black letters. The spiky blonde reappeared a few moments later.

"He'll be right out. Can I get you a drink while you wait?"

"No thanks. I'm on duty."

She winked again. "I won't tell if you won't."

The door swung open again and a man with collar-length glossy black hair and a deep tan appeared. He broke into a huge grin when he spotted Pryce.

"Detective Pryce! Long time, no see."

Rosco Martino was around a decade older than Pryce, which made him about sixty, and he apparently still wore his trademark attire of satin shirt, unbuttoned to mid-chest, and tight-fitting jeans and crocodile-leather pointed-toe shoes.

The hair color and tan were both from a bottle, and his white teeth and gold jewelry were as fake as his charm. He had managed, or owned, various dodgy bars in and around Hollywood for decades. Pryce had known the man since he was a rookie cop busting those places for drugs and bar brawls, back when Rosco went by his real name of Ross Samson. Then it was Rossy Samson, Sammy Samson, and, finally, Rosco Martino. Despite the claims about his exotic heritage, the nearest he'd ever gotten to Italy was Louise's Trattoria along the street.

"Rosco. How you doing?"

"That depends on why you're here, Detective. Business or pleasure?"

"Business."

"This about Doc?"

"How'd you guess?"

"I heard he had taken off. Wasn't sure if he was running from the cops or the missus. She called earlier. Sounded like a real firecracker."

"Mrs. Durrant claims he was working here Saturday night. I need to check out his alibi."

Rosco nodded. "He sure was. Doc was here the whole night."

"Until what time?"

"The last of the stragglers were out the door by half past midnight. Then the staff had a few drinks until around two. Birdie here can back that up."

"Absolutely," the bartender chimed in. "Doc was here the whole time. Left around two a.m. just like Rosco said."

"I noticed you have a camera above the door outside, and I see you have another one inside too." Pryce pointed to a camera behind the bar in the opposite corner from the old TV. "Can I see the footage from Saturday night?"

Rosco crossed his arms across his chest. "You got a warrant, Detective Pryce?"

"I don't, but I can easily get one."

Rosco grinned and pointed his trigger fingers at Pryce. "I'm shitting you, Pryce. 'Course you can see the tapes. Come with me. Birdie, hold my calls."

The bartender rolled her eyes. "Sure thing, Rosco."

Rosco gestured for Pryce to follow him through the door marked "PRIVATE," and led him down a short corridor, past a small, bad-smelling restroom, and into a backroom that doubled as an office and smoking den judging by the stink of cigars. The butt of a fat Cuban was smoldering in a saucer on the desk, the window cracked open to release the telltale smoke.

Rosco took a seat on a ripped leather swivel chair, and opened one of the desk drawers and produced a half-empty bottle of Glenlivet and two glasses. He held them up. "Care to join me? I keep the good stuff back here. None of that cheap crap that's behind the bar."

"It's a little early in the day for me," Pryce said.

Rosco shrugged. "Suit yourself."

He poured himself a measure, threw it back in one go, then started tapping two-fingered on the computer keyboard.

"Let's see . . . Saturday night . . ." He squinted at the screen. "Here we go."

Pryce joined him on the other side of the desk, and leaned over Rosco's shoulder for a better look at the black and white image on the old-model iMac. It was the feed from the camera posted above the front door. Two big, burly men wearing dark suits were visible in the shot. The time stamp showed seven p.m.

Rosco pointed a finger at the screen. "That's Doc right there."

Pryce recognized Durrant from the mugshots they had on file. "Can you fast-forward through the feed?"

Doc Durrant left his post only twice between the start of his shift, at seven, and after midnight when the bar shut. On both occasions, he headed inside to the gents to take a leak, as captured on the security camera above the bar. The same interior feed backed up Rosco's claim that their prime suspect had spent close on two hours throwing back whisky shots with other staff members, including Birdie the bartender, after his shift was over, before he'd booked an Uber on the bar's account to take him home to Cypress Park.

"Dammit," Pryce said.

"I guess whatever you were trying to pin on him ain't gonna fly now, huh?"

Pryce's cell phone buzzed in his pants pocket, and he took it out and glanced at the screen. It was Medina. He rejected the call. Pulled up a photo of Jordana Ford and showed it to Rosco. "You ever see this woman in the bar? Ever see her with Durrant?"

Rosco averted his gaze. "No, I never saw her with him."

"But?"

"But nothing."

"Rosco, you've got that shifty look going on. What aren't you telling me?"

Rosco sighed. "Okay, I never saw Doc with her. I never met her. But I do recognize her. He showed me her photo a couple times. Reckons he was banging her." He chuckled. "I guess when you've been inside as long as Doc was, one woman ain't enough to satisfy the bedroom needs. Why? What's she done?"

"She's dead. She was murdered Saturday night."

"No shit? And you thought Doc did it? No way, man." He gestured to the frozen image on the computer screen of Doc Durrant leaving Rosco's at just past two a.m. "I guess he's in the clear now?"

"I'm going to need a copy of that footage."

"No problem." Rosco opened the desk's top drawer and fished among the mess of pens and rubber bands and paper clips and Post-its before producing a flash drive that was still in the plastic wrapping. "I keep these handy in case we get any hotties in the bar that I want to keep for my personal collection."

Pryce stared at him. "Please tell me you're joking, Rosco."

Rosco rolled his eyes. "'Course I am, Pryce. Jeez, I remember the good old days when you used to have a sense of humor. Wait, no. I'm thinking of your buddy, the one who looks like the Fonz. You'd sure as hell need to have a sense of humor to dress the way he does."

"Just make the copy, Rosco." Pryce threw his card down on the desk. "And email it to me too, while you're at it."

Once he was back outside on Pico, the flash drive safely in his pocket, Pryce returned Medina's call.

"I'm just done at Rosco's," he said, when his partner answered. "Durrant's alibi checks out. I guess we're back to square one, bud."

"Not exactly. We got the DNA results back."

"And?"

"The skin they found under Jordana's fingernails was her own. Looks like she'd clawed at her neck in a desperate attempt to loosen the hosiery. But the DNA from the perspiration on the pantyhose didn't belong to Jordana. That appears to have belonged to our perp."

Pryce barely dared to breathe. "Please tell me we got a hit from the system?"

"Yep."

"Durrant?"

"Nope."

"Shit. Who then?"

Medina paused for effect. Then said, "A family member of one of Travis Dean Ford's victims."

Pryce's elation quickly turned to despair. He closed his eyes and rubbed his temples. "Lou Hardwick."

"Wrong again."

Pryce's eyes snapped open. He started walking toward his car. "Give me the name and address and I'll meet you there. Whoever this sonofabitch is, we got him."

"It's not that simple, bud," Medina said. "Our man is dead. Has been for well over a decade."

29

JESSICA

The Volvo was old and boxy, the color of turned milk, with a big rusted silver grille at the front.

It was far enough back, about fifty yards, that it wasn't nudging the fender on Jessica's truck. Not yet anyway. But another glance in the rearview told her it was the only other car on the road. Ahead of her, there was nothing but blue sky and yellow desert. No houses or trailers or gas stations.

Jessica almost always felt safe in her truck, with its high seats and fat wheels and electric windows firmly locked—not to mention the fully loaded Glock in the glovebox. Now, she was horribly aware of how exposed she really was. How easily her tires could be shot out, or she could be forced off the road, with no one around for miles who could help.

She stabbed at the screen of her iPhone, sitting in the charger on the dash, and saw there was no cell signal.

"Fuck."

Jessica checked the rearview mirror again. The Volvo was still there. Of course it was, there was no place else to go. The sun glinting off the windshield meant she couldn't get a good look at the driver. Didn't know if they were male or female, young or old, a threat or no threat at all.

Her tank was more than half full, after she'd topped up in Palm Desert. She'd bet on the Silverado being able to outgun the old Volvo if it came to it, but Jessica still felt uneasy. She popped the lid on the glovebox, fumbled for the gun, and set it down in the console between the two front seats, within easy reach. Then she applied some more pressure on the gas. Watched the little needle on the speedometer jerk up, along with the beat of her heart.

Still, the Volvo stayed with her.

No place else to go.

As Blythe loomed on the horizon, and the service signs started to appear, Jessica's eyes continued to flick between the road ahead and the car behind her. Maybe the Volvo would peel off onto one of the exit roads for food or gas or lodgings, and she'd laugh at herself for being a paranoid fool who'd gotten so easily spooked.

Jessica briefly considered pulling off the main highway herself but quickly dismissed the idea. She didn't know the area at all and didn't want to risk taking a wrong turn and winding up down some remote dirt track.

The Volvo didn't pull off the main highway either.

Jessica's pickup kept on eating up the miles, Blythe came and went, and then she was crossing the state line. The Colorado River sparkled in the sun like a cluster of precious gems under a spotlight, and the red, white, and blue Arizona sign welcoming visitors to the Grand Canyon State flashed by in a blur. The traffic had increased somewhat since Blythe, and Jessica took the opportunity to floor the gas pedal and overtake a FedEx truck, putting it between herself and the Volvo.

A few moments later, the Volvo was back on her tail, having also overtaken the delivery truck.

"Seriously?" Jessica muttered. She was starting to get pissed now.

After what seemed like forever, a gas station finally appeared up ahead. She waited until the last possible second to take the exit. Sure enough, the driver of the cream Volvo hit their own blinker, still fifty yards back. It followed her onto the forecourt and parked up behind a huge freight truck, as Jessica stopped in front of the gas store entrance.

There was now no doubt in her mind that she'd been tailed since Palm Desert, possibly the whole journey. She could think of only one person who'd be taking such an interest in her. Someone who seemed to be taking too much of an interest in her case. Someone who would welcome the opportunity to put some distance between himself and Los Angeles right now, while keeping Jessica in his sights.

Doc Durrant.

"Okay, asshole. Let's do this."

Jessica shoved the Glock into her big leather bag and hoisted it over her shoulder as she got out of the Silverado. Her legs felt wobbly as a result of both the long drive and a potential confrontation. The automatic doors whooshed open and the coldness of the AC hit her as she entered the store. No one followed her inside. She wandered up and down aisles crammed with potato chips and bags of ice and truck tools and road maps, and noticed there was a back exit.

She glanced around, then pushed down on the metal bar, wincing in anticipation for a fire alarm going off, but nothing happened. There was no ear-splitting screech, no angry staff member rushing in her direction, demanding to know what the hell she was doing. Jessica stepped out into the blistering heat, this time at the rear of the building, where trash bags and cardboard boxes were piled next to some dumpsters. Wide-open, empty desert lay straight ahead to the north.

Sweat dampened her brow and ran down her back as she pulled the gun from her bag and made her way around the side of the building in the direction of the forecourt. The Volvo was still there, behind the freight truck. Jessica crept up stealthily behind the car, her weapon drawn, and approached the driver's-side door.

The window was rolled all the way down and the person behind the wheel was staring straight ahead, watching the automatic doors, no doubt waiting for Jessica to re-emerge.

She could see who the driver was now, and her temper flared.

It wasn't Doc Durrant.

It was Christine Ryan.

Jessica dropped the gun back into her bag and yanked open the door. The woman started so violently that Jessica almost felt bad for her. Almost.

"What the hell do you think you're doing, Christine?" she demanded.

"Jessica, you almost scared me half to death." Christine breathed heavily, a hand went to her throat, and she dabbed at the perspiration on her face with a crumpled Kleenex.

A handgun was sitting on the passenger seat and Jessica gestured toward it. "Just as well you didn't have that thing in your hand," she said. "Or I might've ended up with a bullet hole in me when I startled you."

"I never usually carry a weapon but I was a little nervous about making the trip, especially as I didn't know where we were headed. I thought it'd make me feel safer, what with the car being old and unreliable and me being a woman on my own. It's really quite daunting."

"No shit," Jessica snapped. "Especially when someone is following you."

"You left me no choice," Christine said, defensively. "You wouldn't tell me what was going on or where you were going."

"You followed me all the way from the motel?"

Christine nodded. "I jumped in the car and headed on over to the Strip right after you called. I didn't even stop long enough to pack a bag. Not even a toothbrush."

"Just a gun."

"Right."

Jessica was pissed at Christine but she was even more pissed at herself. If her head hadn't been so full of Connor and Rae-Lynn, she might have noticed she was being tailed for hundreds of miles.

"I'm sorry, Jessica. I just need to know Veronica and Mia are safe."

Jessica sighed. "I know you do but this kind of behavior isn't acceptable, Christine. I told you I'd be in touch as soon as I had anything to report."

"You think they're in Arizona?"

"I don't know. Maybe. It's a long shot."

"But still worth us checking it out?"

"No, not us. Me. You need to turn around and go back home and wait for news."

"I can't go back, not today. It's too far. I wasn't expecting such a long drive. I'm tired, Jessica. I spent most of the night tossing and turning again." She wiped the back of her neck with the Kleenex. "This heat isn't helping either. The car's AC is busted."

Christine's face was even paler than it had been when they'd met in Dustin's, and kind of sickly and pasty with the sweat. She didn't look good at all. Jessica felt a flicker of sympathy, despite her frustration. She was getting far too soft.

"Okay," she said. "We stay overnight in a motel and then you drive back to LA first thing in the morning once you're rested. In the meantime, you let me get on with my job and don't interfere. Deal?"

Christine smiled gratefully. "Deal. Thank you, Jessica. Do we have far to go?"

"An hour, ninety minutes tops. You okay to drive that far?"

"I'll be fine."

"Why don't you head into the store and pick up some toiletries and a t-shirt to sleep in? Maybe one of those little handheld fans and some water for the remainder of the journey?"

"Good idea. You won't drive off without me?"

"I'll wait. Just don't make me regret it."

The Halfway House Inn was about a mile outside of town on a drab, lonely stretch of highway.

It was flanked by a razor-wire-fenced builders' yard on one side and an almost empty RV park on the other. It comprised two single-story terracotta buildings with roofs and trim painted in a lurid green, in what must have been one of the ugliest color combinations Jessica had ever seen—and she had stayed in some butt-ugly motels over the last few years. Dusk was coming on fast and the neon signs were already lit. An "F" in "OFFICE" was burnt out and the "E" was flickering like it might join it any day now.

Christine followed Jessica into the office, which led through to a compact lounge area with a nicely stocked bar. The desk clerk reminded Jessica of a young Brad Pitt. He told them a double room would cost fifty bucks and Christine insisted on paying for both rooms to make amends for tagging along uninvited. Jessica figured Connor would be happy to save on the expense claim, especially when he saw the gas receipts.

Christine counted out the cash, signed the guestbook, and handed one of the keys to Jessica. Their rooms were located in the other building, right next door to each other. There was still a heavy heat in the air as they walked to rooms five and six.

"You want to go get some food?" Jessica asked.

Christine shook her head. "I'm totally beat." She held up the plastic bag with the gas station logo on front. "I think I'll have a shower and change into my cool 'I Heart Arizona' tee, then go lie down for a while."

"When did you last eat?"

"Breakfast."

No wonder the woman looked so rough.

"I'm going into town," Jessica said. "Why don't I bring you back a sandwich and soda and leave them in front of your door for you? You might be hungry later."

Christine smiled tiredly. "Sounds good, thanks."

Jessica showered and changed into a fresh pair of jeans and t-shirt that were only slightly crumpled after being shoved carelessly into the overnight bag during Connor's unexpected visit. His announcement about the wedding and the baby had thrown her enough that she'd forgotten to pack her evidence board but, thankfully, Jessica kept a small portable printer stored in the Silverado's flatbed.

There was limited cell signal in the motel and the free Wi-Fi was spotty, only connecting to one device at a time. Jessica hooked up the printer to the laptop and the laptop to the Wi-Fi and printed off a few copies of the farmhouse photo from The Lonely Hearts Club's website. She still had the photo of Veronica saved on her cell phone. It would have to do in the absence of the original, which was taped to her evidence board back in LA.

The plan was to show both photos to the desk clerk, see if he recognized either the woman or the building, but the counter was unmanned. He was probably in the john or on his dinner break. Jessica considered helping herself to a drink from the bar while she waited but her belly had other ideas and growled loudly. She decided food was more important than booze.

She'd check in on Brad Pitt again later when she got back from town. Maybe have that drink too.

30

JESSICA

Halfway was home to 3,051 souls scattered over forty square miles of dirt, dust, and rock. It was surrounded by huge red-rock buttes the color of medium-rare steak that seemed to watch over the town.

Downtown covered six square blocks and was dominated by a main street with a post office and a hardware store and a bank and a mini-mart. They were all shuttered for the night and the streets were empty.

She spotted a hazy beam of yellow spilling onto the sidewalk from one of the stores and pulled over. It was a cab office. She nosed into one of two spots designated for taxis. Walking into the cramped office was like walking into 1987. The color scheme was brown and cream and nicotine. A redhead with a bad dye job sat behind a cheap walnut-effect desk smoking a cigarette. She was about sixty and heavily made up with hard black eyeliner and crimson lipstick that had bled into the tiny smoker's lines around her mouth. Her clingy top was cut low enough to display the crepey tan skin on her décolletage under a big gold locket.

There was no computer. An ancient radio system sat on the desk in front of her and hissed and crackled and spouted mysterious codes and addresses. A phone on the desk shrilled loudly and the redhead held up a finger at Jessica and picked up the receiver.

"Cabby Shack. Uh-huh. How many people?" She placed the cigarette carefully on the edge of an amber glass ashtray, picked up a pencil with a chewed end, and started scribbling on a legal pad. "Uh-huh. Number twenty-five, you say? Uh-huh. Should be around fifteen to twenty minutes. That okay, hon? Good."

The woman slammed down the phone and picked up the radio mike, pressed a button on the side, and put out a call for the hire at 25 Lilac Road. There was some more hissing and crackling, then a man's voice identified his cab number and said, "Roger that, Ramona. Over."

The redhead—presumably called Ramona—picked up the burning cigarette and stuck it in the corner of her mouth. She leaned over toward a metal sheet on the wall and moved a magnetic peg to a new location on an engraved map of the town.

Just when Jessica was beginning to think Ramona had forgotten all about her, the woman finally turned to her and gave her the once-over. "Can I help you?"

"That's the plan."

"Where you headed?" Ramona blew smoke up toward the yellowed popcorn ceiling and stubbed out the cigarette in the ashtray. She picked up the pencil again. "I'll see what we've got available."

"I don't need a cab."

Ramona unwrapped a stick of gum and folded it into her mouth. "I'm not sure how to break it to you, hon, but this is a taxi office. If you ain't after a taxi, there ain't a whole lot I can do for you."

Jessica withdrew the printout of the farmhouse picture from her bag. "I'm looking for this place. Do you know where it is?"

Ramona snapped the gum and stared at her. Eventually, she held out her hand. "Give it here."

Jessica gave her the sheet of paper and the older woman put on a pair of reading glasses that had been hanging on a chain around her neck. She squinted at the picture, then looked up at Jessica. "It's a farmhouse."

"Yes, it is. Do you recognize it?"

"Sure, I recognize it."

"Really?"

"No, not really. It looks like every farmhouse I ever saw."

"I meant specifically in this town. I think it's in Halfway someplace."

"It looks like every farmhouse in this town, and the next one, and the one after that."

Ramona shrugged and returned the sheet of paper.

"You work in a taxi office in the middle of town," Jessica said. "Surely you must know all the places around here?"

Ramona regarded her over the rims of the glasses, her lips a thin scarlet slash. "That's right, I work in the taxi office. I don't drive the taxis."

"Do you think any of the drivers might know where the farmhouse is?"

"I have no idea, and I sure as hell ain't dragging them all the way across town to look at some picture. They've got work to do, genuine fares to pick up."

"I'll book a taxi then."

"No, you won't. You already said you didn't need one."

"I changed my mind."

"It'll be at least an hour's wait."

"You told the last caller fifteen minutes."

"We just got busier."

Jessica showed her the photo of Veronica Lowe. "What about her? Do you know this woman?"

Ramona sighed but took the phone and pushed the glasses back up the bridge of her nose. Her eyes narrowed when she looked at the screen. "Why are you looking for her? What'd she do?"

"She didn't do anything. An old friend is trying to track her down."

Ramona held out the phone to Jessica. "I've never seen her before."

"Are you sure? Have another look. It's an old photo from around twenty years ago so her appearance would have changed by now."

"I don't need to take another look. I already told you, I don't know her."

Jessica thought the woman was lying, that there had been a flicker of recognition when she'd seen the picture of Veronica. Did Ramona know something? Or was she simply wary of a stranger with a New York accent showing up in town and asking after someone who might be one of the locals?

The phone on the desk began to ring again and Ramona snatched it up.

"Cabby Shack. Uh-huh." She put a hand over the mouthpiece. "I don't know the farmhouse and I don't know the woman." She removed her hand from the mouthpiece again. "Sorry, can you repeat the address?"

"Food," Jessica said loudly.

Ramona held the receiver to her chest. "What now?" she snapped.

"Where can I find some food around here?"

"Kaplan's Diner, a half mile or so down the street." She made a shooing motion with her hand. "Now get the hell out of my office."

◆ ◆ ◆

Jessica carried on down the street, passing a pet food store and an auto shop and a barber. They were all shuttered. So was a video-rental place on the corner, but Jessica wasn't sure if it was closed for good or if folks in Halfway still owned VCRs.

She spotted a square of light across the street and thought she'd found Kaplan's. But it wasn't the diner; it was a laundromat. Jessica could see rows of big silver washing machines and dryers with detergent and powder stacked on top through the window. Two women were chatting and sorting huge bundles of clothing into neat little piles.

Jessica was starting to think she'd missed the diner completely when a blur of pink neon appeared up ahead. Right at the end of Main Street, standing on its own on a patch of muddied land, was a fifty-foot-long metal trailer. The sign on top of the roof screamed "Kaplan's Diner" in an eye-watering fuchsia script.

"Bingo."

The restaurant was all lit up and the red "Open" sign on the door confirmed it was, indeed, one of the few businesses in Halfway that didn't pull down the shutters by seven p.m.

There were three vehicles in the lot: a dirty green pickup, an orange Toyota wagon, and a tan soft-top Chrysler LeBaron with a mismatched gray wing panel. Jessica pulled in next to the convertible, the space closest to the front entrance, and cut the engine. She jumped down from the Silverado's cab onto hard mud and took the three metal steps to the front door. A bell tinkled quaintly overhead.

If entering the cab office had been like jumping into a DeLorean for a trip back to the '80s, stepping inside Kaplan's was the '50s equivalent. Blue leather and white Formica booths lined the window side, while matching high-backed stools fronted the gleaming chrome counter. A Fender guitar hung on the wall at the far end of the trailer, and a Wurlitzer played "Crystal Chandeliers" by Charley Pride at the near end.

The interior was spotlessly clean and too new to be authentically retro. Jessica realized the styling was 1950s but everything inside the trailer—right down to the napkin holders—was modern replicas.

She chose the booth right at the back, which offered the best view of the rest of the room. Not that there was a whole lot to see. There was just one other patron, a mustachioed guy sitting at the counter eating a fat burger. He wore blue jeans and a plaid shirt and dirty work boots. A Stetson was on the counter next to his plate.

An image of Rae-Lynn and her pink sparkly cowboy hat flashed into Jessica's mind and she pushed the thought away. Connor had finally stopped trying to call, or maybe the cell signal was so spotty he couldn't reach her. The man's boots were tapping in time with the song against the stool's footrail. Jessica guessed he was the owner of the green pickup and the one who'd just fed the jukebox.

Jessica perused the options on the menu. A waitress—who'd been behind the counter, occupied by a cell phone—approached the table. She was petite in her powder pink uniform and white tennis shoes. "Katie" was stitched into the material above her left breast in the same fuchsia font as the sign outside. The waitress was about college age, with big eyes the color of melted chocolate and shiny, ponytailed brown hair. She had a quick smile and a burst of freckles across her nose.

"Hi, I'm Katie." She produced a notepad and pencil from her apron pocket. "What can I get for you on this fine evening?"

"I'll have the mac and cheese with a side of fries and a Diet Coke. Can I also have a sandwich and soda to go?"

"Hungry tonight, huh?" Katie grinned.

"The sandwich is for a friend. I have a big appetite but not quite that big."

"I believe you. What kind of sandwich?"

Christine Ryan hadn't mentioned any dietary requirements, and Jessica had never met a veggie or vegan who didn't offer up that information at every opportunity, so she guessed her client was a carnivore like herself. She decided to split the difference by ordering tuna mayo and cucumber on brown.

"Anything else?" asked the waitress.

"A moment of your time to look at some photos."

"Sounds intriguing."

Jessica found the image of Veronica on her phone and handed it to the waitress.

"I don't suppose you recognize this woman?" she asked. "The photo was taken a long time ago so she'd be around twenty years older now."

Katie took the iPhone and looked at the screen and frowned. She shook her head. "I don't think I know her." She pinched the screen to zoom in on Veronica's face. "Nope, she's not familiar."

"Are you sure?" Jessica asked. "I thought she might live around here."

"If she does, she sure doesn't eat in here. Not only do I know pretty much everyone in town, but I also know what most of them like to order. It's a special skill."

"The woman's name is Veronica," Jessica tried. "Sometimes goes by Roni."

Katie chewed her bottom lip and tilted her head to one side. "There's a Vanessa who lives over on Torrance and a Victoria who was in the year below me at school, who went by Tori, but no Veronica. There is a Ronnie who comes in here a few times a week, but he's a man. Sorry."

Katie returned the phone and Jessica gave her the printout. "How about this farmhouse?"

This time the waitress nodded but she appeared uncomfortable suddenly. "Why are you asking about this place?"

"You recognize it?"

"Are you a cop?"

Jessica smiled in what she hoped was a reassuring way. "Definitely not a cop."

"I didn't think so. Most of them eat breakfast in here. If you're not a cop, who are you?"

"I'm a PI."

Katie hesitated. "It's about a mile or two outside of town."

Jessica's pulse jackhammered. "Do you know the family who lives there?"

"No one lives there. It's derelict. Has been for years."

Jessica felt the glimmer of hope deflate. "You're sure you're thinking of the same place?"

"One hundred percent." Katie glanced over her shoulder at a serving hatch that was open partway and lowered her voice. "It's where the high-school kids go to party, if you know what I mean. So yes, I'm sure it's the same place. The rope swing is still there. My dad would totally freak if he knew I'd been out there."

"Your dad?"

Katie jutted a thumb toward the hatch. "He's back there in the kitchen. He owns this place."

Right then a pudgy hand appeared and pushed the hatch door all the way back, and a cheerful, ruddy face appeared. "Katie, honey?"

"Yes, Pops?"

"Are you going to give me the lady's order or are you going to spend all evening chatting to her instead?"

"Sorry, Pops. Be right there."

"And don't call me Pops. It makes me feel old."

"You are old! How about Mr. Kaplan instead? Or Frank? Either of those any better?"

"Even worse. 'Dad' will do just fine, thank you." He closed the hatch again.

Jessica laughed. "Sorry if I got you into trouble with your dad."

"Don't sweat it. He's a far bigger chatterbox than I am. Won't be long for the food."

Katie pushed the order slip through the serving hatch, then went back to the counter and her cell phone, thumbs flying across the screen. Boyfriend texts or Candy Crush? There was the occasional pause, as though the girl was reading a response, before the frantic tapping resumed. Definitely boyfriend texts.

While she waited for her dinner, Jessica thought about what the waitress had told her. Veronica wasn't from around here but the farmhouse, where the old snap of Bibi and Doc Durrant had been taken, was. It might even have been the place where Veronica and Mia had vacationed once, but it seemed like Jessica was wrong about them being in Halfway now.

Katie returned with the food and Jessica asked how long the farmhouse had been derelict for, and if a woman and her daughter had ever lived there.

"It's been empty for as long as I can remember," she said. "Nothing there but old mattresses and beer crates and bongs. I don't remember anyone ever living out there. When I was a kid, there was a rumor it was haunted, but I think that was just something the older kids said to keep the younger ones away from the place while they were out there getting high and having sex."

"Who's getting high and having sex?" Frank Kaplan called from the hatch window.

"Not you!" Katie yelled back, with a grin. She put a brown paper bag with the takeout order on the table, along with the check, and told Jessica to enjoy her meal.

Charley Pride had been replaced on the Wurlitzer by "Stand By Your Man" by Tammy Wynette. Jessica tucked into the mac and cheese and tried not to think about Matt Connor.

A wind was getting up when she left the diner. As she drove back along Main Street, Jessica spotted the waitress in her rearview mirror, pacing outside the diner, talking animatedly on her cell phone.

She frowned. Definitely *not* a boyfriend.

31

PRYCE

Back at Hollywood Division, Medina had pulled the file that had been flagged on the system by the DNA from the Jordana Ford crime scene.

"Tell me about Tom Palmer," Pryce said, pulling his chair over to his partner's cubicle.

"One glance at Palmer's rap sheet and anyone would be forgiven for thinking the guy was your typical lowlife," Medina said. "More DUIs than I've had hot dates. Assault convictions, mostly for bar brawls that got out of hand. A dozen drunk and disorderly charges."

He pushed the rap sheet across the desk toward Pryce.

"Looks like someone with serious addiction and anger issues," Pryce said. "But I'm guessing Palmer wasn't your garden-variety criminal?"

"Not even close," Medina confirmed. "Until spring of '89, he'd never had so much as a speeding ticket. The guy had been a walking advert for the American dream. Pretty wife who he'd married straight out of college, two beautiful and smart daughters, nice home on a nice street in Newbury Park, two cars in the drive. A good job as a construction site manager for a big firm. Never missed a day in twenty years. Lots of friends at work, as well as being popular in the neighborhood."

"Sounds like a standup guy," Pryce said.

"He was, by all accounts. A bit too square for me obviously, but Tom Palmer seemed like the kind of guy you'd have been buddies with, Jase. You know the type. The neighbor you'd chat with over the back fence while mowing the lawn, or the coworker you'd meet for a beer on the weekend while watching the game. Then everything changed."

"His daughter was murdered," Pryce supplied.

"Right," Medina said.

Pryce went back to his own desk and rummaged in one of the boxes Grayling had given them during the briefing. He found the blue ring binder with Devin Palmer's name stuck on the front. He took the murder book to Medina's cubicle and opened it on the desk in front of them. Read aloud from the pages that had been punched and filed inside even though he didn't need to; he already knew every detail by heart.

Pryce had made a point of getting to know the stories of all the victims after Grayling had instructed them to read up on the Valley Strangler case. They'd all hit hard but Devin Palmer had hit hardest of all. She was the one closest in age to Dionne, the one who brought him out in a cold sweat and who had robbed him of sleep.

Pryce said, "Devin Palmer. Murdered March 10, 1989. At eighteen years old, she was the youngest victim of the Valley Strangler. She was supposed to be meeting her older sister in a bar in Van Nuys, but the sister didn't show. Devin's car was still in the lot outside the next day. Her body was found in Stoney Point Park not long after she was reported missing. She had been strangled with her own pantyhose. According to eyewitnesses, she left the bar alone. We still don't know if Travis Dean Ford forced her into his vehicle or coerced her somehow. The latter seems more likely, considering what we do know about him and how he operated."

He flipped the page to the clear plastic folder holding the photo of Devin that had appeared on the front pages of all the newspapers and had made the lead story on the evening news every night for weeks. Pale skin, long red hair, slim build. Just like the others. But also, not like the others. Each of these women had been a person in her own right, not merely a composite of the perfect victim.

Pryce urged Medina to pick up his story about Tom Palmer.

"The first time he got in trouble with the cops was a few weeks after Devin died," he said. "He got smashed in a bar, started mouthing off, and got into a fight. Came off a whole lot worse than the other guy. Palmer was big and strong as a result of his job, but he wasn't a brawler by nature.

"The cops knew what had happened to Devin and let him off with a warning. Figured the hangover and black eye and fat lip would be punishment enough. It was the start of a downward spiral. The drinking became more frequent. He started getting pulled over while drunk behind the wheel. He lost his license, then his job, and then his wife."

Pryce thought of Lou Hardwick and his bitterness toward Mary Ellen's mother, and how his ex-wife had been able to move on with her life after the murder of her daughter.

"Any idea what happened to Devin's mom? Is she still alive?"

Medina nodded. "I asked Rodriguez to check her out. She divorced Palmer in '91 and remarried in '94. Has two stepkids and lives in Monterey Park. No criminal record. Ditto the husband. Around the time she was hooking up with future hubby number two, Palmer was being court-mandated to attend AA meetings but it looks like he never got past the first few steps. Jail time followed. Nothing major, though. A few weeks here, a month or two there. He was a drunk who lost more fights than he won."

"You said he died more than ten years ago?" Pryce said.

Medina consulted his notepad. "The booze was always going to get the poor bastard. It was just a question of whether it would be a long, slow death that ended with a fucked liver or it would be fast and violent."

"Which was it?"

"Fast and violent. Seems like Palmer got good and hammered, then got behind the wheel and did a Thelma and Louise off a cliff with a hundred-foot drop on the other side. Didn't stand a chance. Investigators reckon he must've been doing at least seventy to smash right through the crash barrier the way he did. The car, or what was left of it, was like a concertina file."

"Accident or suicide?" Pryce asked.

"Officially? Undetermined. But I'd say it was no accident."

"Why's that?"

"The date it happened."

"Which was?"

"A few days after they fried Travis Dean Ford."

"They didn't fry him, he died by lethal injection. But—*damn*."

"Yep." Medina held up a mugshot of Tom Palmer and tapped it with his finger. "The point is, our man here went off a cliff less than a week after his daughter's killer was executed. That doesn't seem like an accident to me."

"I guess we'll never know for sure."

Pryce took the photo from Medina. Palmer was gaunt, with hollowed-out cheeks, and greasy hair, and heavy bags under eyes that had a haunted look about them.

"Now this guy's DNA has shown up at our crime scene?" he asked. "How the hell is that even possible?"

Medina shook his head. "Uh-uh, that's not what I said, Jase. The DNA on the pantyhose flagged Palmer's name—but the DNA wasn't his. The DNA profile was female."

"What? How does that work?"

"You followed the Golden State Killer case, right?"

"Sure."

"They caught him through familial DNA. Same kind of thing here."

"What do you mean?" Pryce asked.

Medina said, "I mean there's no way Tom Palmer could have killed Jordana Ford—but a female relative of his did."

32

JORDANA

Jordana had just opened a bottle of Merlot when the doorbell rang.

Her first thought was that it was Doc making another unexpected visit. The memory of the night before, those precious couple of hours spent together, made her smile. It was exactly what she'd needed after the altercation with Lou Hardwick. Maybe Doc was playing hooky from the bar this evening so they could enjoy a date night. Drink some wine, watch a movie. Just as quickly, she realized Doc wouldn't show up on her front doorstep; he'd text to say he was coming over and use the key for the back door, just like he'd done last night.

Jordana's cell phone was on the kitchen counter next to the bottle of wine. There was no text.

The doorbell rang again.

Jordana made her way down the hallway and looked through the peephole. Dusk was setting in and she could only just make out the faint shape of a woman. She groaned inwardly. Did those fundraisers really call on people this late on a Saturday evening now? Jordana decided it'd be best to be polite but firm, rather than pretend there was no one home. Make it clear she didn't want whatever charity it was showing up at her door again.

She undid the security chain and opened the door a few inches.

"Hi, Jordana," the woman said cheerfully.

Jordana recognized her but, seeing her out of context, it took a beat for her to place the visitor's face. The TV producer who wanted to sign Jordana up for a new true-crime documentary about Travis. Jordana couldn't remember her name. More to the point, she had no idea what the hell she was thinking, showing up at her home on a Saturday night; how she even knew Jordana's address.

"Can I help you?"

"You do remember me, don't you?"

"I do, but I'm a little confused as to what you're doing here. How do you know where I live?"

The woman looked embarrassed. "Oh, God. Nadia didn't tell you?"

Nadia was Jordana's agent's assistant. The girl was lovely but very ditzy. "No, she didn't. She told you to come here this evening?"

"That's right. She said you were reconsidering the project we discussed at the coffee shop. I did think it was a little odd when Nadia suggested we meet at your house, but when she explained how busy your schedule was with the promotion for the new book—well, I guess it kind of made sense. I'm so embarrassed, Jordana."

Jordana was pissed. She'd made it clear to her agent she wasn't interested in the documentary after she'd been accosted by the producer—what the hell was her name?—while having coffee. Her agent was, understandably, upset that Jordana was stepping away from the true-crime stuff. It would mean a big loss in commission, even if Jordana wrote some fiction books under a nom de plume. But to have Nadia send this woman to her house and try to railroad

Jordana into the documentary was unacceptable. Even so, it wasn't the woman's fault.

"I guess you'd better come in." She swung the door open and stepped aside. "Sorry, you'll have to remind me what your name is."

"It's Jane." She patted her oversized shoulder bag. "I have all the info on the documentary right here. I won't take up too much of your time."

They went through to the living room.

"I'm afraid you've had a wasted journey, Jane. I'm still not interested. Nadia shouldn't have sent you here. I made it quite clear to the agency that I wouldn't be signing up for any more projects involving Travis."

"Can I ask why not?"

"It's just time to move on. I was about to have a glass of wine. Can I pour you one?"

"No, thanks. I don't drink alcohol. My father was an alcoholic."

Great, Jordana thought. An over-sharer. Just what she needed. Well, Jordana was having some wine whether Jane approved or not.

"Coffee, then? Water? Soda?"

"I'm good, thanks."

"Take a seat. I'll be back in a moment."

Jordana went into the kitchen. Her cell was still on the counter. She tapped out a text to Nadia, not really expecting a response until Monday morning. It was the weekend and the girl was probably out on a date.

Not happy about you setting up meetings without asking me first, and really pissed that you gave out my home address.

She poured a large glass and was surprised when a new message flashed up on the screen almost immediately.

Hi, J! Sorry, I don't understand. What meeting? We never give out our clients' home addresses without permission. Hope everything is okay!

Now Jordana was really angry, this time with Jane. Persistence was one thing; lying your way into someone's house was something else altogether.

Jordana returned to the living room. Jane was still standing in the middle of the floor, hadn't sat down on the couch. She was clutching the big bag protectively to her chest.

"I think it's best if you leave, Jane. I'm not going to sign up for the documentary. There's no point in wasting both our time."

"I haven't even told you what it's about yet."

"I don't care. The answer is still no."

"It's about women who fall in love with monsters. Bundy, Ramirez, Bianchi, Ford. They all had women throwing themselves at them, writing them, sending them photos, degrading themselves. Even marrying them. This project will be an exploration of just how sick and desperate people like you really are. Not to mention the lack of thought and consideration for the victims and their families."

"Get out of my house."

Jane didn't move, just stared at Jordana defiantly.

"Maybe you didn't hear me. Let me show you the way out."

Jordana walked past Jane in the direction of the hallway. She heard a rustling sound behind her, followed by a sharp snap, then another. Before she had the chance to turn around, white-hot pain shot through her skull. Stars exploded in front of her eyes and her legs gave way beneath her. She flopped onto the carpet like a marionette with its wires cut. She felt a warm wetness run down the back of her neck. Then, a voice in her ear.

"Where is Veronica Lowe?"

Veronica.

Always intruding into Jordana's thoughts, even now.

The guilt over the stalking and the reporting back to Travis. Telling him where Veronica lived, where she worked, who she was dating. Just so Jordana could get close to Travis, gain his trust, earn his love. All these years, she'd tried to convince herself that Maurice Wayland's murder had been a coincidence, that it'd had nothing to do with the information she had passed on to Travis just days earlier . . .

Now, as she lay fighting for her life, Jordana wondered if this was her punishment.

"Help me," she pleaded.

Jordana tried to get up but her body had stopped working. All she could focus on was the pain. She had to stay conscious, fight the blackness at the edge of her vision. Fight the urge to close her eyes.

"Tell me where Veronica and Mia are. If you do, I'll call 911. You'll live."

"I don't know."

"Tell me."

"I swear, I don't know. Please, you have to help me."

Jane didn't help her.

Jordana felt rough nylon brush against her throat. It grew tighter until she couldn't breathe, couldn't force any air into her lungs. Her fingers tried to claw at the fabric, at her neck, but she was too weak.

Jane's voice was in her ear again.

A different name this time.

"This is for Devin."

Then Jordana surrendered to the darkness.

33

JESSICA

It was very dark by the time Jessica returned to the Halfway House Inn.

The fizzing red sign outside the office reflected on the tarmac like a pool of blood. The mountains were completely obscured by the black sky. It was late evening but felt like the middle of the night.

A handful of rooms had pale lamps burning behind gauzy drapes. The lights were off in Christine's room. Jessica knocked lightly on the door and waited, listening for any sounds of movement. All she could hear was the low drone of a TV set farther down the block and an electrical hum in the air. When there was no response, she left the takeout bag and soda on the doorstep.

The office was still unattended, but Jessica spotted the cute desk clerk behind the bar in the lounge. A couple sat at a corner table, engaged in low conversation and hand-holding, a bottle of red wine between them. Otherwise, the place was empty. Jessica took a seat at the bar. She shrugged out of her leather jacket and folded it over the back of the next stool. Placed her cell phone on the bar and noticed it had one bar of signal. There were no new messages.

The desk-clerk-slash-bartender-slash-town-heartthrob sauntered toward her. She opened her mouth to ask for a drink but, before she could utter a word, he held up a hand to silence her. "Let me guess—Pinot Grigio, right?"

"Wrong."

"Pinot Noir?"

"Nope. And I'm getting thirstier by the second."

He grinned at her and snapped his fingers. He was very cute when he grinned. "A nice, cold beer. Tell me I'm right?"

"Scotch, please. On the rocks. Large."

"That was going to be my next guess."

He reached for a bottle of Jameson and Jessica stopped him. "Not that one. That's Irish, not Scotch. I'll have the Talisker."

He lifted down the correct bottle from the shelf. Cracked the seal and poured a large large, without bothering to use a measure. He placed the drink on a napkin in front of her.

"First day on the job?" Jessica asked. "I guess you never went to bar school?"

"Cheeky. I like that. I'm Dacre."

"Jessica."

She guessed Dacre was around her own age. He had side-parted blond hair that brushed his collar and blue eyes and tanned skin and white teeth, but was just rough enough around the edges, with a light beard and dirty fingernails, to stop him coming across as an aging jock. The short sleeves of his Hawaiian shirt, worn open over a white tee, offered a glimpse of a black Celtic tattoo on one arm.

"Nice to meet you, Jessica. Nice tatts." He wasn't looking at her inkwork when he said it.

Jessica smirked. "I want you to take a look at a photo."

Dacre raised an eyebrow and leaned in toward her. "If this is the part where you show me a pic of you in your underwear so you can get free drinks all night, then I'm here to tell you I have an almost full bottle of Scotch with your name on it and I'm completely on board with that plan."

Jessica motioned him closer. "This is the part where I show you a photo of a missing woman and ask if you recognize her, before I settle up my own bar tab."

Dacre straightened up with a sigh. "That's no fun at all. Why are you looking for a missing woman?"

"Someone's trying to find her."

"If anyone was missing around here, I'd know about it. The whole town would. The closest Halfway gets to excitement is when the convenience store runs out of fresh milk."

Jessica pushed the cell phone toward him with her finger. "Take a look."

She drank down some whisky, while Dacre picked up the phone and expanded the photo of Veronica Lowe in the same way Katie Kaplan had. "Yeah, I know her."

Jessica almost choked on the liquor. "Seriously? You're sure?"

"No, I'm not sure," he said, giving her the cell phone back. "The woman I'm thinking of is older, but the girl in the photo looks a lot like her."

"This is an old photo," Jessica said. "It was taken around twenty years ago."

"Yep, makes sense. Could be the same person."

"And this woman lives in town?"

"I don't know where she lives."

"How do you know her?"

"She used to work in a bar in the next town over. If it's the same person, that is. This was a few years back."

"What bar? What town?"

"I could show you," Dacre offered. The grin was back. "I get off at eleven."

Jessica had been jazzed about Dacre recognizing Veronica Lowe but now her guard was up. The guy was clearly a flirt and she wasn't sure if he was trying to help or just hitting on her. She threw back some Scotch. "I'll think about it. While I'm thinking, I'll have another drink."

Dacre topped off her glass and poured a small measure for himself. Jessica bit back a smile as he winced when he drank it. "Is this woman a friend of yours?" he asked. "Family member?"

"No, I'm a private investigator. I've been hired to find her."

"That is so fucking cool. Sure beats a missing milk delivery at the store."

"Tell me about the farmhouse where kids go to party."

Dacre looked confused. "What farmhouse?"

"The derelict building outside of town where the high-school kids go to get drunk and get high and get laid."

"I have no idea what you're talking about, Jessica."

"How old are you?"

"Twenty-six."

Dacre was younger than Jessica had initially thought and was well within the age demographic that would've partied at the farmhouse, based on what Katie Kaplan, the diner waitress, had told her earlier.

"Don't take this the wrong way, Dacre, but were you a bit of a dork at school? Didn't get invited to many parties?"

"I was captain of the soccer team, played bass in a local band, and was voted homecoming king my senior year. Sweetheart, there was no such thing as a party back then unless Dacre Nevin was invited."

Jessica unfolded the increasingly grubby printout of the farmhouse. "Did any of those parties ever take place here?"

He shrugged. "Maybe. If their folks were away for the weekend."

"No, I'm not talking about a house party. At least, not the usual type. The place I'm interested in is abandoned and derelict. Has been for years. Kind of a spooky vibe going on. Apparently, there were even rumors it was haunted."

Dacre frowned. "Jessica, I've never seen this place before. It's not well known around here."

"So there's no place in town where the cool kids go to party?"

"Sure there is. You know the RV park next door? Way at the far end, there's a couple old Airstream trailers. *That's* where the youth of Halfway go to party. Has been for as long as I've been old enough to make out with cute girls and drink lukewarm beer from a keg."

"And the redhead?" Jessica asked. "You weren't shitting me when you said you recognized her? This is important, Dacre. I just drove for more than five hours from LA. I'm not in the mood for messing around."

"It's like I told you—it might be the same person; it might not be. She wasn't a redhead, though. Her hair was brown, and it was shorter. But it looks a lot like her. I'm definitely not shitting you."

Jessica nodded slowly. "Okay. What time did you say you get off again?"

34

JESSICA

The Last Chance Saloon was a sports bar in Echo Ville, the next town over from Halfway. They rode together in Dacre's car. Jessica would have been happy with companionable silence, but he was determined to chat the whole way. She zoned out after the first mile.

It was Tuesday night, so the bar wasn't packed but it wasn't empty either. The clientele was a mix of all ages, both men and women.

There were six flatscreens under a huge red plastic Arizona Cardinals banner. A dozen tables were scattered around two pool tables as though those shooting pool were the entertainment when there wasn't a game on-screen. There was lots of corrugated iron and Bud Light and Coors Light beer signs. One corner housed a small stage area for a live band, but no one was playing tonight. The TVs were showing a rerun of a football game.

They found a table and Dacre suggested he buy the drinks and do the talking with the bartender. He asked Jessica to hand over her cell phone with the photo of Veronica Lowe, as well as the farmhouse printout.

She shook her head. "No way. I've been a PI for a long time, you know. I think I know how to do my job by now."

"It's better if I speak to him."

"Why?" she demanded. "Is it because I'm a woman? You think he won't take me seriously, is that it?"

"No, Nancy Drew, that's not it. It's because you're not from around here. Folks in small towns don't like strangers showing up asking questions."

"You didn't seem to mind."

Dacre grinned. "Not everyone is as friendly as me. I know the guy. Trust me, there's a better chance of getting the information you're after if I do the talking."

Jessica sighed and surrendered the phone and the printout. "Fine."

"Scotch on the rocks? Large, right?"

"No, I'll have a nice, cold beer."

He shook his head and laughed. "Whatever."

She watched Dacre approach the bar and order two pints of beer, then show the bartender the photo on the cell phone. The bartender was a big man, more fat than muscle, with gray hair buzzed close to the scalp. He wore a blue t-shirt that seemed unintentionally snug, the words "I'm drinkin' in the Last Chance Saloon" printed on the back. The t-shirts were on sale for ten dollars.

A conversation between the two men followed, with lots of nodding and shaking of heads. Jessica couldn't gauge whether the guy knew Veronica or not. Then Dacre unfolded the printout and the bar guy spoke for a while, before Dacre folded the sheet of paper again and tossed it onto the tray with the drinks.

"Well?" she asked.

He returned the cell phone. "I added my number to your contacts on there. It's saved as 'Hot Dacre.' I know you wanted to ask for it but were too shy. Also, it's two-dollar PBR drafts tonight so beer was a good call."

"Will you just tell me what the bartender said and quit fooling around?"

"What's it worth, Nancy Drew?"

"Stop calling me that."

"Do I get a kiss first?"

"What? No, you damn well don't."

"Can't blame a guy for trying. Yeah, he knows her. Says it's the same chick who worked here a while back, just as I thought. She didn't last very long though. Could pull a pint and she knew how to waitress—was able to carry a ton of plates in one go—but her social skills weren't up to scratch. Not very chatty, according to Big Howie."

She knew how to waitress.

Jessica felt a flicker of excitement. "Did he have a name for her?"

"What did you say her name was again?"

"I didn't. It's Veronica Lowe. Sometimes she called herself Roni."

Dacre took a pull of beer and wiped foam from his lips. "Different name altogether. Big Howie says her name was Ruth. Ruth Kaplan."

Jessica stared at him. "Kaplan? Like the diner in Halfway?"

"I guess so. Although I only know Frank and Katie. No Ruth."

"How well do you know them?"

"About as well as anyone knows the staff in a diner. 'How's your day going? You want fries with your burger? Looks like rain later.' That kind of chat. It's not like I'm best buds with them or anything. Katie is a kid and Frank is, like, sixty or something."

A thought occurred to Jessica. The eye color and hair color were all wrong but that meant nothing in a world where hair dye and colored contact lenses were so readily available, where it was easy to completely change your appearance with not a lot of effort. Especially if your eyes were the same bright blue as a famous serial killer.

"You don't know how old Katie is?" she asked.

"Yeah, she's nineteen. She was in the same class as my sister."

The same age Mia Ford would be now.

"It was Katie who told me the farmhouse was derelict. That kids went there to party."

Dacre said, "If I tell you something really interesting, will you let me take you out to dinner?"

"No, but I'll let you buy me another two-dollar beer."

"Big Howie recognized the farmhouse."

"And?"

"It's where Ruth Kaplan lived."

That flicker of excitement was now a flame. "He's sure?"

"Yep. He dropped her home one night after work. Her car wouldn't start and it was going to be at least an hour for the nearest auto shop to send someone out to have a look. Big Howie offered her a ride and she got real antsy, said she'd call her husband to come pick her up instead. Big Howie told her not to be silly—it was one a.m. and there was no point waking the husband if he was in bed already. She reluctantly agreed. Didn't say a word for the whole journey home.

"The thing is, Big Howie has owned this bar for years. He's well known—and well liked—by everyone in Echo Ville and Halfway, so it's unlikely she was worried about him trying to get fresh with her or some such other ungentlemanly conduct. He thought maybe her house was a real dump and she was embarrassed but, when he got there, it was just a normal farmhouse. She never showed up for her next shift. When he called her, she told him she'd found another job."

Jessica's gut was telling her Ruth Kaplan was Veronica Lowe and Katie Kaplan was Mia Ford. It was almost midnight. Too late to head on over there now to find out for sure. She'd have to wait until morning.

They had another beer and Jessica asked Dacre to drive her back to the motel. When they pulled up outside, Dacre said, "I did good, huh?"

"You did better than good."

Jessica impulsively leaned over and kissed him on the cheek.

"I'm guessing you want me to come in for a night cap?"

"Don't push your luck, pal."

Jessica got out of the car and slammed the door shut. Dacre made a "call me" gesture and she laughed and shook her head. As she passed by Christine's room, she noticed the lights were off but the sandwich and soda were gone.

Once inside her own room, exhaustion hit her like an eighteen-wheeler. It'd been a long, long day. Jessica took off her leather jacket and kicked off her sneakers. Decided she'd lie down on the bed, just for a minute, before taking off the rest of her clothes and removing her makeup and setting the alarm on her cell. As her eyelids began to droop, she was vaguely aware of a faint smell in the room that hadn't been there before. It was a heady, old-fashioned scent.

Then Jessica was fast asleep.

35

PRYCE

Devin Palmer may have been dead for more than three decades, but it was her sister who had become a ghost.

After establishing that the DNA on the hosiery that had been used to strangle Jordana Ford was from a female relative of Tom Palmer, his other, surviving daughter was top of the list of people Pryce and Medina wanted to take a closer look at.

Erika Palmer had had a driver's license in the state of California since the age of seventeen. The most recent provided them with a photo, physical description, age, and address. She had shoulder-length dark blonde hair, blue eyes, and a thin face. A lot of people didn't smile in official photographs but there seemed to be a real sadness about Erika Palmer—or maybe Pryce's perception of her was colored by his knowledge of her tragic past. Erika was a year older than the age Devin would have been if she'd still been alive today. Her home address was in Echo Park in central LA.

However, when Pryce and Medina had paid a visit to the bungalow on Santa Ynez Street the day before, a woman in her thirties, who bore no resemblance to the driver's license photo, had answered the door. She'd introduced herself as Melanie Cox and told them she and her husband Aaron had bought the house six months earlier.

Melanie had invited them in for coffee and they'd seen for themselves the work the Coxes were in the middle of carrying out. The tiles had been stripped off the walls in the kitchen, cupboards had been ripped out, and there was dust everywhere. They had their drinks in the living room, where Melanie filled them in on what she knew about the previous owner.

As far as the Coxes could tell, Erika Palmer had lived alone. She wasn't an old woman, fifties would've been Melanie's guess, but the house was pretty rundown, the furniture was basic, and not a lot of effort had been made to modernize the decor. It was the kind of place you'd expect to inherit from an elderly relative.

When they'd viewed the property as prospective buyers, the owner had been a little odd. Not rude exactly, but distant, not particularly friendly. When the Coxes had asked, conversationally, where Erika was moving on to, she'd been cagey. All she would say was she was selling up because she had some family business to take care of.

There had been no forwarding address. Their new neighbors said Erika had kept to herself and had never shown an interest in socializing with them. Had never once attended a neighborhood party or barbecue.

Medina had shown Erika's driver's license to Melanie and she had confirmed it was the same person, although her hair had been much shorter and blonder than it was when the photo had been taken.

Back at the station, Pryce and Medina had done some more digging on Erika Palmer. She'd never been married. She didn't appear to have any kids. She'd worked as a claim handler at an insurance company for twenty-some years but had quit six months ago—around the same time she'd sold the Echo Park house.

According to her former boss, Erika had been sick for a while and had had some time off work. Then she'd unexpectedly offered her resignation and had declined to work her notice period. As far as her boss was aware, none of her coworkers had spoken to Erika since she'd left.

In short, Pryce and Medina had no idea where Erika Palmer was or what she'd been doing for half a year.

The harder it was trying to track the woman down, the more the bad feeling in Pryce's gut intensified. She didn't have a criminal record, but neither did Jordana Ford's killer, which is why only Tom Palmer's name had been flagged by the partial DNA hit.

One of the few pieces of information they did have on Erika was that she had not attended the execution of Travis Dean Ford. Neither had her mother. According to the list of victims' family members in attendance back in January 2006, only Tom Palmer had been there to represent Devin and witness Ford meeting his end in the San Quentin death chamber.

Before finishing up for the evening, Pryce had put in a call to Erika's mother out in Monterey Park. The answerphone had picked up. He had explained he wanted to speak to her about her daughter Erika and had left his cell phone number as well as the direct line at the station. Jackie Sanders still hadn't returned the call.

Now it was Wednesday morning and Pryce and Medina were back at their desks trying to formulate a new plan of action to track down the elusive Erika Palmer. It was just past eight a.m. when Pryce's landline rang. It was Erika's mother.

"Mrs. Sanders," he said. "Thanks for getting back to me. I appreciate it."

Medina looked up from his notepad and gave Pryce a thumbs up.

Jackie Sanders said, "Apologies for the delay in returning your call, Detective Pryce. My husband and I were with friends for dinner last night and it was very late when I picked up your message."

"That's no problem at all," Pryce said. "I won't keep you long. I wanted to ask you about your daughter, Erika."

"I don't think I'll be much help, I'm afraid. I haven't been in touch with Erika for a very long time."

"How long?"

"Since the day I walked out on my first husband," she said, matter of factly. "May I ask what this is all about?"

"Erika's name has come up in connection with a case we're working on and we'd like to speak to her, but we're having some difficulty locating her."

"Maybe she's dead."

Pryce was taken aback by the bluntness. "We don't believe that to be the case."

There had been no death certificate registered in Erika Palmer's name.

"Does this have something to do with my other daughter?"

Pryce hesitated. "Possibly. We don't know for sure yet."

"Then I guess you know all about what happened to Devin?"

"We do. I'm very sorry for your loss, Mrs. Sanders."

"So you'll know it's Erika's fault that my little girl is dead."

Pryce was stunned into silence. When he didn't respond, Jackie Sanders went on, "I know how harsh that sounds, Detective Pryce. But it's true. It's a simple fact that Devin would still be alive today had her sister not left her alone in a bar, in a strange town, at the mercy of a killer—all while Erika was sneaking off with some boy and getting up to goodness knows what.

"Believe me, I tried to forgive her. I tried my hardest to keep on loving her in the weeks and months after it happened. I'd already lost one daughter; I didn't want to lose them both. But every time I looked at Erika, all I felt was resentment. I couldn't hide it from myself and I couldn't hide it from her. I think Tom resented her too. His answer was to crawl inside a bottle so far he couldn't get out again. Mine was to leave."

"You haven't been in touch with Erika at all since—when? The early nineties? No phone calls, Christmas cards, letters. Nothing?"

"That is correct."

"And you have no idea where we might be able to find her? No family members she might be staying with or old friends she could be in contact with?"

"None that I'm aware of."

"You will let us know if Erika does contact you?"

"Of course—but she won't. My husband and I are in the book. We're not difficult to find. But Erika has never made any attempt to reach out to me over the years and I certainly have no desire to reach out to her. As far as I'm concerned, both my daughters are dead."

Pryce ended the call and recounted the conversation to Medina.

"Man, that's cold," he said. "Turning your back on your own daughter like that? Sure, Erika made a mistake—a big one—but she was a kid back then, doing what kids do. There's no way she could've known what would happen to Devin."

Pryce nodded his agreement. To be blamed by your own mother for the death of your sister and to then watch your father kill himself—whether intentionally or not—with booze . . . What did that amount of grief and guilt do to a person? What did it make them capable of?

Just then, Rodriguez came over to Pryce's desk with the information he'd requested about The Lonely Hearts Club and its members. His gut was telling him Jordana Ford's murder had more to do with a family's desire for revenge and less to do with a pen-pal club, but he knew he had to cover all bases. He took the list from Rodriguez. It was a long list.

She said, "Those are all the women I've been able to establish were members of TLHC and, where possible, the period they are believed to have been active members. Those highlighted in green have a criminal record, while those highlighted in red are deceased."

Pryce skimmed through the pages. More than two dozen had spent time in prison themselves, their crimes including theft, assault, drug possession, and trying to smuggle prohibited items into jail for their lovers.

He turned his attention to the names in red. Eleven had died. Cancer, heart attack, car accident. There had been three homicides, including Jordana Ford. One was a woman named Tonya Brooks. Her husband had been convicted of beating her to death in a jealous rage back in 2001, after finding out she'd been writing other men in prison and sending them lingerie snaps.

Pryce looked at the other name and felt a jolt of recognition. Where did he know the name from? Then the answer came to him and a cold feeling of dread washed over him.

He called Rodriguez over and pointed to the name. "Is this correct, Silvia? You're sure this woman is dead?"

She took the list from him and compared the name highlighted in red to a sheet of paper stapled to the back of the bundle.

"She sure is," Rodriguez confirmed. "Home invasion gone wrong. They still haven't caught the guy. A copy of the report is attached."

Pryce read through the crime report, the feeling of dread growing by the second. The woman had died five months ago. She was supposed to have been on a weekend break out of state with her husband. He was a pharmaceutical rep who had been attending a conference in Portland. The wife was going to tag along, do a bit of sightseeing while he was working. But she'd been called in to the hospital where she worked as a staff nurse to cover illness, and she'd had to cry off the trip at the last minute.

The woman had been home alone when an intruder had gained entry to her house, possibly believing the property to be empty. She had likely disturbed him during a burglary. She was stabbed with one of her own kitchen knives and had bled out by the time she was discovered by her distraught husband more than a day later.

The place was in disarray and some jewelry had been taken but more expensive items had been left behind. The theory was the burglar had freaked out after the stabbing. Or, Pryce thought, the incident had been made to look like a home invasion gone wrong. The husband was in the clear; he had a rock-solid alibi provided by dozens of attendees at the conference in Oregon. Just as Rodriguez had said, the killer hadn't been caught and the cops investigating the case seemed to have hit a brick wall.

The woman's name was Christine Ryan.

Jessica Shaw's new client.

36

VERONICA—PRESENT DAY

It was around six months ago that Veronica started to get real worried.

Not that she'd ever stopped worrying. Not really. Not even after all this time. But, with every day, week, month, and year that had passed, she'd begun to relax a little bit more.

Then Christine's letter had arrived.

For almost two decades, Veronica had been Ruth. First Ruth Martin, then Ruth Kaplan after she'd married Frank. Katie knew the truth. How she'd been born Mia Ford, the daughter of a serial killer. Frank didn't. Veronica hated lying to him but she knew it was for the best.

Only three people knew that the woman who used to be Veronica Lowe was now living in Arizona as Ruth Kaplan.

Only two—Bibi and Doc Durrant—knew exactly where in Arizona.

It was Bibi she'd turned to, the night she'd fled Los Angeles after discovering what Travis Dean Ford had done to Maurice Wayland. They had driven through the night, across state lines, to the farmhouse owned by Bibi's aunt where Bibi had spent summers as a kid. The aunt was in a nursing home and the farmhouse was empty and isolated. Veronica had vacationed there with Mia and Bibi just months earlier. Once they'd arrived in Halfway, it was simply a case of lying low for a few days until Doc's contacts supplied the necessary paperwork.

Then Veronica Lowe and Mia Ford had become Ruth and Katie Martin.

Ruth homeschooled Katie until she was a teenager, before deciding it was safe for her daughter to attend the local high school and lead as normal a life as possible. Katie was a smart kid; she understood the importance of keeping her identity a secret. They agreed she would wear colored contact lenses outside the farmhouse, same as Ruth did. Her fair hair had naturally darkened over the years but if anything was going to connect Katie to Travis Dean Ford, it was those electric blue eyes.

Ruth's savings hadn't lasted long. She'd needed a job so she'd started waitressing at the local diner soon after landing in Halfway. She'd figured out pretty quickly that the owner was sweet on her. Frank was older, and there'd been no thunderbolt moment for Ruth, but he was a good man. Another safe option. Katie adored him and that was the clincher.

After the wedding, Frank moved into the farmhouse, and Ruth and Katie took his surname. It was another step away from their old lives as Veronica Lowe and Mia Ford; another layer of deception. The thing with the contact lenses was explained away as "girls being girls" and wanting to keep up with the latest trends, including the most popular eye color. Frank never really questioned it. Why would he?

His income meant Ruth no longer had to waitress at the diner and spend so much time in town. They were also able to buy the farmhouse from Bibi's aunt a year or so before the old woman passed. A while back, when they'd hit a rough patch financially,

Ruth had taken a job at a bar in Echo Ville. But the boss was too nosy and asked too many questions. She'd quit after Big Howie insisted on driving her home one night. Ruth didn't like strangers knowing where she lived.

Even Christine didn't know her address. She wrote to "Ruth Kaplan" care of a PO box in Phoenix. Ruth made the trip to the city twice a month to do a big grocery shop and pick up her mail. It wasn't that Ruth didn't trust Christine—of course she did—it was just safer for her best friend if she didn't know where Ruth and Katie were if anyone ever came asking. But no one ever did.

Until six months ago.

Christine's correspondence was usually light-hearted and humorous. She'd recount funny stories about patients on her ward or what she and Richard had gotten up to on their most recent mini break, or go into far too much detail about a show or a movie she'd loved or hated.

Her last letter was different.

A TV producer had shown up at Christine's house asking about Veronica Lowe. She was making a documentary film about Travis Dean Ford and wanted to track down his past loves. She had been very persistent but Christine had told the woman—her name was Jane something—that she hadn't been in touch with Veronica Lowe for years. Christine was sure it was nothing to worry about—after all, plenty of other shows had been made about Ford over the years—but she thought Ruth should know about the visit anyway.

But Ruth *had* been worried.

Worried enough to call Christine's cell phone from a payphone on her next visit to Phoenix; to want to find out more about this mysterious "Jane" and why she was going to the trouble of showing up at people's homes. That didn't seem to Ruth like something a professional filmmaker would do. Christine's line had been disconnected.

Ruth had then gone to the nearest public library and booked out a computer for a half hour and searched for Christine's name with a growing sense of dread. Her social media pages were filled with messages of condolence. According to a report in the local newspaper, Christine had been stabbed in a home invasion gone wrong while Richard was out of town. Her best friend was dead. And, just like Maurice Wayland's death, Ruth was sure there was more to it than the cops thought.

The question was—who was responsible this time?

Travis Dean Ford was long dead.

Jane?

Who was Jane?

Then, two days ago, Bibi had called the farmhouse. Bibi never called the farmhouse unless it was an emergency. A private detective was looking for Veronica and Mia. She was young, around thirty, blonde and punky, with a lot of tattoos. Her name was Jessica Shaw. Doc had warned her off, Bibi said, had told her Veronica was dead and she should drop her investigation.

Jessica Shaw hadn't dropped her investigation.

According to Katie, the PI was in town last night, showing an old photo of Veronica. Asking about the farmhouse.

Jane.

Jessica.

Were they the same person?

Ruth had to assume so. And she had to be ready for her when she came. Because she would come. There was no doubt about it.

Frank had left before dawn to prep for this morning's breakfast crowd. Katie was expected to join him later at the diner. Then a haboob had swept in, quick and unexpected, meaning Katie was holed up in the farmhouse along with Ruth. She'd told her daughter to stay in her room, while Ruth had taken up position at the living-room window.

She watched now as dust and grit battered the glass and the wind howled and shrieked and rattled the decaying wooden frames. Only a lunatic would be out driving in these conditions. Only a lunatic would kill to find Veronica Lowe. Sure enough, the twin beam of headlights finally pierced the wall of dust a quarter mile down the barren dirt track that led to the farmhouse.

Frank didn't approve of firearms, didn't allow them in the house. He didn't know about the SIG P365 Ruth kept in a shoebox at the bottom of her closet.

The car pulled in next to Katie's LeBaron. A blonde got out, straight into the storm, and threw a blanket over her head and made a dash for the farmhouse. She darted up the porch steps and banged on the front door. It was like a cop's knock. Loud and insistent. A knock that said the visitor wasn't taking no for an answer; that they weren't delivering good news.

Jane.

Jessica.

Ruth tightened her grip on the gun and crossed the living room to the hallway. She looked through the peephole and frowned. The woman standing on the porch was older, late fifties, no tattoos, not punky, quite frail-looking. She was coughing hard and rubbing grit from her eyes.

Not Jane/Jessica.

Ruth slipped the gun into the waistband of her pants, under her t-shirt. She opened the door a crack.

"I'm so sorry to bother you," the woman said between fits of coughing. She was very pale and her eyes were red. "I got lost and suddenly my car was being pounded by a ton of dirt. I saw your light on. I have no clue what's going on."

"It's a haboob," Ruth said. "A dust storm. It'll pass soon."

The woman was being buffeted by the wind and struggling to keep the blanket around her. The dust was blowing into the house.

Ruth opened the door fully. "Look, you'd better come inside until it's over."

The woman was staring at her in a very intense way. "It *is* you, Veronica."

Ruth's hand quickly went to her waistband.

The woman pulled a handgun from under the blanket.

The wind screamed and the sound of gunfire exploded in the farmhouse.

37

JESSICA

Jessica's eyes flew open. She was briefly disoriented before remembering she was in a motel room in Halfway, Arizona. She was lying on top of the bed sheets and she was still fully clothed. The waistband of her jeans dug into her belly and last night's makeup felt dry and crusty around her eyes.

The curtains were still open. It was daylight but not bright sunshine. A strange sort of gloom blanketed the town. Her phone told her it was after nine. There was no cell signal.

Then she remembered the farmhouse.

"Shit."

Jessica's plan had been to wake early and check out the lead from last night's visit to the sports bar in Echo Ville, see if her hunch was right, that Ruth and Katie Kaplan were Veronica Lowe and Mia Ford. Instead, she had overslept.

Another memory from last night lingered just beyond reach. Something important. Then Jessica remembered: the faint aroma of perfume in her room. A scent that she'd recognized.

Christine Ryan's perfume.

Jessica sniffed the air now. Nothing. Had she dreamt it? Why would Christine have been in her room?

She opened the settings menu on her phone and connected to the motel's Wi-Fi. Stood up and looked around. Overnight bag, laptop, printer, toiletries. Something wasn't right. Her eyes did another quick inventory and stopped on the printer. The little green light was no longer green. It was blinking red. She crossed the room and saw the alert was because the paper tray was empty. The paper tray hadn't been empty when she'd printed off the photos of the farmhouse last night.

Unless . . .

Someone had used the printer since then.

Jessica opened the lid of her laptop and hit the space bar. The password prompt appeared on-screen. She was confident her files and emails hadn't been breached. But access to the laptop wasn't necessary to find out what Jessica had last sent to the printer. All someone had to do was hit the print-queue button on the machine and the images of the farmhouse would've spewed right on out.

"Shit."

Jessica's cell phone pinged with a voicemail. She put the phone on speaker, while pulling on her sneakers. The message was from Pryce and had been left around a half hour earlier. He sounded agitated. Jessica froze as she tied the laces of her Converse. She listened to the message again. What Pryce was telling her was impossible. But, at the same time, it had to be true. Pryce didn't make those kinds of mistakes.

Christine Ryan was dead.

So who the hell was Jessica's client?

Who was this woman who had followed her to Arizona, had apparently broken into her motel room, and had then stolen print-outs of the farmhouse?

Jessica tried calling Christine's number. It went straight to voicemail.

She shoved the cell phone into her back pocket and put on her jacket. Picked up her bag from where she'd dropped it on the floor the night before and found her keys. Outside, Christine's car was gone. Jessica made her way to the office where an elderly man was behind the check-in desk. If Dacre was every teenage girl's secret crush, the old guy was everyone's favorite grandpa.

"The woman in room six," Jessica said. "Have you seen her this morning? Did she check out already?"

The desk clerk consulted the guestbook, then peered at her over half-moon glasses. "Yes, she was here a short while ago to check out. Just the one room though. She'd paid for two."

"The other room is mine."

He gave her a disapproving look. "So, you're the one who lost the room key."

"Huh? What are you talking about?"

"When I came on shift last night, your friend mentioned you'd lost your key and asked for the replacement. I checked the guest-book against her ID and saw that she'd paid for both rooms so I gave her the spare for room five. You owe me ten bucks for the replacement key by the way."

The spare key. That was how Christine—or whoever she was—had accessed Jessica's room. Then another thought occurred to her—how was the woman able to produce ID if she wasn't Christine Ryan?

Jessica grabbed the guestbook and spun it around to face her.

"Hey!" the desk clerk protested. "You can't do that."

The old guy was fast losing his favorite-grandpa appeal.

She ignored him and ran her finger down the page until she found the entry from the night before. Both rooms had been signed for by an Erika Palmer.

Jessica returned Pryce's call, told him what she'd discovered. There was silence on the other end of the line. She checked the signal. The motel's Wi-Fi was still connected.

"Pryce? Are you there? Did you hear me?"

"I heard you." His voice was serious. "Jessica, Erika Palmer is a suspect in the murder of Jordana Ford. We've been trying to find her. Her sister was one of Travis Dean Ford's victims."

"Fuck. And now she's going after Veronica and Mia."

"Jessica, listen to me. Call the local cops. Let them find her. Don't get involved."

"I'm already involved. I led her straight to them."

Jessica disconnected and turned her attention back to the desk clerk. She was trying—and failing—to suppress the bubble of panic blooming in her belly. He was watching her with an expression that was someplace between confused and wary.

"Did my, uh, friend ask about a farmhouse?"

"She did," he confirmed. "Now, about that ten-dollar charge for the key."

"Forget about the damn key. I have it right here. It isn't lost. Tell me where the farmhouse is."

His eyes widened. "You can't go there right now."

"Why not?"

"Did you not see the sky? How dark it is? There's a haboob on the way. It's not safe."

"A ha-what?"

"A dust storm. They're dangerous. You should wait here in the office or go back to your room until it passes."

"How long will that be?"

He shrugged. "It depends. Could be a few minutes, could be a few hours."

"I don't have that long! This is important. I need to know where that farmhouse is."

"Miss, please, calm down. I already told you, it's not safe to drive."

"You told Erika Palmer where the place is, so now you can tell me."

"I didn't know about the haboob then. These things can come on fast."

"The lives of two people are in danger. If you don't tell me where the farmhouse is, I'll get in my truck anyway and drive around town until I find the goddamn place. That'll mean a lot longer on the road than if you just give me the directions."

He gave her the directions.

Jessica got into the Silverado and turned onto the highway and almost slammed on the brakes when she saw the incredible spectacle in front of her.

A wall of dust that seemed to be a mile high was rolling in the distance against the kind of pink and lilac sky an art lover would admire in a watercolor painting. Jessica took a deep breath, pressed down on the gas pedal, and drove toward the storm. The dust wall appeared to be moving in slow motion but, by the time she hit Main Street, fine, grainy particles were already smattering the windscreen.

Cars were pulling off the road in a haphazard zigzag, hazard lights flashing, their horns blaring as she passed by them. Jessica jumped as a sudden long, loud whoop shattered the quiet of the truck's cab. She realized it was coming from her cell phone where she'd tossed it into the center console. Her eyes went to the screen.

Emergency Alert. Dust storm warning in your area. Avoid travel. Check local media for updates.

Jessica knew she should pull over and join the other vehicles at the curb. She also knew she'd never forgive herself if something happened to Veronica and Mia. She just hoped she wasn't already too late.

Dust and trash and leaves and everything else being picked up by the swirling winds was now pelting the windshield hard. She put the wipers on high and the headlights on full beam. She was forced to slow to a crawl, leaning all the way forward in the seat in a desperate attempt to improve visibility. Jessica had traveled all over the country but she'd never experienced anything quite like this haboob. She kept on going. Eventually, through the dusty curtain of gloom, she saw what looked like the dirt road described by the grandpa back at the motel.

Jessica signaled for the turn, even though there was no other traffic around, and gently eased the truck onto the narrow road. Up ahead was the silhouette of a building. Lights burned behind the windows.

The farmhouse.

She continued her slow crawl along the track until the building came fully into view and she slowed to a stop. Erika's cream Volvo was parked next to the Chrysler that had been in the lot outside the diner last night. Katie Kaplan's car. The old tire swing from the photo twirled violently in the powerful gusts and battered against the trunk of an ancient tree.

The front door was wide open.

Jessica found a fresh disposable face mask in the glove compartment, then rummaged in her overnight bag for a t-shirt and tied it around her face, adding an extra layer of protection to her nose and mouth. She put on sunglasses. She took off the leather jacket and threw it over her head. Then she got out of the truck and made a run for the porch, her head down. The blast of dust particles in her face and the strength of the winds were almost overpowering.

Piles of dust were packed into the corners of the porch like mini sand dunes. A thick trail had been swept inside the house.

The front door swung back and forth. Jessica dumped the shades and stepped over the threshold. The rising panic was making it difficult to breathe under the mask and tee. There was something else among the dirt.

A pool of blood.

Jessica moved farther into the hallway and saw the body of a woman lying unmoving on the floor.

38

ERIKA—SIX MONTHS AGO

It had been a Saturday morning in March 1989 when a phone call changed Erika Palmer's life forever.

She'd still been in bed, not asleep, just lying there lazily thinking about the night before. Relishing the memory of making out in Todd's car, remembering the feel of his hands on her body, knowing it was only a matter of time before they went all the way. They'd shared a six-pack of beer too and her head felt a little fuzzy, but a hangover was a small price to pay for such a great night.

The landline rang loudly in the hallway and Erika hoped Cindy or Debbie would pick up. She knew at least one of them was awake already. She'd heard the shower going and the tinny voices of the radio earlier.

"Erika!" Cindy yelled. "It's for you. It's your mom."

Erika groaned and threw back the sheets and got out of bed. The headache was worse than she'd realized. She padded gingerly down the hallway to where the receiver was sitting on top of the little wooden telephone table.

"Hey, Mom."

"Hi, honey. Did you have a good night last night?"

Erika's eyes widened. Why was her mom asking about her date? "Um, yeah. I guess."

"You girls had fun, huh? I'm glad. Devin was so excited about seeing you. Can you put her on, please? I need to know what time she'll be home with the car. I have a few errands to run later."

Erika's heart stopped and her face burned. How could she have forgotten about drinks with Devin? Dread clawed at her gut. "I'll call you right back, Mom."

She replaced the receiver on the handset and went into the living room, where Cindy was sitting on an armchair, eating cereal and laughing at kids' cartoons. The sofa was empty. No spare pillows or folded-up bedding. No Devin.

"Did Devin stay over last night?"

"Nope. But she called. Sounded like she was in a bar."

The hours that followed passed by in a blur.

Their mom's old Ford Pinto—which Devin had borrowed for the drive over to Van Nuys—was still parked in the lot outside Mike's Tavern. The bar staff were called in and interviewed. One waitress remembered serving Devin several cocktails. She'd also seen the girl leave and was sure she'd been on her own.

The car didn't have any flat tires. The engine turned over at the first time of asking. So why was the Pinto still in the lot? Where was Devin? The logical explanation was that she'd called a cab after drinking too much alcohol. But none of the taxi companies in the area had any record of a pickup at Mike's where the passenger matched the description of Devin Palmer.

The Palmer family was worried. The cops were even more worried. A young woman had been found dead in Stoney Point Park just days earlier. The Chatsworth crime scene was around eighteen miles from Mike's Tavern. The victim, Mary Ellen Hardwick, had looked a lot like Devin Palmer. The cops had a pretty good idea where to look next for the missing girl.

That hunch led to the second phone call that shattered Erika Palmer's life.

Her daddy never recovered from identifying the body, seeing his baby girl lying there on a cold mortuary slab. Jackie Palmer never forgave Erika for leaving her sister alone in a bar, easy prey for a killer. Erika never forgave herself either. She quit college and moved back home. Her mom then quit her older daughter and her husband. Erika looked after her dad as best she could while he surrendered to the liquor bottle, knowing it was the least she could do.

More girls died. A community lived in fear. Everyone was a suspect. The Palmers stopped being newsworthy when the media moved on to the family of the next victim, and then the next. While her dad lay passed out drunk, Erika frequented bars late at night. She willed the Valley Strangler to take her too. But she was blonde and curvy, whereas Devin and the others had been slim with red hair. She left lots of bars with lots of men but none of them were *him*.

Then *he* had a name.

Travis Dean Ford.

Erika should have been happy, or as close to happy as she remembered. Justice for Devin, closure for the families. But she felt cheated. Erika didn't know what she craved more—the chance to kill the Valley Strangler herself or to be killed by him, just like Devin had been.

Travis Dean Ford didn't look like a murderer. He looked like a movie star. He should have been reviled, despised, hated for what he'd done. Instead, women stood in line for hours outside the courthouse to attend his trial, as though they were waiting for a glimpse of an A-lister on the red carpet at a premiere. They wrote him in prison and sent him photographs and underwear and marriage proposals.

One gave birth to his child.

Another married him.

Veronica Lowe.

Jordana Ford.

They disgusted Erika but she disgusted herself more.

She didn't attend Travis Dean Ford's execution. She knew her mother wasn't the only one who blamed Erika for Devin's death. She was a coward. She couldn't put herself in front of the media's glare again; couldn't endure the barely disguised contempt and the whispered accusations. Erika knew what they'd said about her back then: the slut who'd left her sweet, innocent little sister at the mercy of a monster while she'd been out getting drunk and horny in the back seat of a car. She knew that witnessing the death of her sister's killer would do nothing to ease her own guilt.

Then her dad had gotten good and loaded and driven his car off a cliff, and Erika had felt . . . relieved. Her mother was gone, her father was dead, and maybe now Erika had a chance to reclaim her life. No more daily reminders of the grief and despair and heartache she had inflicted upon her family. No more trying to pretend her daddy didn't blame her every bit as much as her mother had. He'd just hidden it better, had salved the rough edges of his resentment with booze. But Erika hadn't been able to move on. She hadn't lived; she'd merely existed.

Then, a few days ago, the third phone call that changed her life.

They'd found a lump in her breast a while back. She'd had grueling chemo, shed a lot of weight and lost her hair, but the cancer was gone. Now it was back and, this time, it was incurable. Her doctor discussed treatments that might prolong her life but not save it. Erika had said no. Like her father's suicide, the diagnosis had been a relief. The guilt had eaten her up long before the cancer ever did.

Six to eight months was all she had left.

It was enough time.

Veronica Lowe.

Jordana Ford.

And the biggest prize of all—Travis Dean Ford's daughter.

Evil flowed through the genes of that family like a poisoned river, and Erika was going to end it before it destroyed anyone else. It would be Devin's legacy. Whenever anyone spoke of Travis Dean Ford in the future, they would also speak the name of her sister. Devin Palmer would not be forgotten like the other fourteen victims. Erika would make sure of it.

Veronica Lowe.

Jordana Ford.

Mia Ford.

The three great loves of Travis Dean Ford's life.

Now all Erika Palmer had to do was find them.

39

JESSICA

Jessica crouched down next to Veronica Lowe.

She was lying on her side. Blood oozed from a bullet wound below her rib cage. Her skin was waxy, and damp hair stuck to her forehead. Her eyes were closed and she didn't appear to be breathing.

Jessica pressed two fingers lightly to her neck, hoping—but not expecting—to find a pulse. She felt the faintest throb and almost wept with relief. Veronica's eyes opened and filled with terror. Jessica tore the t-shirt and mask from her face. Shook dust off the t-shirt and pressed it against the wound, and moved Veronica's hand to hold it in place to stem the blood flow.

Jessica's cell phone had a single bar of signal. It was a miracle. She punched in 911 and told the dispatch operator to send police and an ambulance to the farmhouse.

"There's a dust storm right now. I'm not sure how long—"

Jessica cut her off. "A woman has been shot. An armed person may still be in the house. Send help as fast as you can, please."

She tossed the phone into her bag and pulled out the Glock.

"Is she still here?" she asked.

Veronica's voice was the shadow of a whisper. "I think so. Katie . . . Help her . . ."

"Where is Katie?"

"Her bedroom. Down the hall."

The farmhouse was one story but spacious. Jessica made her way slowly down the hallway, gun raised in front of her. The lamps flickered. Hot winds blew through the open front door. Jessica's eyes and lungs burned from the exposure to the haboob that continued to rage outside.

She kicked open each door, while leading with her weapon.

A living room.

A family bathroom.

An office.

The master bedroom.

Then—a teenage girl's room.

It had a queen bed, and a desk with an iMac on top, and a dressing table with lots of makeup, and a closet with one door open exposing a rail stuffed with jeans and blouses and dresses. A pair of chunky Beats headphones were on top of the bed, hooked up to a cell phone that was still playing music.

Katie Kaplan stood next to the bed, cheeks wet with tears, her bright blue eyes wild, her body rigid with fear.

Erika Palmer was at the other end of the room, a gun pointed at the girl.

"Put the gun down, Erika," Jessica said.

"So, you finally figured it out, huh?" Erika kept her gaze fixed firmly on Katie. "Took you long enough. I'd say you were a crappy PI but you did exactly what I paid you to do. I wanted you to find Veronica and Mia and here we are, so I guess I should be grateful."

Jessica edged farther into the room. "I know why you're doing this, Erika. I know about Devin. But this isn't the answer."

"You don't know shit, Jessica. Don't come any closer. I mean it. I'll shoot the little bitch if you do."

Katie flinched and Jessica stayed where she was. She was about equal distance away from each woman. She kept her gun on Erika, who kept her own weapon on Katie.

"Travis Dean Ford killed Devin," Jessica said gently. "Katie has done nothing wrong. Come on, Erika, she's just an innocent teen girl, like Devin was."

"She's not Katie," Erika spat. "She's Mia and she's exactly like him. She's just like his father was too. Don't you see, Jessica? I'm trying to do the world a favor. Kill the evil before it has a chance to kill other people. Do something good for once, before I'm dead myself."

"What do you mean?"

"Cancer. I've got nothing left to lose."

Fuck.

"Katie has done nothing wrong." Jessica tried to keep the desperation out of her voice. "Put the gun down, Erika. Let Katie go."

"Stop calling her that! Her name is Mia Ford, not Katie."

"The police are on the way. An ambulance too. Don't make this any worse than it has to be."

Erika gestured to the bedroom window with a nod of her head. Dust pounded against the glass like fists trying to gain entry. "There's a storm outside, in case you hadn't noticed. No one is coming to help. No cops, no paramedics. It's too late for Veronica Lowe and it's too late for *his* daughter."

Katie moaned and grasped at the bed frame for support. "What did you do to my mom?"

"Your mom is dead."

"No, you're lying. Please, God. No."

"Yes."

Then, Erika Palmer did something Jessica didn't expect.

She threw the gun at Katie. It landed on the bed in front of her. The girl's eyes widened, then she grabbed the weapon. Jessica could see how Erika's plan had changed and the alternative ending to this nightmare wasn't a whole lot better.

"No," she said.

"Your mother is dead," Erika repeated. "I killed her. Now you have the chance to kill me. Go on, Mia. I know you want to. It's in your blood. Prove me right."

Katie raised the gun and pointed it at Erika Palmer. The weapon shook dangerously in her hands. She undid the safety catch.

"Katie, no!" Jessica shouted. "Don't do it. Don't let her win. Your mom is still alive."

Tears streaked a river down Katie's face. "If my mom is still alive, then where is she?"

"She's badly hurt but she's still breathing," Jessica said. "Help is on the way."

The wind shrieked outside in apparent contradiction of that statement.

"She's lying," Erika said. "Veronica is dead. Do it, Mia. Take your revenge. Shoot me."

"Don't pull the trigger," Jessica said. "Do not prove her right."

"I'm sorry, Jessica," Katie said.

Then she pulled the trigger.

Jessica didn't stop to think; her instincts took over.

She launched herself at Katie, knocking her onto the bed as the gun discharged. Jessica's ears rang from both the blast and Erika's piercing scream before the woman fell to the ground. Blood stained the white wall behind where she'd stood. She'd been hit. Katie lay dazed on the bed, Jessica on top of her. She gently took the gun from Katie's hand, and pushed herself up off the bed. Holding both weapons, she walked over to Erika. There was a lot of blood. She wasn't moving. Then her eyelids fluttered and Jessica saw the slight rise and fall of her chest.

"Is she dead?" Katie asked in a small voice.

Jessica shook her head. "No."

Erika was alive. For now.

Jessica prayed that she'd stay that way—for Katie's sake.

40

JESSICA

One storm had replaced another by the time Jessica made the long drive back from Arizona. A biblical thunderstorm instead of dust.

For the second time in two days, she found herself hunched forward on the seat, wipers pumping furiously, headlights on full beam. Only, this time, she was trying to see through a sheet of rain.

Lightning split the dark sky and thunder boomed like the gods were real pissed.

Katie Kaplan had fired the gun but she hadn't killed Erika Palmer. Erika had escaped with a minor gunshot wound to the shoulder rather than a fatal one to the heart. She was recuperating in hospital in Phoenix, under arrest and under the watchful gaze of an armed guard.

She'd been charged with the homicides of Christine Ryan and Jordana Ford, as well as the attempted murder of Veronica Lowe, but she wouldn't live long enough to go to trial. The woman was very sick. She had weeks left to live, at best. Exposure to the dust storm, and its deadly particles getting into her lungs, had only contributed to her deteriorating health.

Jessica had fared better. No real damage from the storm other than some irritation to her eyes. She'd been lucky. What she'd done had been stupid and desperate. Once she'd given her statement to the cops, she'd gotten a slap on the wrist for her "reckless decision" to drive through the haboob. But Jessica knew if she hadn't, two lives could have been lost. As it was, no lives were lost.

Veronica Lowe—or Ruth Kaplan as she was now—had undergone surgery lasting several hours. It had been touch and go for a while. But she'd survived and the signs looked good. Jessica was glad, not least because Katie was going to need her mom to help her deal with the trauma of what she'd been through. It was unlikely Katie would face charges for discharging a weapon and causing injury to Erika. The woman—having already committed two murders—had trespassed on the Kaplans' property, she'd shot the owner, and then she'd threatened the life of the owner's daughter. The Halfway Police Department had no desire to prosecute Katie Kaplan.

Doc Durrant was also unlikely to face charges back in LA. Jordana Ford's lover had been found holed up in a motel in Nevada after Medina had tracked him down using CCTV images. The starting point had been the cameras on the Strip after Durrant's visit to Jessica's motel. He remained a free man, but only time would tell whether his marriage to Bibi would survive his infidelity.

The wipers continued to battle the torrent and Jessica's cell phone lit up with an incoming call.

It was Connor.

He'd been trying to reach her the last couple of days but Jessica didn't want to speak to him. Maybe once the wedding was over, they'd talk then. Right now, she had to quiet a pulsating itch. The small square of unmarked skin on the inside of her right wrist that had yet to feel the sweet relief of the tattooist's needle.

She came off the 10 in Indio and found a tattoo parlor on Golf Center Parkway which accommodated walk-ins. A half hour later, she walked back out again, the wrist bound tightly with Saran wrap. The throbbing had been sated for now, replaced by a deliciously sharp sting. Under the clingy film was a brand-new red heart with a jagged thunderbolt slicing through the middle.

Jessica didn't know if the choice of tattoo had anything to do with Connor.

If it was the halves of two different hearts.

Or one heart split in two.

A lonely heart.

Maybe that's exactly what Jessica was and what she would always be.

Friday night found Jessica in a bar in West Hollywood with Pryce and Medina.

They were enjoying celebratory drinks after closing another case. One less killer on the streets of Los Angeles for the city to worry about. Jessica didn't feel much like celebrating. She thought of Katie Kaplan, and the years of therapy that no doubt lay ahead of the young woman. And she thought about Erika Palmer. A whole life destroyed because a teenage girl had done what a million other teenage girls did all the time and had gone on a date with a boy—only, Erika's actions had had tragic consequences. Jessica didn't believe Erika was to blame for what happened to Devin—only Travis Dean Ford was responsible for the death of her sister—but her actions over the last six months had been unforgivable.

No, Jessica didn't really feel like celebrating, but she was a trooper so she bought another round of drinks and pasted on a smile and ignored the calls that kept on coming from Connor.

Pryce bowed out around ten, figured he should go home and spend some time with his wife. He'd barely seen Angie for days while working the case. By now, the booze was doing its job and Jessica was starting to relax and enjoy herself. When Medina asked if she wanted another beer, she realized she really did. While he was at the bar, her cell phone vibrated. It was Connor. Again. Jessica sighed and answered.

"Connor."

"Finally! I was beginning to think you were avoiding me."

He sounded drunk. Jessica could hear the bells and pings and jingles of a dozen slot machines in the background.

"So, you made it to Vegas," she said.

"Yup, it's my bachelor party, if you can call it a party when the groom's the only guest. Are you in a bar?"

"Yes. I should go. I'm with someone. I'll speak to you on Monday."

"Who are you with? Are you on a date?"

"That's none of your business, Connor."

"Jessica?"

"What?"

"Tell me not to go through with it."

"What are you talking about?"

"The wedding. Tell me not to marry Rae-Lynn and I won't."

"I'm not going to do that," Jessica said. "What I am going to do is tell you to stop throwing liquor down your neck, go to bed, and sleep it off. You don't want to ruin the wedding photographs."

She turned off the phone as Medina returned with two more beers and some whisky chasers.

◆ ◆ ◆

Saturday morning.

Jessica woke to blinding sunshine streaming through the motel window. She noticed a smear of blood on the white sheets. The Saran had come off in the night and the tattoo had yet to heal. She reached for a glass of water on the nightstand and took a sip. She picked up her cell phone and turned it back on. It was almost eleven.

There was a missed call from Connor, and he'd left a voicemail. But it wasn't more drunken ramblings. The call had been made this morning. Jessica listened to the voice message. The wedding was off. Rae-Lynn had lied to him. She'd visited his hotel room at dawn and told him there was no baby. She'd planned on trying to get pregnant as soon as possible after the wedding and then fudge the dates. When he'd asked her why she'd lied, she said she'd known it was the only way Connor would agree to marry her. She'd been afraid of losing him. Connor said Rae-Lynn was right. He didn't want to marry her. He was in love with Jessica.

Jessica deleted the voicemail.

She felt an arm slide around her waist, and soft lips kiss her shoulder, and a warm body press up against her own.

"Someone important?"

"No," she said. "No one important."

Jessica put the cell phone back on the nightstand and turned around.

Vic Medina smiled at her. "Hey."

Whenever they'd been in each other's company in the past, Pryce's partner had always been a little flirtatious and Jessica had suspected he might have a crush on her. But Medina had a crush on everybody, so she'd still been surprised when he'd made a move on her outside the bar last night. Surprised and flattered. And badly in need of some fun after all the shit with Connor. Right now, she didn't know if this was a one-night thing or the start of something. What she did know was that she didn't have the usual regrets that accompanied the hangover after a drunken one-night stand.

Jessica returned Medina's smile. "Hey yourself."

Then she pulled him toward her and kissed him.

ACKNOWLEDGMENTS

Thank you for reading *Lonely Hearts*—I really hope you enjoyed Jessica's latest adventure. It's because of you, the reader, that I get to do my dream job every day. I'm hugely grateful to each and every one of you.

My name is the one on the front cover but, of course, it takes many people to turn an idea into a book. Huge thanks go to everyone at my publisher, Thomas & Mercer. To my former editor, Jack Butler, for believing in this book from the start, and to my new editor, Victoria Haslam, for your enthusiasm and encouragement. Once again, the input and insight of developmental editor Charlotte Herscher has been invaluable.

I'm very fortunate to have the best agent I could ask for, so a million thanks to Phil Patterson for all that you do. And thank you to the rest of the brilliant team at Marjacq, including my foreign rights agent, Sandra Sawicka, who has done an amazing job of helping to bring Jessica Shaw to new readers around the world.

Lonely Hearts was written during a very strange and challenging time for everyone, when it wasn't always possible to see the people who are important to us as often as we would have liked. But the support and encouragement of friends has been as strong as ever. Particular thanks go to Lorraine and Darren Reis, and Danny Stewart.

Thanks, also, to all the bloggers and reviewers who have helped to spread the word about my books—I'm forever grateful.

As always, my biggest thanks go to my family. Mum, Scott, Alison, Ben, Sam, and Cody—thank you for always being there for me, for believing in me, and for your love and support. And to my dad, who is always in my thoughts, and who was proud of everything I did.